THE COMPLETE
ADVENTURES OF
ERIC TRENT
VOLUME 2

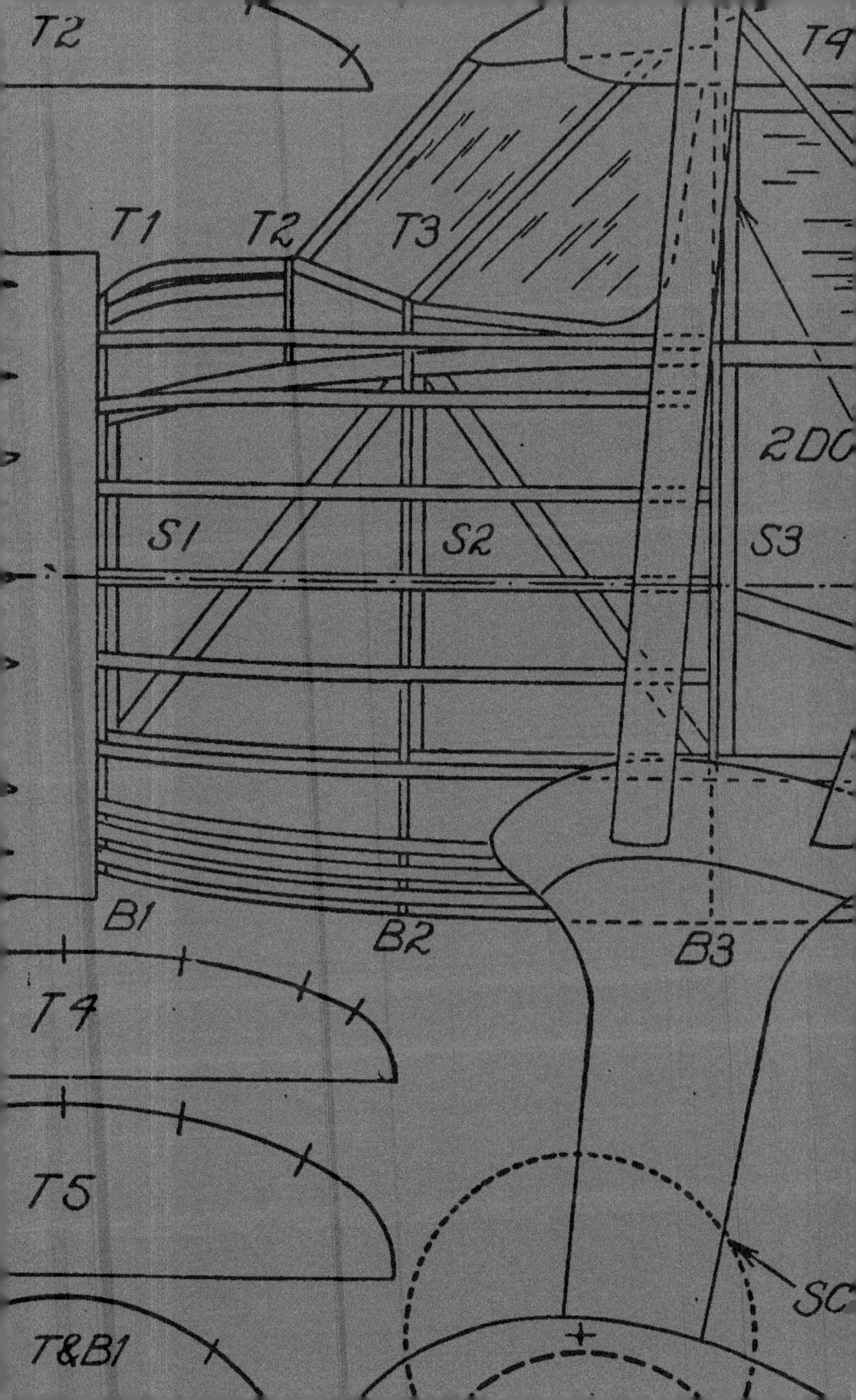

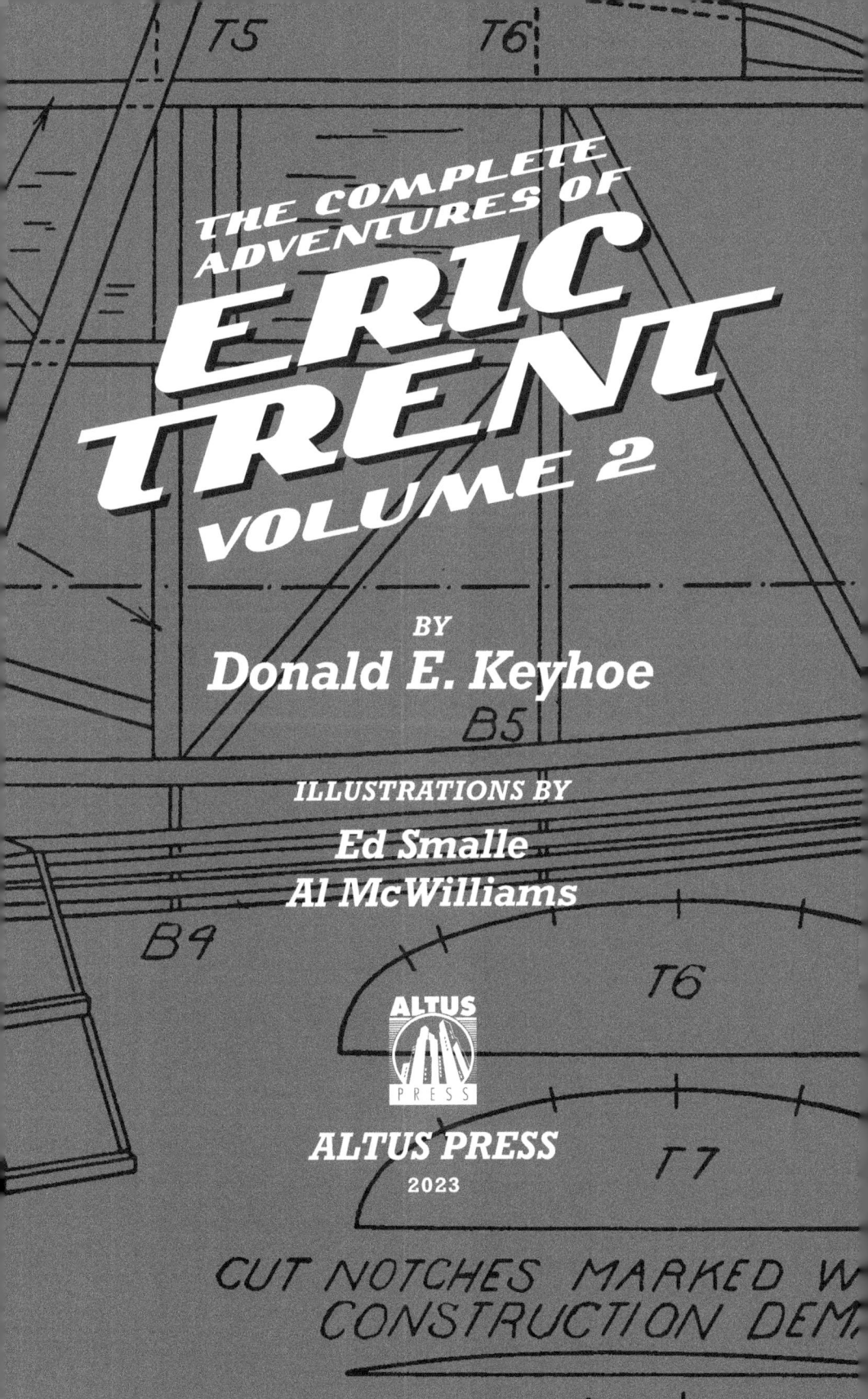

THE COMPLETE
ADVENTURES OF

ERIC TRENT

VOLUME 2

BY

Donald E. Keyhoe

ILLUSTRATIONS BY

Ed Smalle
Al McWilliams

ALTUS PRESS
2023

© 2023 Altus Press, an imprint of Steeger Properties, LLC • First Edition—2023

PUBLISHING HISTORY

"Squadron of the Dead" originally appeared in the April 1941 issue of *Flying Aces* magazine (Vol. 38, No. 1).

"Lure of the Liberators" originally appeared in the June 1941 issue of *Flying Aces* magazine (Vol. 38, No. 3).

"Death Dives the Douglas" originally appeared in the August 1941 issue of *Flying Aces* magazine (Vol. 39, No. 1).

"Ryan Retribution" originally appeared in the November 1941 issue of *Flying Aces* magazine (Vol. 39, No. 4).

"Death Flies Blind" originally appeared in the January 1942 issue of *Flying Aces* magazine (Vol. 40, No. 2).

"Death Flies the Beam" originally appeared in the May 1942 issue of *Flying Aces* magazine (Vol. 41, No. 2).

"On Haunted Wings" originally appeared in the July 1942 issue of *Flying Aces* magazine (Vol. 41, No. 4).

Visit *altuspress.com* for more books like this.

TABLE OF

Contents

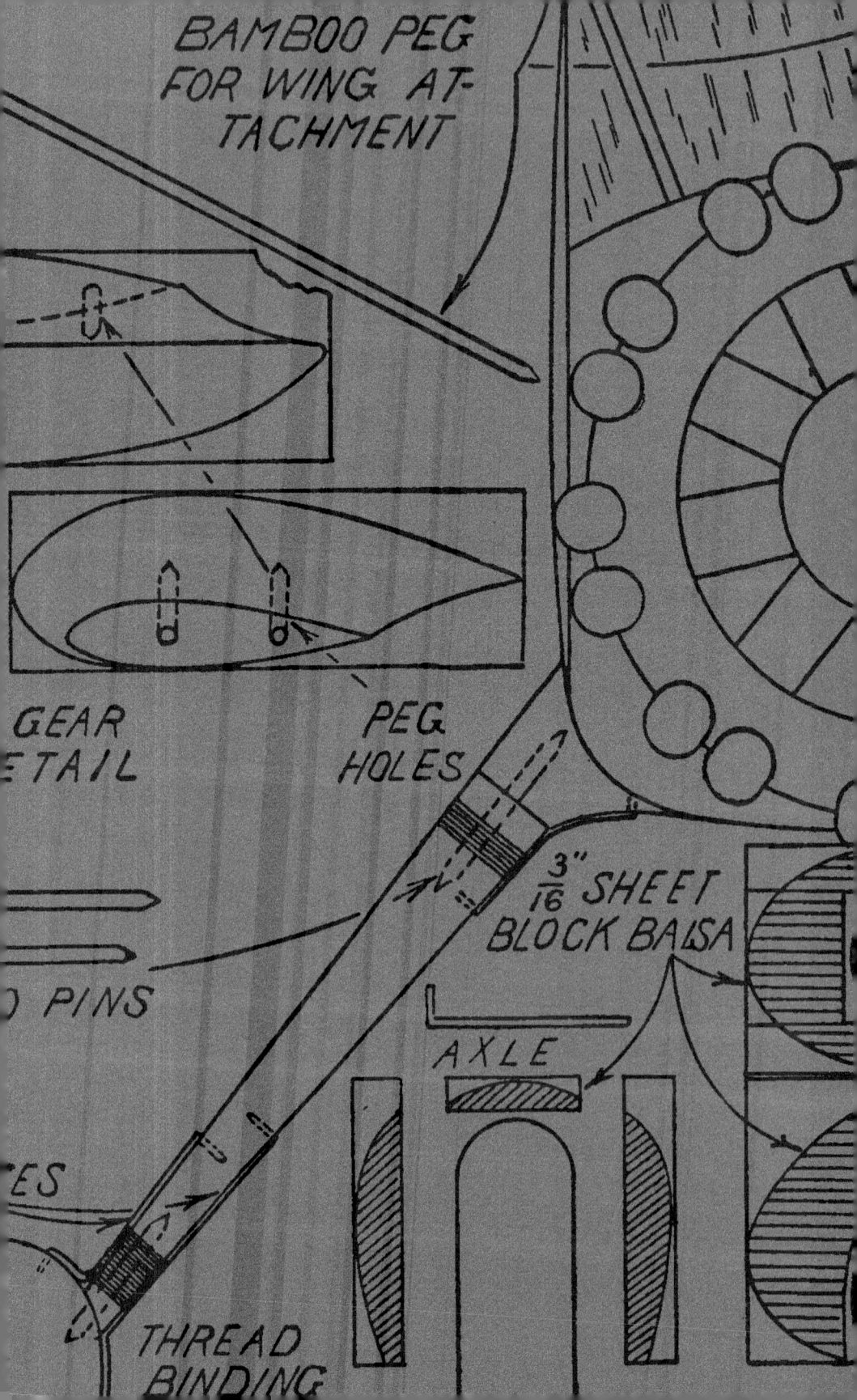

BAMBOO PEG
FOR WING AT-
TACHMENT

GEAR
ETAIL

PEG.
HOLES

PINS

$\frac{3"}{16}$ SHEET
BLOCK BALSA

ES

AXLE

THREAD
BINDING

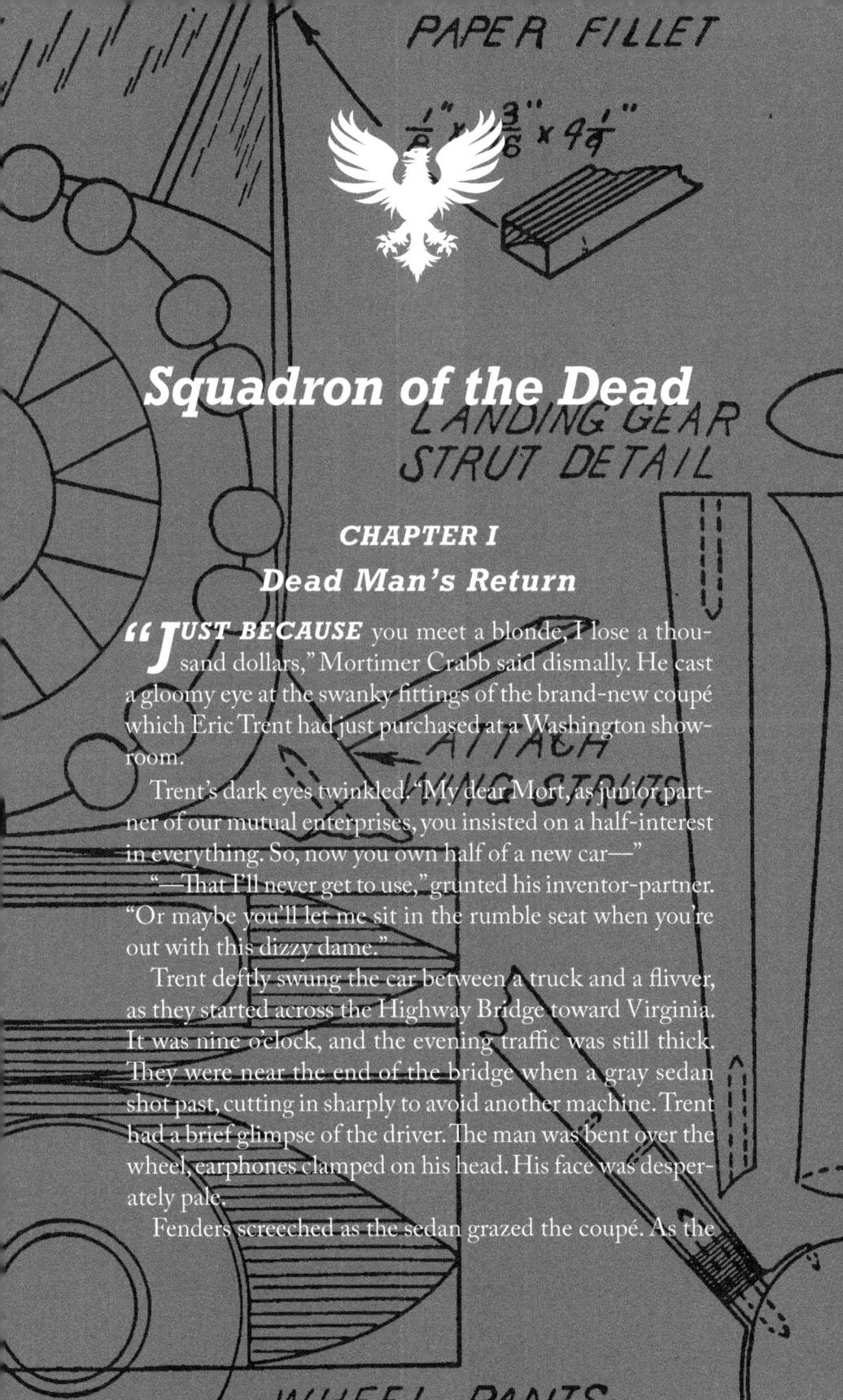

Squadron of the Dead

CHAPTER I

Dead Man's Return

"**JUST BECAUSE** you meet a blonde, I lose a thousand dollars," Mortimer Crabb said dismally. He cast a gloomy eye at the swanky fittings of the brand-new coupé which Eric Trent had just purchased at a Washington showroom.

Trent's dark eyes twinkled. "My dear Mort, as junior partner of our mutual enterprises, you insisted on a half-interest in everything. So, now you own half of a new car—"

"—That I'll never get to use," grunted his inventor-partner. "Or maybe you'll let me sit in the rumble seat when you're out with this dizzy dame."

Trent deftly swung the car between a truck and a flivver, as they started across the Highway Bridge toward Virginia. It was nine o'clock, and the evening traffic was still thick. They were near the end of the bridge when a gray sedan shot past, cutting in sharply to avoid another machine. Trent had a brief glimpse of the driver. The man was bent over the wheel, earphones clamped on his head. His face was desperately pale.

Fenders screeched as the sedan grazed the coupé. As the

gray machine sped away, Trent raced after it. The sedan cut in front of an oncoming car, plunged down into the Memorial Highway through a "Do Not Enter" lane. Trent followed, with a grin at Mortimer Crabb's anguished yell. The other car stopped suddenly and the driver sprang out, jerking off his earphones.

"Here—I'm sorry—emergency call!" he said hoarsely.

Trent saw the carrier's superstructure
loom out of the darkness as he
kicked rudder. Then the Vultee
crashed with a deafening roar!

He thrust a crumpled twenty-dollar bill into Trent's hand, wheeled to re-enter his car. Abruptly, words cracked from the dangling earphones:

"W-64! Cover old field, with W-19… If landing is made—"

The message ended sharply, as though a switch had been

thrown. The driver slammed the door, turned the sedan, and headed westward along the boulevard. Trent whistled softly.

"Mort, there are more interesting things than blondes. I think we'll just follow our excited friend."

"If you take my advice for once," Crabb said acidly, "you'll mind your own business. He paid you, didn't he?"

"Entirely too much. And those earphones—did you notice how quickly that message ended? There was some one down behind the front seat, operating a short-wave set, or my gray-matter is off a mite."

"A mite? They've got saner people in padded cells," grated Crabb. "The trouble with you, you've got a hangover from those crazy jams you got us into in Europe. That was probably just some radio 'ham' trying an experiment—" he broke off and Trent braked to a quick stop as a droning roar came from up in the night.

"Fighters!" said Eric Trent. There was an eager glint in his eyes. "Mort, we *have* run into something."

ABOVE THE howl of diving ships came the unmistakable chatter of machine guns. The long beam of a searchlight poked up from Bolling Field, was joined by another from the Naval Air Station. In a moment a furious dog-fight was outlined in the sky.

Trent threw the coupé into gear and drove swiftly to a point beyond the railroad bridge, from which they could watch the battle. Three planes were whirling in and out at less than two thousand feet. Circular cocardes showed on the side of a two-seater as it whipped into a tight turn.

"That's a British ship!" Crabb ejaculated. "What are they doing over here?"

Trent stared up at the machine. The nearest was a Blackburn dive-bomber. It was charging in with both the cowl and rear-pit guns blazing at a Dutch Koolhoven F.K. 58 fighter, as the Dutch ship desperately darted back and forth in an attempt to reach the Naval Air field. A blast from the Koolhoven's guns raked across the cockpit enclosure of the Blackburn, and for an instant Trent thought the two-man crew had been killed. But the Blackburn slued off on one wing, came back in a steep bank. The Koolhoven plunged toward the field, but the third job, a French Dewoitine D.373 fleet fighter, dived swiftly to intercept it. The Dewoitine's Chatellerault guns pounded in a long burst, and Trent saw the tracers strike into the Koolhoven's wing.

The Dutch ship staggered, lurched around in a last attempt to meet its attackers. The Oerlikon cannons in its upper wing flamed for an instant, and the Dewoitine zooming too late, was caught squarely. Fire gushed from the French fighter's cowl, and the craft pitched down headlong at the Potomac. But the Koolhoven was finished. Almost out of control, it went down in a whistling sideslip toward the Virginia side of the river, with the Blackburn roaring after it.

The Koolhoven ruddered out of the slip at a hundred feet, plummeted down onto the new and still unfinished Washington airport. The Blackburn swung back for a strafe of the wrecked ship, then pulled up hastily as a Grumman streaked across the Potomac from the Naval Air Station field. Trent had already started the car and was speeding toward the airport entrance. He flicked a sidewise glance at Mortimer Crabb. The inventor's long and mournful countenance had a dazed expression.

"Don't let it sink you, Mort," said Trent. "Those jobs were actually there."

"It's the craziest thing I ever saw!" Crabb gaped up at the fleeing Blackburn. "An English ship and a French fighter ganging up on a Dutchman—and here in the U.S.A.! The war's over for Holland and France—"

"Somebody doesn't seem to have heard the news." Trent sent the coupé bouncing onto a runway, ignoring a uniformed watchman running to stop them. The Koolhoven had crashed about a hundred feet from the other end of the runway. As they stopped and jumped from the car, an ashen face turned toward them from the wrecked cockpit.

"Good Heavens, it's Rene Lareau, France's leading ace!" Trent exclaimed.

Crabb's eyes bulged. "I thought he was dead—shot down in the Nazi invasion."

"So did I." Trent ran toward the ship, with Crabb at his heels. The French ace groaned as Trent tried to free him from the cockpit.

"It is no use—I have only a few minutes," he gasped. Then his pain-racked face suddenly changed, with a look of dread. *"Mon Dieu,* it is a trick! You have been sent here by them!"

"What's he mean?" whispered Crabb.

Trent shook his head. Lareau looked at them, with an agonized doubt in his eyes, then his expression changed.

"Non, non!" he said, almost to himself. "You would have killed me—"he caught feverishly at Trent's arm. "It is not too late! Find Captain Benson—American Naval Intelligence—tell him Rene Lareau says—" a fit of coughing shut off the words, and blood came to his lips. But he drove himself on. "The *Bearn*—Martinique—they'll use 'chutists—"

"Eric! Look out!" Crabb broke in hastily. Trent spun around, then jumped aside and plunged his hand inside his coat. The gray sedan was rolling to a stop on the runway. Poked through the opened rear window was the snout of a Tommy-gun.

The .38 in Trent's armpit holster seemed to have leaped out into his magician-trained fingers. The Tommy-gun gave a brief, clattering roar—then the man behind it toppled from sight with Trent's bullet in his head. The driver, with his earphones still in place, rasped the gears into mesh and fled as Trent pumped three more shots at the gray car. Crabb scrambled to his feet, from beside the wrecked Koolhoven.

"They got Lareau!" he said in a sick voice.

Trent threw a swift, pitying look at the dead ace. "Come on." His voice had a new, hard note. "We're going to catch that devil."

BUT LUCK was against them. The gray sedan had a head

start and it raced out onto Memorial Highway, its lights off, and was quickly lost in the snarl of traffic that had followed the battle and Lareau's crash. Trent slowed, to avoid attention, as a green Park Police car charged through the tangle of cars, siren screeching.

"We'd better get out of here," Crabb mumbled. "That airport watchman probably got our number. They'll have us behind the bars—not that it'd be anything new, after what I've been through with you."

"They can't get a dragnet out for the car right away," answered Trent. "We're going to Benson's house. Maybe he'll be able to fit the pieces together."

"The *Bearn*—that's a French aircraft carrier, isn't it?"

"Right. And it's at Martinique, down in the West Indies. But how that fits with a French ace who's supposed to be dead, and that Dutch plane fighting those others, is beyond me. Too bad I didn't nail that driver."

"You can be thankful you got the other bird," Crabb said grimly. "A second more and we'd have been back there with Lareau."

"I took the sedan's number," said Trent. "Benson can get quick action on that. He's assistant chief of Naval Intelligence. I met him a month ago, when I reported the details of that Alaska television affair. He was over at G-2 for a conference."

"Where's he live?"

"Somewhere in Chevy Chase. We can look it up in a phone book."

Half an hour later Trent parked the car a block from Benson's residence. It was Thursday, maid's night out, and Benson answered the bell himself. He was a small man, with a dried-up, leathery face, but his eyes were shrewd and alert.

"Captain, we've got to see you a minute," Trent said crisply. "Did you know Rene Lareau?"

Benson looked surprised. "Yes, he was air attache at the French Embassy before the war. Why?"

"He was killed in an air fight forty minutes ago while trying to reach Anacostia. Before he died, he gave us a message for you."

The Intelligence officer's mouth was wide open.

"But Lareau was shot down in France when—" a startled look suddenly came into his face. "Good Lord, don't tell me it's happened again?"

Then before Trent could answer he hurriedly motioned them inside and closed the door.

"Come into this room where we can be alone." He shut the library door, and Trent saw the agitation in his eyes, "Now let's have it."

Trent told him briefly, but omitting no important detail.

"Another 'ghost'!" muttered Benson. "It's getting more fantastic every time."

"You mean there have been other fights like this?" Crabb interjected.

Benson turned to the phone. "Wait till I call the police. That sedan should be found as quickly as possible. And they may have discovered something helpful when they searched Lareau's body."

He made the call, sat down again, gazing into space for a moment. "It's been kept a carefully guarded secret, but I'm going to tell you the whole thing. After what you two did at the Canal and in Alaska, I know it will be safe. And you may know something that will fit in.

"Our first report of these 'ghost planes' came in about a month ago. One of our Neutrality Patrol destroyers caught a message in straight German code sent by the captain of a U-boat. He was flashing an SOS and a message to Kiel that he was being attacked by German planes of the former 129th Squadron. If you remember, the 129th was a Stuka outfit, and it was totally destroyed during the mass air-raids on England in September of 1940."

Trent nodded. "That was when the Nazis lost about two

hundred ships a day, until they found day-raids were too costly."

"Especially for Stukas," said Benson. "Well, here was a puzzle: A German sub commander reporting that he was attacked by not only Nazi machines, but planes that didn't exist. We thought it was a trick—until the destroyer found a huge oil slick at the spot where the sub had radioed. Then a Portuguese freighter which was secretly bringing some French and Dutch refugees to America, along with whatever jewels and money they'd been able to save, was sunk in mid-Atlantic by French and Dutch planes. One of the Dutch ships had the stork-and-bomb insignia of a famous ace named Vroom.

"We learned this from a survivor who was found half-conscious on some floating wreckage after one of our Patrol vessels caught their SOS. Since then, there have been a dozen rumors and several confirmed stories of a 'ghost squadron'— the pilots all supposed to have been killed in the European war. The last case, until tonight, was that of a British ship captain whose vessel was attacked by English planes two hundred miles East of Bermuda. I've been thinking it was some Nazi trick, but that doesn't add up, in spite of what Lareau said about the *Bearn* and parachutists. The Germans certainly aren't in any condition to be dropping 'chutist forces onto Martinique. Our Navy could get them out of there, anyway, though it would mean open war."

BENSON STOPPED as the telephone rang. He answered it, gave a start. "Commander Webb? But that's impossible— unless it was stolen."

He listened for a few minutes. Just as he put down the phone, there was a muffled sound outside the French doors opening onto the enclosed side-porch. Trent wheeled, but before he could reach for his gun one of the leaded-glass doors burst open and a man sprang inside.

It was the driver of the gray sedan, and there was a .45 automatic in his hand.

"Webb!" Benson cried incredulously. "Have you lost your mind?"

"I'm sorry, Captain," the other man said thickly. Trent saw that his lips were trembling. "But these men—you'll all have to come with me."

Benson started to lunge for the gun, but Trent seized his arm.

"No need of that, Captain. I think the commander will abandon his little murder-plan when he knows the police have him spotted."

Webb turned on him with a snarl. "That's a lie! They never followed me—"

"You fool!" snapped Benson. "Trent took your number and I had the police look it up. They've already broadcast a pickup description of you."

Webb's face went white, then he crumpled, staggered to the nearest chair. The .45 dropped from his grasp, thudded to the rug.

"It's the end," he whispered. "Poor Jeanne—she'll know everything now."

Trent bent to retrieve the .45. Webb, his hands shaking, opened a cigarette case. There was only one cigarette in it.

"Benson—try to help Jeanne—make it as easy as you can—" he thrust the cigarette to his lips, bit down hard. There was a faint crunching sound. Trent tried to snatch the cigarette away, but it was too late. A horrible grimace distorted Webb's lips and he stiffened convulsively. Then he slid to the floor and an awed silence filled the room.

For a while, no one moved. They all bowed their heads silently. Benson finally got up and turned.

CHAPTER II
The Invisible Empire

"**I'LL GET** a doctor," Benson said hoarsely. He turned to the phone, but Trent, on his knees beside the commander, shook his head. "It won't do any good. He had a capsule of the cyanide in the tip of that cigarette. There was enough to kill ten men, from the size of the capsule."

"This is awful." Benson looked down at the dead man and shivered. "Webb was the last man I'd ever have believed a traitor."

"He was in Naval Intelligence?" asked Trent.

Benson nodded. "My right-hand man. And his wife— that's Jeanne Webb—is a close friend of our family. It's going to be terrible telling her."

"We'd better search him," offered Trent. "There might be something linked with Naval Intelligence you wouldn't want the police to handle."

Benson shuddered. "I couldn't do it."

"After what happened to Lareau, I think I can force myself to it," Trent, said dryly. He emptied Webb's pockets, placed his wallet, handkerchief, and key-ring on the floor. In a vest-pocket he found something wadded up, a short newspaper clipping wrapped around an object the size of a hickory nut. The thing proved to be a small carving, a head with four tiny faces. The detail was surprisingly accurate. Benson and Crabb had gone into the hall. He followed them and held the carved head close to a table-lamp. The four faces were identical, each with a look of brooding menace. He heard Benson draw in his breath sharply, looked up to see the captain staring at the carving.

"The Four Faces!" Benson whispered. "How in Hades did they ever get hold of Webb?"

"Then you know what this thing means?" asked Mortimer Crabb.

"It's the symbol of the most ruthless criminal organization this world has ever known," Benson answered. "Have you ever heard of the Invisible Empire?"

Both Trent and Crabb shook their heads.

"It's been pretty quiet since the war started. We thought perhaps they'd been put out of business. It's a world-wide criminal empire, headed by four men whose identity has never been completely established. There's been a rumor that one is Lowenstein, the European banker who was supposed to have fallen to his death from a plane over the English Channel some years ago. Zaharof, munitions king, supposed to have died mysteriously, is also thought to be one of the Four Faces.

"Their aim," Benson went on, "is to force all large criminal groups under one control, by blackmail or murder-threats or bribery. Before the war they were known to have members from court circles down to the lowest sneak-thief in most European and Asiatic nations. We encountered them half a dozen times here in America. Richard Knight, probably the smartest secret agent in our service, tangled with them and discovered two of their hide-outs, as well as their communication network in this country. But Knight's in the hospital and we can't count on help from him."

"I met Knight once," said Trent. "Chap named Doyle was with him. But I thought they were just a couple of aerial globe-trotters."

"That's a cover-up. But what Knight and Doyle found out about the Four Faces won't help us much now. They've evidently built up a new system. And if they got Webb, there's no telling what else they've done." Trent looked at the scrap of newspaper. It was a brief interview with a Belgian refugee. The man's name had been circled and at one side was penciled "W-19."

"Webb must have been W-64," said Benson, as he bent

over the item. "I've a hunch the 'W' stands for their Washington roster. And that refugee must have been the man you shot. The Four Faces probably saw a chance to plant him here along with real refugees. They've a special killer group, according to Knight, and this man was undoubtedly one of them."

"Knight never saw the Four Faces enough to identify them?" queried Trent.

"I think he unmasked one of them, but he's never been sure who it was. You see, they keep their faces hidden from all but the innermost circle. At one meeting, where all four were present, they wore full-face masks identical with the features carved here. I've seen the symbol before; one of their killer men had it tattooed on his arm, apparently so they could always prove who he was. Webb must have been carrying this thing tonight to identify himself to W-19."

TRENT LIGHTED a cigarette, stared at the carved faces. "I wonder what they had on Webb."

Benson hesitated. "He had some trouble with a Russian girl, on Asiatic Station. I've heard he was infatuated. He may have been lured into some devilment, and the Four Faces heard of it and blackmailed him. Or he might even have been married to the Russian. She disappeared, and he may have married Jeanne without being too careful to know he was free. But what counts now is this Martinique affair. We've some consuls there, but they're not trained in counter-espionage—"

He stopped, looked shrewdly at Trent and Crabb.

"Now, wait a minute," said Crabb, but Trent straightened up briskly.

"Captain, I think you've sold a bill of goods. Never mind Mort, he's an old-fire-horse when the bell rings."

"Then you'll take this job?" asked Benson, relieved.

"If you'll explain matters to the police. They'll be asking questions that otherwise might be embarrassing when they check up on our car number. And I've an aversion to jails."

"You've been in enough to feel at home," Crabb retorted acidly.

"I'll call the police and we'll get the questioning over," muttered Benson. "Thank God my wife's out tonight. She'd be scared stiff at this thing—and I wouldn't blame her."

It was two hours later when Trent and Crabb left Benson's house, after Webb's body had been removed and the homicide squad had finished their investigation.

"A fine thing," Crabb said gloomily. "You take me out to meet a blonde, and I almost get killed. And then some bull-necked cop takes me over the hurdles for an hour. You'd think I had a criminal record the way that fellow acted."

"The poor chap was naturally disappointed," said Trent. "When he came, he took you for the captured murderer, with that mournful expression."

"You'll be more than mournful before this thing is over, or I miss my guess," Crabb dismally predicted. "That Four Face mob sounds tough."

"No argument there." Trent paused beside the coupé. "I've met a lot of two-faced people before, but four faces is a new one."

"Remind me to laugh at that," Crabb said sarcastically, "if I'm still alive a month from now."

ONE HUNDRED and twenty miles west of Martinique, a Vultee Torpedo Seaplane droned through the dark above the Caribbean. As Eric Trent checked the course to the French island, Mortimer Crabb's dismal voice came hollowly through the intercom phones.

"Why is it nothing ever turns out the way it's planned when *you* get hooked up with it? Everything was set for us to pull this fake forced landing in the daytime—and here we are all balled up again,"

Trent laughed. "Is it my fault the skipper of the *Richmond* got an order to put us over the side and scoot for St. Thomas?"

"Trouble just naturally gravitates to you," grumbled Crabb. "It's going to make those Frogs suspicious, coming in there at ten o'clock at night. They'll know we'd have had to take off from St. Thomas at sundown, and what sense would there be in that, when we're just supposed to be delivering this job to Brazil, and no rush about it?"

"Stop worrying." They'll simply take us for a couple of eccentric Americans. We can put on a little act to help it along."

"You won't have to. Just act natural," retorted Crabb.

"That's what I like about you, Mort," chuckled Trent. "You bolster my ego, just when I think I'm sinking into the rut of conventional behaviour."

"I still think it's a crazy stunt," complained the inventor. "Even if that trick valve I fixed up does keep them believing we've got some mysterious engine trouble, they're going to be watching us every time we move around Martinique."

"They'll be watching you," said Trent. "You'll be the front man and I'll pull a sneak act. And that reminds me. If I should happen to use my old magician tricks, don't bother explaining to everybody within earshot. It spoils the illusion."

"If you're referring to Miami, or that stunt you tried on the captain of the *Richmond*, I still think you're nuts. In another minute, those Miami cops would have locked us up—what's the matter?"

Trent had switched off the already dimmed instrument board light, was staring through the Plexiglas enclosure and beyond the left wing.

"I thought I saw something—there it is again!"

It was only a blur in the night, a shadow flitting alongside the Vultee. Trent ruddered away, but Crabb gave a hasty cry of warning.

"Hold it, Eric! There's something on this side, too!"

Almost immediately, a tiny red light glowed from the darkness above. It flickered, began to wink out a message in Continental code.

"D-o n-o-t u-s-e r-a-d-i-o i-f y-o-u w-i-s-h t-o l-i-v-e."

"Swing up those rear guns, Mort!" Trent said swiftly. He

switched on the landing-lights, started a tight chandelle. The lights fell on the wing of a Blackburn dive-bomber, less than sixty feet above. Trent whipped into a sharp turn, almost collided with another Blackburn on his left. A stream of tracers flared over the Vultee and he jerked around, saw a third dive-bomber riding above the tail. Farther back, and a trifle higher, he could make out two French Potez 63's, like ghostships out in the gloom.

"They've got us dead to rights!" groaned Crabb. "There goes another signal."

The red wingtip light on the first Blackburn was blinking again.

"F-o-l-l-o-w c-o-u-r-s-e e-l-e-v-e-n d-e-g-r-e-e-s."

Trent banked, picked up the heading. "As you were on those guns, Mort, this doesn't seem to be the moment for it."

"Don't worry," Crabb said gloomily through the intercom. "I'm not fool enough to argue, with a dozen machine guns trained on my back. Let's see you get out of this, Mr. Magician."

"What bothers me is how they picked us up in the dark. Even if we do pull a disappearing act, they'll be able to find us again."

"Maybe they've got some trained cats flying with them," Crabb said with heavy irony.

"Never mind the sarcasm," replied Trent. "Just keep your trigger-finger set."

"You idiot! It's suicide to try anything now!"

"And just a slower brand of suicide if we don't," said Trent.

The landing-lights were still on. Evidently the unknown pilots preferred to leave the captive plane well illuminated, in spite of their ease in finding it in the dark. Trent looked into the cockpit rear-view mirror which showed the tail area. His dark eyes shifted from the reflection of the Blackburn, now riding aft, to the maze of instruments before him. It would be a tight thing.

His hand was on the flare-pull when another curt order winked from the leader's Blackburn, overhead,

"G-l-i-d-e t-o c-a-r-r-i-e-r s-i-x m-i-l-e-s n-o-r-t-h. L-a-n-d a-l-o-n-g-s-i-d-e."

Simultaneously, the lights of an aircraft carrier came on in the darkness ahead. Trent nosed down, then with a yell to Crabb he jerked the flare-pull and hauled the Vultee into a furious zoom. The Blackburn overhead whipped into a frantic chandelle. Trent blasted a fusillade after it, rolled out of the top of the loop, and swiftly cut off his landing-lights. Tracers were wildly stabbing at the seaplane, and the enclosure beside him crackled under a close burst. But the gunfire ceased as his lights went out, and the mystery ships twisted hastily away from under the parachute flare.

CRABB FLUNG a blast at the nearest Potez. The fighter skidded, dived under the Vultee. Trent saw the pilot plunge at the flare, but his hurried turn was not quite in time. Bullets tore into the parachute torch and the glowing fragments hurtled down toward the sea.

A searchlight speared up at the twisting planes, was followed by another. Trent made out the flight-deck and superstructure of a huge carrier, but he had no time to identify it. The attacking planes were charging in from three directions. He twisted away from the searchlights, charged back as one of the beams silhouetted a Potez. For an instant, the once-familiar emblem of the French 83rd showed in the glow. Trent stared. The 83rd had been one of the ill-fated squadrons hurled into the hopeless last battle against the Nazi air hordes. It had been reported completely wiped out.

"Another ghost ship!" he muttered. He thumbed the stick-button, threw a three-second burst at the French ship. But the fighter whipped out of the light just as he fired, and the tracers went wide. One of the Blackburns loomed swiftly out of the shadows. Trent snapped the Vultee into its wingtips and caught the dive-bomber squarely under his guns.

His tracers struck into the tail and mid-fuselage as the

Blackburn's pilot desperately tried to zoom clear. The dive-bomber lunged into a skidding turn and Trent's bullets ripped on through the cockpit enclosure to the two men huddled inside. The pilot slumped and the Blackburn plunged steeply toward the sea.

A Potez darted in furiously, was blasting through Crabb's hasty return fire. The other French ship was almost in range, and the two remaining Blackburns were spreading out for converging dives.

Without warning, the Vultee's engine abruptly went dead. Trent dived away from the lights, swiftly cut off the fuel-valve to prevent fire, and then cut the switch. One of the searchlights swung toward them. Trent ruddered to one side, put the Vultee in a forward slip—straight toward the deck of the carrier.

"Are you crazy?" Crabb howled. "You haven't got any wheels on this ship."

"It's our only chance, Mort," Trent flung back. "They've got a couple of planes lined up on deck. If we can scrape through the crack-up, maybe we can grab one of them."

Machine gun fire suddenly flamed up at them from the carrier's superstructure, and the searchlights pawed at the Vultee. Trent slued out of the tracer storm with a kick to the right, then dived under the nearest searchlight beam. For an instant, the Vultee was in half-shadow. He jerked the nose back toward the carrier, thumbed the stick-button.

A murderous torrent blasted from the Vultee's forward guns, raked across the carrier's deck defenders and on to the superstructure. The Vultee was down to three hundred feet and Trent was still firing, with the panicky gunners below fleeing for the hatches, leaving their dead and wounded behind.

The belts ran out, just as one of the searchlights went dark under Trent's final burst. He banked swiftly into the wind, fishtailed to kill his speed as the seaplane moaned in toward the flight deck. The remaining searchlight tilted, trying to catch them. Mortimer Crabb unleashed a brief barrage from the rear-pit guns, and the light went out hastily.

In the resulting blackness, Trent for a moment could see nothing. He leveled off, braced himself against the impact. The rear tips of the pontoons scraped across the deck. He pulled the stick back, holding the ship off till the last second. Suddenly the left pontoon hit solidly, and the Vultee lurched around. Trent saw the superstructure loom out of the dark as he kicked the opposite rudder. Then with a deafening crash the seaplane struck it and stopped.

CHAPTER III
Ghost Ship

TRENT HAD thrown his hands before his face, and his arms took the shock as he was slammed against the instrument board. The jerk of the safety-belt took half his breath, but he managed to gasp a question to Mortimer Crabb.

"Mort, are you Okay?"

"I guess so," Crabb said shakily.

"Make for that Koolhoven escort-fighter up to the right! They'll be out here in swarms—"

The clattering roar of a machine gun cut him off. Tracers flashed within a foot of his head as he jerked open the Plexiglas hood. Then Crabb opened up with an answering burst, and the other machine gun ceased firing. A hulking figure appeared from around the edge of the superstructure as Trent leaped to the deck. He recognized the weird fire-proof helmet and bulky asbestos suit of an emergency-fireman, the type known in the Navy as a "hot papa." The man had an automatic held clumsily in his gloved fist. Trent's right hand flashed under his coat, and the two guns roared almost as one. Trent's left helmet earphone shattered as a slug grazed it.

The fireman staggered, tried to raise his gun again, then pitched headlong beside the wrecked plane. Another blast of fire flamed through the dark toward the Vultee. As Crabb fired back, Trent hastily bent over the man he had shot. It was a ten-to-one shot. If he could make the change quickly enough, he might trick those devils into thinking the fireman had captured Mort, that he himself had been killed...

The helmet came off, and he tore at the bulky asbestos suit. There was a brief, ominous lull in the firing.

"Eric!" Crabb said hoarsely. "Where the hell are you?"

"Down here—got to put on an act, or we'll never reach that ship—hold them off another minute!"

The suit was hard to handle. Trent struggled, with frantic haste, knowing the odds were mounting every second. The Four Face gunners were stabbing quick, short bursts from two directions, drawing Crabb's fire. In another second or two the Vultee's rear guns would be empty.

"Get ready to jump, Mort!" Trent said swiftly. "Run toward the Koolhoven. I'll chase after you—fire a couple of shots and try to fool them. When we get to the ship you stand them off with the tourelle guns while I start the—"

Crabb's guns broke into his hasty instructions. Two Four Face gunners wilted behind the piece they had dragged up from beyond the superstructure. And just as Crabb's guns went dead, another flurry of tracers sparkled from a position farther aft. The inventor leaped from the wrecked ship, started to run for the Koolhoven. He had not gone ten feet when the flashing tracers struck into the nose of the Vultee and a geyser of flame leaped up.

The puff of fire which whirled out from the gas-soaked wreckage momentarily cut off Trent's view. He plunged through the flames, with fire crackling around his diver-like helmet, then groaned in sudden dismay. Blinded by the glare, Crabb had started to run in the wrong direction. Trent ran after him, but the bulky suit slowed his steps and the helmet drowned his shout.

Half a dozen men in dungarees erupted from the super-structure hatchway, dashed after Crabb. Trent groaned. There was not the slightest chance now of their escaping in the Koolhoven. His only hope was of continuing in the role he had planned for only a few tense moments.

He spun around to the blazing ship as the Four Face crewmen seized Crabb. The flames had spread across the gas-covered deck, almost hiding the body of the fireman. As Trent stepped into the holocaust, a muffled explosion sent fiery fragments in all directions. The burning ship settled halfway across the now blackened form of the dead fireman. Trent stumbled back, turned his helmeted head away from the glare as several dungaree-clad figures ran toward the spot. A man in khaki uniform shouted something at him in English.

"He's dead—I shot him!" Trent yelled back through the insulated helmet. The sooty smoke from the burning gas had partly obscured the special glass eye-slits, but he had a taut moment as the man's pale blue eyes met his. This was evidently one of the Four Faces' senior officers. He wore four black stars on the collar of his uniform, and his gaunt face had the look of one accustomed to command.

"You fool!" the officer flung at him. "They wanted him alive."

Trent made a desperate gesture. "It was my life or his."

"Tell them that, not me!" snarled the other man. "You knew the orders."

By now, a dozen men were spraying fire-extinguishers at the blaze. As it began to subside, a loudspeaker roared:

"Captain Borhel! Orders from Command Station. Prepare to land planes."

THE GAUNT-FACED man turned, and Trent knew that he was Borhel. He was glad of an excuse to slink back into the shadows, away from those pale eyes. He saw Mortimer Crabb, held captive by two huskies in khaki. Nearby were several men in varied uniforms. Some wore the tunics of RAF pilot officers; two were French Air Service flyers; one was Belgian, and Trent thought he saw two Polish airmen. Their manner was plainly different from that of the men in khaki. Most of the pilots' faces had a hopeless, beaten expression; two or three were merely sullen. The men in khaki, the men with the black stars on their collars, were more brisk. But Trent saw, too, that their faces were harder, with a grim determination.

The Four Face planes began to land, the Blackburns coming first. The last ship had barely been swung into "alerte" position beyond the superstructure when the loud-speaker came on again. This time it was a different voice, oddly tone-less.

"Captain Borhel, report to Command Station. The remaining prisoner will be questioned by Lieutenant Ganet."

A hush fell over the now shadowy flight deck. Trent saw Borhel peering around and knew the man was looking for the supposed fireman. He drew back into the deeper shadows, and Borhel motioned curtly to Crabb's guards.

"Take him to Detention. See that he is secured before you leave."

He strode away and the guards marched Crabb toward the aft hatchway of the superstructure. Trent Waited until they had disappeared inside, then cautiously followed. He had no gun. In the moment before Borhel had confronted him he had tried to slip his pistol inside the fire-proof suit, but the clumsy gloves had balked him and he had dropped it rather than risk the man's quick suspicion.

Crabb's guards took him two decks down, turned to the starboard side of the vessel. Trent, still wearing the cumbersome helmet, followed as quietly as he could. As he started across the deck he saw a man in khaki glance out from a cabin labeled "Communications." The man stood up, addressed him sharply.

"What are you doing down here, fireman?"

Trent had loosened the helmet. He lifted it partly as he mumbled the answer. "Captain Borhel told me to report to Lieutenant Ganet."

"Very well," the man said gruffly. As he turned back, Trent heard a voice from inside. "I don't like this. The *Richmond,* is still circling back."

"They must have become suspicious about those orders, and double-checked," said the first man. "What's her distance now?"

"Thirty-eight knots—too close for comfort unless we change course."

"Try that detector-meter again. She was over fifty knots north the last time I checked."

"They've increased speed. I'm going to report to Command. If they should know about us—"

"How could they suspect a ship they don't know is afloat?"

Trent did not hear the answer, for Mortimer Crabb's guards were reappearing in the doorway to a compartment not far ahead. He barely had time to dart into the conceal-ment of a companionway ladder when the door opened wide and light shone out. A slightly-built, pasty-faced man in the uniform of a French lieutenant stood there, looking at the two guards.

"That's all Borhel told us," growled one of the men. "If you need help to make him talk, you can send word."

They lumbered forward into a passage illumined only by dark blue war-lamps. Trent left his hiding-place as swiftly as he dared, pounded at the locked compartment door they had entered.

After a moment the door opened and the pasty-faced Frenchman stared at him.

"Lieutenant Ganet?" Trent asked. "Captain Borhel told me to help you—" he was inside with a sudden leap, his left hand whipping the door shut behind him. Ganet sprang back in alarm, but before he could make a sound Trent's hands were at his throat.

"KEEP STILL or I'll kill you," he muttered. He spun the Frenchman around against the bulkhead, locked the door. Then he saw Mortimer Crabb across the barren compart-ment. A dozen sets of handcuffs and leg-irons were secured to the aft bulkhead, and standing gloomily in one set of irons was the inventor.

"Get him out of those!" Trent said in a hard undertone.

Ganet was deathly pale now. As Trent tightened his grip, the Frenchman moaned, produced a key. Trent quickly took off the helmet as Ganet freed Crabb.

"A lot of good this'll do," Crabb said morosely. "We'll never get off this tub alive."

Ganet stared from Crabb to Trent in sudden horrified understanding.

"You—you are the other man! The one they thought was killed."

"A bright deduction, mon ami," Trent said. "Mort, I'm sorry I messed things up. But we're not sunk yet."

"You think to escape from here?" Ganet said hoarsely. "You're insane. No one has ever escaped from this hell-ship—and lived. They would follow you to the ends of the earth—"

"The way they followed Rene Lareau?" Trent said softly.

"You know—you knew Lareau?" whispered Ganet.

"I saw him murdered by one of this damned Four Faces mob. That's why we're here." Trent was watching Ganet's tortured face. "What have they got on you?"

"What does it matter? It is enough that I can never go back. I am a slave, like the rest—as you will be."

"I'll take a rain-check on that," said Trent. "I'm going to give you a chance. Help us out of here and tell what you know about these devils—and I'll see you're in the clear, if I have to call out the Navy."

Ganet shrank back. "No, no! You don't understand. When they once force you into the Invisible Empire, death is the only way out. This is a pirate ship—manned by men who are supposed to be dead, by men who might as well be dead—"

"I know the Four Faces system," Trent cut in. "But how they ever were able to put this over is too much for me. What ship is this?"

"The British carrier *George V.* Even the English think it was sunk at sea by Nazi U-boats. The Four Faces planted their agents on board, had them release poison gas one night. A freighter was waiting with a secret crew—most of them men like me, blackmailed into the Invisible Empire, some of them criminals willing to take the risk. The Four Faces directed it all through Borhel, until they came aboard in a special plane three nights ago, from where nobody knows."

"How did they get those planes?" demanded Trent.

"I think they have a secret air base somewhere. They must have been building up their air fleet for a long time, mainly by forcing pilots to steal the ships—pilots they'd tricked into something criminal, or some treachery to their country. They even kept on with it during the war, Lareau said. They had proof—falsified documents—that would have made him seem a traitor, and he followed their orders to disappear and join us. We were off the African coast then. They've a special detector system that will pick up the sound of a plane a hundred miles away, or any kind of vessel, even a U-boat. They simply change course and keep out of range.

"They've captured tankers to refuel the ship, using the planes to put their radio out of commission before they could reveal the secret. Except for that, and getting food supplies, all they want is to prey on all sides during the war. They've got agents everywhere, flashing them word in code about ships with valuable cargoes aboard. So you see—it's hopeless. They've thought out everything!"

"Never mind that," said Trent. "They're up to something about Martinique. And that doesn't sound like piracy. I think you're lying."

He knew most of the story was true, but he also knew better than to trust this hopeless derelict. If Ganet could trick them, turn them over to the Four Faces, it would raise him in the eyes of his sinister masters...

"I'm not lying!" Ganet said thickly. "But there's something about this Martinique plan that is known only by the Four Faces and their high officers, like Borhel. I heard Borhel tell one officer they'd like to see America drawn into the war to keep Hitler from winning and controlling the world. But they seem only to want the *Bearn*—"

Ganet choked off, trembling, as a sharp knock came at the compartment door. Trent's gloved hands shot to his throat.

"Ask who it is! Tell him you're busy."

Ganet obeyed, in a shaking voice.

"Open the door!" came the harsh answer. "The Fourth Face wishes to see the prisoner!"

CHAPTER IV
The Fourth Face

"**M**ORT, BACK** in those irons! Pretend they're fastened!" Trent flung at the inventor. Then his hand loosened on Ganet's throat, "Unlock it—but if you make one sign to warn him I'm back of the door, I'll get you if it's my last act on earth."

The sharp knock was repeated and Trent heard a voice, oddly muffled, then the harsher one roared out another order to Ganet. The Frenchman staggered to the door, turned the bolt. Trent had stepped to one side, so that the door hid him when it opened. The heavy fireproof helmet was lifted in his hands, almost over his head, when he heard the strangely muffled voice again.

"The guards will remain outside. Petty officer, inform Command Station of my presence here."

Ganet's ashen face held a look of frantic warning despite Trent's threat, but apparently the Fourth Face had turned to give his orders. The door swung shut, and Trent had a glimpse of a black-robed figure with a Roman numeral "IV" for identification. He saw a sinister, dead face which he recognized instantly as a shell-mask. The man's eyes, back of the slits in the mask, seemed to be sunk deep in his head.

As the eyes of the Fourth Face fell on Ganet, the robed man stiffened in sudden alarm. He wheeled toward Trent, jumped back with a strangled cry as Trent leaped. Ganet's mouth opened for a shout to the guards outside, but Crabb, letting the irons fall with a crash, hurtled against the Frenchman and knocked him to the deck.

Trent's fist thudded to the solar plexus of the masked figure, to stifle further outcry. The Fourth Face doubled over, sagged to his knees with a groan. Trent sprang to the door and flipped the bolt as an anxious voice sounded outside.

"Excellency! *Que est?*"

Trent took a chance, answered in muffled French.

"I am teaching the traitor a lesson. Don't interfere!"

Ganet lay motionless where his head had struck the desk. Crabb had let go of the Frenchman, was bending toward the Fourth Face. The robed figure twisted around on one knee, and the muzzle of a small air-pistol appeared as he threw the robe back. Trent dived in between Crabb and the Fourth Face just as the man pulled the trigger.

There was a hiss, and a short, thick needle hit the glass eye-piece of the helmet. Trent seized the man's wrist, shoved the air-gun upward as the Fourth Face made another desperate attempt to fire. The weapon hissed again, and a tiny, dark spot appeared on the man's throat, above his robe. The Fourth Face gave a convulsive jerk, and dropped the air-gun. One black-gloved hand clawed wildly at the spot where the poisoned needle had entered his throat. Then with a hoarse, rattling breath he slumped back and lay at Trent's feet. Trent hurriedly removed the fireman helmet.

"Good Lord, that was close!" Crabb said huskily.

"Must have been Malay *lakta*, the stuff they use on poison darts," murmured Trent. He threw a backward glance at the door. "We're in a tough spot. Our only chance is for me to make them think I'm that devil—long enough to order those guards away. Play up when I start firing questions at you—it'll cover the time while I'm getting ready?"

Crabb shook his head gloomily, but went back to the bulkhead and gave the manacles a rattle. Trent held his voice to a muffled tone, but one which he knew could be heard outside, as he stripped off the asbestos suit.

"Now, you meddling Yankee, talk quickly—or you'll meet the same fate. Whom were you to meet in Martinique?"

"Nobody," mumbled Crabb. "That, is, not at first. If we couldn't find out anything, we were to look up the American consul."

"How did you know about this vessel?" Trent hissed through his teeth.

"We didn't know," Crabb answered dismally. "All we knew was that something was going to happen at Martinique."

"If you're lying, you'll regret it!" Trent threatened. He took the black robe and the Four Face mask from the man on the deck. A lined, swarthy face was revealed, the face of a man over sixty, with a grim jaw and a mouth like a trap. Trent recognized Zarahoff, the munitions king who was supposed to have died two years ago at his guarded villa in France. The man was still breathing with laboring gasps, but he was plainly in a coma and sinking fast.

"He won't trouble anybody again," Trent whispered to Crabb. Then he said aloud, "Our secret reports show that you and your fellow-meddler Trent made a small fortune in tricking the Axis during the last two years. What is the amount, and where is it banked?"

Crabb gave him an agonized look. "It's not much over a hundred thousand," he groaned. "Part of it's invested in my laboratory and plant in Vermont."

"You will be ready to give me a detailed statement when I return," Trent said coldly. Then he added, in a swift undertone: "Get into those chains again. Lock the door after I get them away from outside, and don't let anybody in until I signal with four quick taps."

HE HAD the robe now, and it hid his clothes. He adjusted the mask shell, which was held in place by its own weight and the snugness with which it fitted down over his head. There was a thin strip of metal gauze fastened back of the mouth-slit. Also, there was a narrow deflector evidently intended to change the natural tone of the wearer's voice.

He gave a last look at Ganet, unconscious on the deck, and the Fourth Face, his head now concealed within the fireman-helmet, the asbestos suit arranged over him so that from the doorway it would seem that he was in it. Then with a quick gesture to Crabb he unlocked the door, gripping the poison-needle pistol in his left hand, under the robe.

One of the Four Faces officers, a heavy-set man with two black stars on his khaki coat, was waiting outside with two armed guards. All three men stiffened to attention and the officer saluted. Trent saw their eyes shift past him into the room, saw their morbid curiosity change to a puzzled surprise at sight of Ganet lying there beside the supposed fireman. He flicked a quick glance back as he closed the door. Crabb was standing with the manacles over his wrists and the leg-irons about his ankles; he was a picture of gloom and despair. Trent shut the door.

"No one is to go into that room," he said in a voice as near like that of the Fourth Face as he could make it. "I wish the American to be left alone to look at my object lesson."

The officer saluted again. Trent noted an expectant look on his face. The guards made no move to leave.

"Escort me to the flight-deck," Trent ordered. "A plane is to be prepared for a special mission at once."

The officer looked at him blankly. "But, Excellency, the deck has just been secured by order from Command Station. All lights are off, crews at stand-by, and the radio has been shut down except for receiving. We are on approach to Martinique."

Trent covered up swiftly, before suspicion could enter the man's mind. "The special mission must have been countermanded just after I left Command."

"That must be the answer, Excellency. They are waiting for you. Captain Borhel and the staff are already assembled for the final orders."

Trent silently cursed himself. He should have anticipated this.

"Very well," he muttered. "Escort me to Command."

The guards faced the dim-lighted passage, and Trent started into its blue shadows, the officer at his left. Two more guards appeared beside a watertight steel door. The officer stepped to a microphone.

"The Fourth Face!" he announced in a subdued tone.

A bright light went on above the door and Trent saw a tilted mirror behind a heavy glass panel. Evidently he was being scrutinized through a periscope system. There was a click and the steel door slowly opened. As he stepped inside, it immediately closed behind him.

He had entered a long, narrow compartment shut off from a larger one facing it by a barrier of bulletproof glass. The glass came down to a steel bulkhead about three feet from the deck, so that the men in the large compartment were easily visible. But it was the three black-robed figures before him who took Trent's instant attention.

THEY WERE attired exactly as he was, with, identical masks. They sat in big leather chairs before a long, flat desk like a judges' bench, on which were four microphones, a small loud-speaker, several switches and knobs, and a litter of papers and charts. The robed man at the farther end of the compartment, with a Roman numeral "I," was just lifting his hand from the switch which obviously controlled the steel door.

The masked men glanced at Trent briefly as he took the empty chair near the door, and the Third Face leaned toward him.

"What did you learn?" he said. He spoke French, but with an unmistakable English accent. Trent noticed that the other two men were listening.

"They knew even less than we thought," he answered. "They knew only that we were planning something at Martinique. There is no danger there. And Trent's death has shaken the other man, Crabb, so he will tell anything we ask."

"*Tres bien,*" said the First Face. Trent recognized the sinister, toneless voice which had given Borhel his orders. "We will examine him in detail later."

He turned back to his individual microphone, pressed a

button. "Captain Borhel," he said emotionlessly, "you will complete your report on final preparations."

Trent gazed out through the glass barrier. Borhel and at least sixty of the khaki-clad officers were packed into the other compartment. He saw a sprinkling of pilots with foreign uniforms. Several microphones dangled from the overhead, to pick up the officers' reports and questions.

"Dive-bomber pilots have been assigned to targets where our agents ashore have not been able to penetrate," Borhel stated. "Gas grenades will account for two-thirds of the island defenders—"

"Confine yourself to your own attack details," the First Face interrupted. "We are aware of all the plans at Martinique. Suffice to say, for benefit of those present, that the majority of the French defenders will be paralyzed or killed by poison-gas at one minute before the air attack is scheduled."

Trent's eyes shifted hurriedly across the long desk as the First Face was speaking. He saw a knob with a safety-catch, labeled "Gas—Main Chamber," beside a switch marked "Main Chamber Lock." Both of these were located in front of the First Face, as well as a small switchboard through which the microphone-speaker units could be connected with any part of the ship.

"The dive-bomber attacks will spread poison-gas at the shore positions marked '1' on all maps," Borhel continued. "The *Bearn* will be a primary target for the Dewoitine gas-layers and the Koolhovens. Any gunners ashore or on the carrier who are not overcome by the gas will be attacked at low altitude by the gas-layers the instant they open fire.

"Martinique and the *Bearn* will be taken within five minutes, by final estimate, and parachutists with machine guns and oxygen-masks will be dropped ashore and on the carrier exactly five minutes after the attack begins. By this time it is expected that the American Neutrality Patrol destroyers outside the harbor will have rushed their crews to battle stations. They will be attacked by dive-bombers with high explosive and gas and sunk as swiftly as possible after their crews are gassed. This carrier will approach the harbor as soon as resistance has been ended, and a skeleton crew will be transferred to the *Bearn,* to prepare her for sailing the instant the cargo is aboard."

"One moment," said the First Face, as a light flickered on the switchboard. Trent watched him make a connection, and again he saw the gas and main-chamber lock controls. If that outer compartment were the main chamber, then this must be some secret protection scheme the Four Faces had created against a sudden mutiny by a group beyond the glass barrier. Gas would act before mutineers could break through the glass with sledges or axes and reach their masters.

"Communications!" said the First Face. He snapped his microphone switch. "Captain Borhel, detail some one to find why Communications called and now fails to answer!"

Borhel gestured to one of the junior officers. As the man started for the exit, the First Face switched off the main-chamber lock. His sleeve dislodged several papers at his left, and Trent saw one headed in large type, "Report on Gold Stored at Martinique, by Agent M-17." A newspaper story on the millions in gold bullion rushed to Martinique from France, just before its surrender, flashed back into his mind. So this was the chief objective of the Four Faces!

The seizure of the *Bearn* was only secondary—but in this ruthless piracy they would set off a war. America would be blamed, accused of a raid on Martinique to steal both the gold and the carrier, to keep it from Nazi hands. France would declare war, at Hitler's order, and the United States would enter the battle.

THE REALIZATION of that grim result momentarily drove from his mind all thoughts of his own peril. But a shout, carried to his ears by main-chamber microphones, jerked his thoughts from this angle. The door was open, and a wild-eyed Four Faces officer had sprung inside.

"Captain Borhel! The *Richmond*—they've got our position—this damned American got into Communications—" he whirled around, and Trent froze. There, at the entrance, gripped by the two guards who had been in the passage, was Mortimer Crabb!

"You imbeciles!" the First Face cried hoarsely. He was on his feet, snarling into the microphone. "Whoever let that man free will die! Borhel—get to the bridge! I'll flash an order to change course to due west, full speed!"

Borhel leaped through the doorway, two officers at his heels.

"Bring the prisoner inside!" rasped the First Face. "We'll soon know what he told—"

He broke off with a stifled oath as Trent dived past the other masked figures and hurtled into him. Just as Crabb's captors started to shove him inside, Trent hit the lock-switch, and the main-chamber door whipped shut. Before the First Face could recover his balance, Trent jerked the poison-needle gun from under his robe.

"Stand up! Get against the bulkhead!" he ordered.

"Good God, he's gene mad!" the Second Face cried.

"You fool, that's not Zarahoff!" shouted the man Trent had knocked over. "We've been tricked!"

Out in the main chamber the assembled men were milling around wildly, some of them trying to break down the locked door. The First Face snatched at the lock-switch. Trent slammed a left to his jaw, and the man sprawled across the desk. As he fell, his black-gloved hand caught the gas-release knob. Instantly a steamy yellow vapor began to swirl down into the chamber outside from concealed outlets overhead. Screams of terror came through the loud-speaker behind the glass.

Trent swung the air-pistol to cover the masked men. All three cowered back, apparently stunned as much by the horror beyond the glass barrier as the threat of the poison-needles. Trent hastily plugged the microphone circuit to the socket marked "Bridge."

"Emergency order! Have a Blackburn started, put in take-off position immediately!"

The Third Face lunged as though to shout into the mike before him, shrank back as Trent twitched the gun at him. Trent pulled out the plug, then with one fierce jerk ripped the communications cable from the switchboard. Measuring the distance to the exit, he pressed the button-control. The steel door swung open. Just as it reached its full arc, he hit the toggle switch a blow with his fist, to close the circuit and break off the toggle.

The door instantly started to shut. He leaped past the cringing Third Face, slammed against the steel panel. A robed figure plunged after him, but he was through and the door clanged shut before the man could stop him.

"Excellency!" a voice gasped. The officer who had escorted him ran up from a connecting passage. "What has happened? I heard screams inside the Command Station!"

"We discovered three traitors had been working with Ganet!" Trent said harshly. "Where is prisoner?"

"The men are taking him to Detention. I thought—" the words died in a gurgle as Trent's left hand suddenly flipped his automatic from its holster. All in one move, Trent raised the gun and thudded it against the man's head. The officer collapsed without a sound, and Trent raced toward the Detention compartment, pulling the black robe above his knees to aid his speed. The two guards were about to handcuff Crabb.

"Get your hands up!" Trent flung at them. Dazedly, the two men backed away.

"GRAB THEIR guns, Mort!" Trent ordered. One of the men, suddenly realizing the deception, clawed at his pistol. Trent put a bullet through his arm, wrenched his gun away. Thirty seconds later, the two guards were manacled to the bulkhead and Trent and Crabb were running for the flight-deck ladder.

"Never mind how I made it!" Trent said breathlessly. "We're not out of the woods yet. If only they don't turn on the lights—"

The roar of an engine was audible as they came out on deck. Guided by the glow of the Blackburn's exhaust flash, Trent hauled the inventor toward the ship. A huge mechanic in dungarees jumped aside as he saw the black-robed figure loom alongside.

"Pull the chocks!" Trent said swiftly. He gave Crabb a boost, sprang toward the front pit. He was half-way inside when a siren screamed wildly above the drone of the engine. A spotlight lanced down at the Blackburn from the bridge. Trent gunned the engine, and the dive-bomber thundered down the deck. A machine gun came to life as the ship swept off the deck, and Trent nosed down to get speed. As he went into a tight turn Crabb cut loose with the rear guns.

Trent threw a hurried look back. Mechanics were frantically starting up the planes already on deck. He saw a Dewoitine race into the air, just as the carrier's elevator brought up a twin-motored Lockheed command-plane.

"Get on the radio and try to raise the *Richmond*. Warn them—planes with poison-gas!"

The Dewoitine drilled up steeply as Trent swung back toward the carrier. He reached out to pull the flare-release, so that he could see his target more clearly. But a furious burst from the French fighter drove him to hasty defense. He thumbed a blast at the Dewoitine, saw tracers carom from the side of the fuselage.

The lights had gone out on the carrier, but suddenly a searchlight poked up, some miles to the east. Trent banked for another attempt at bombing the carrier. That searchlight must be from the *Richmond*. If any of those Four Face gas-planes got off, the men on the cruiser would be doomed.

The Dewoitine charged in to head him off, and by the

glare of the searchlight he recognized Brohel in the cockpit. The captain was bareheaded, his face grim. Trent kicked out of the tracers, dived at the carrier. He was almost in line when Brohel plunged down furiously to force him aside. With a boot at the rudder, Trent flung a lightning burst at the French ship. Borhel crumpled as the Blackburn's guns gouged through the cockpit and Trent swung back, with the dive-bomber's blunt nose aimed dead on the carrier.

The Blackburn leaped as he snatched at the bomb pulls. Seconds, later, flame blossomed out below. He stared down. There was fire, and with, it a steamy yellowish vapor. High explosive and gas!

As he pulled up and away from that inferno where trapped pilots and deck crews were dying, shells began to blaze from the *Richmond's* guns, raising huge fountains around the carrier. He looked back at Mortimer Crabb, and the inventor nodded with gloomy satisfaction.

"I told them to give her the works!"

Trent climbed, banked abruptly as a plane loomed on his right. In the glare from the carrier's deck he had a glimpse of the Lockheed command-plane turning steeply to head east. A rigid, dead face and the dark shoulder of a black-robed figure showed at one window. The remaining three heads of the Invisible Empire had escaped, from the Command Station, as he had known they would. To open the jammed switch had probably taken little over a minute.

He thumbed the stick-button and the Blackburn's guns thrashed out a brief fusillade before the belts ran empty. The Lockheed swept into a chandelle, its mid-turret guns hurling a fiery stream of tracers across the dive-bomber's path. And before Trent could get into position for Crabb to use the rear guns, the Lockheed had vanished in the night.

He looked after it for a moment. At least, he had lopped one head from that four-headed monster of crime. Perhaps they would meet again. He turned, gazed down at the carrier.

Almost the whole deck was ablaze now, as the ship listed under the impact of the *Richmond's* shells.

"Call the cruiser, Mort," he shouted back at Crabb. "Tell them we'll put down on the water near them, and to have a boat waiting to pick us up."

Crabb looked down at the ill-fated carrier. "Too bad she can't be saved. Maybe I shouldn't have told them to open up, but I was afraid some of those gas-planes would get off."

"It's better this way," said Trent. "There'd be too many ghosts aboard her if they ever put her back into service."

They were silent a moment as Trent flew toward the cruiser. The glare from the burning ship suddenly began to fade.

"There she goes!" exclaimed Crabb. "She's half under, going down plenty fast!"

Trent took one last look at the doomed ghost-ship. Then, as the vessel's bow went down for its plunge to oblivion, he reached up and took off the Four Face mask. With a grimace, he tossed it out into the deepening shadows. It fell toward the sea and was quickly lost from sight.

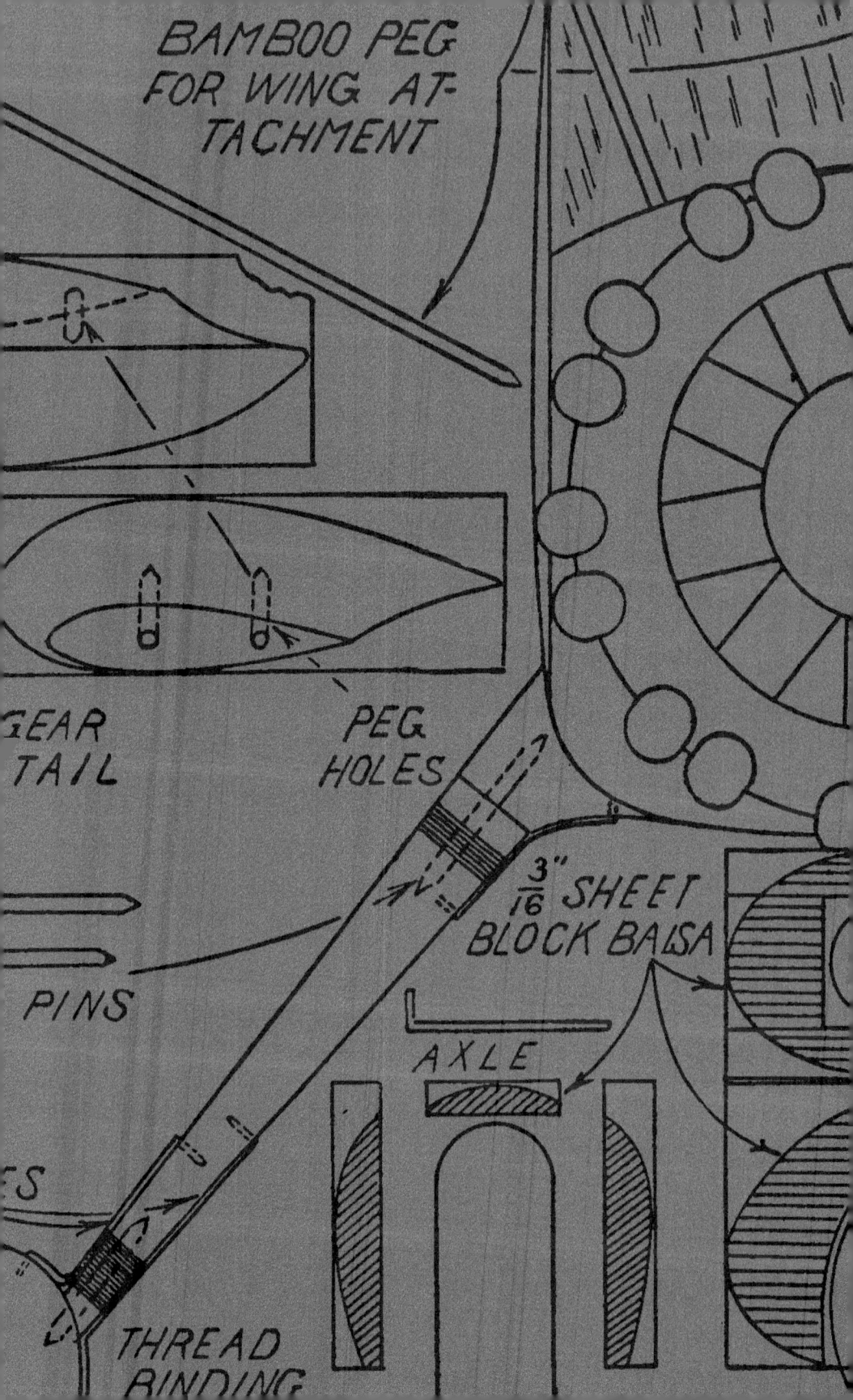

BAMBOO PEG
FOR WING AT-
TACHMENT

GEAR
TAIL

PEG
HOLES

PINS

$\frac{3"}{16}$ SHEET
BLOCK BALSA

AXLE

ES

THREAD
BINDING

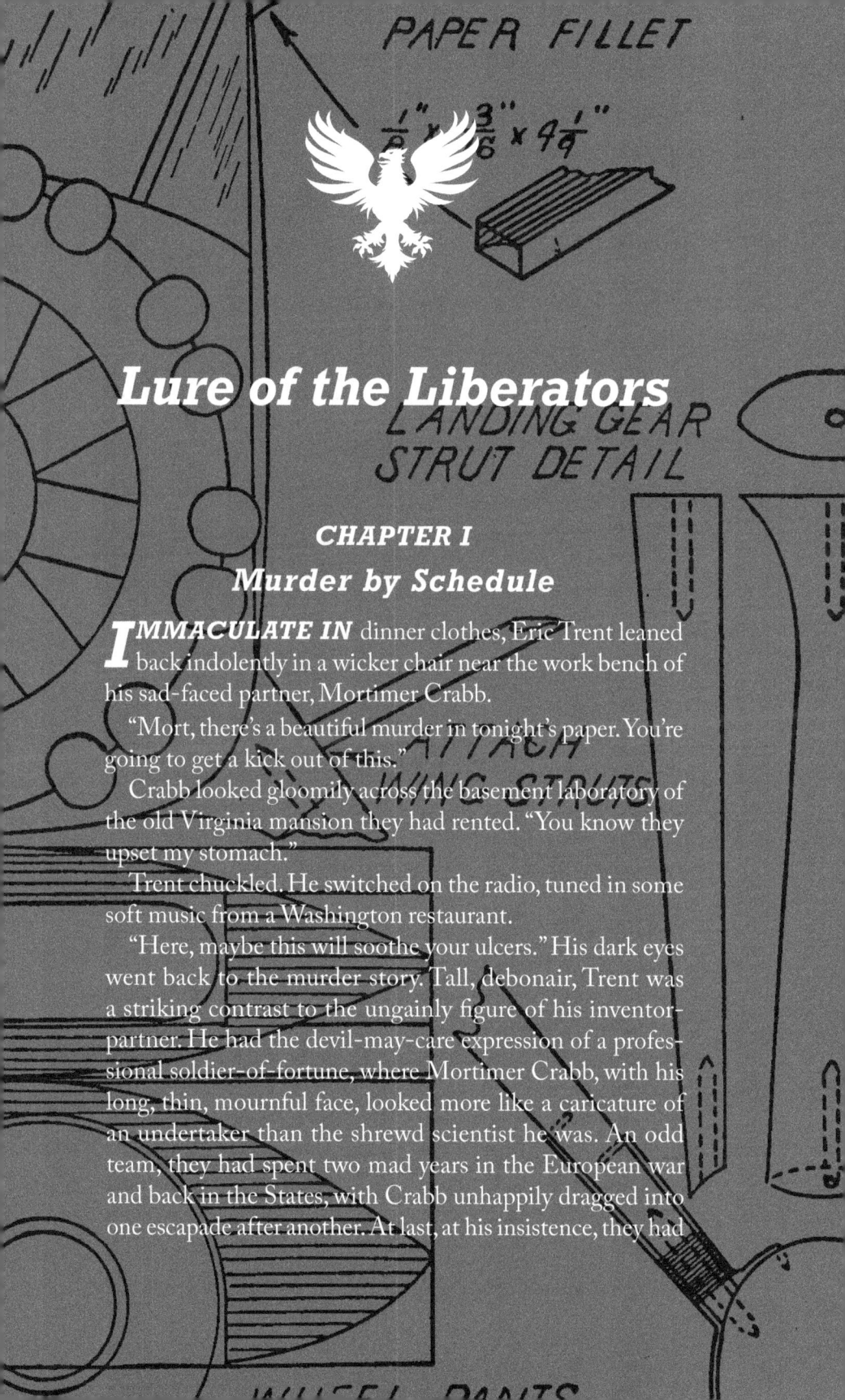

Lure of the Liberators

CHAPTER I
Murder by Schedule

IMMACULATE IN dinner clothes, Eric Trent leaned back indolently in a wicker chair near the work bench of his sad-faced partner, Mortimer Crabb.

"Mort, there's a beautiful murder in tonight's paper. You're going to get a kick out of this."

Crabb looked gloomily across the basement laboratory of the old Virginia mansion they had rented. "You know they upset my stomach."

Trent chuckled. He switched on the radio, tuned in some soft music from a Washington restaurant.

"Here, maybe this will soothe your ulcers." His dark eyes went back to the murder story. Tall, debonair, Trent was a striking contrast to the ungainly figure of his inventor-partner. He had the devil-may-care expression of a professional soldier-of-fortune, where Mortimer Crabb, with his long, thin, mournful face, looked more like a caricature of an undertaker than the shrewd scientist he was. An odd team, they had spent two mad years in the European war and back in the States, with Crabb unhappily dragged into one escapade after another. At last, at his insistence, they had settled temporarily at this Virginia retreat.

Only a few miles across the Potomac from Washington, the old Mansion had belonged to a recluse who had built a high wall, topped with spikes and barbed wire, and a heavy gate with special electric control. To discourage any determined visitors from climbing the wall, Crabb had electrified the barbed-wire with enough current to shock without killing.

Trent read on for a minute, absently practicing a coin-trick, then looked up again.

"This is peculiarly interesting, Mort. Sure you don't want to hear it?"

Crabb wiped his hands on his linen duster, inserted a valve at the end of a metal hose. "All I'm interested in," he said morosely, "is getting this smoke-screen release fixed. I promised the Army I'd give them a demonstration tomorrow—and stop practicing those infernal magic tricks. You make me nervous."

Trent brought the gyro around quickly
to give Mort a clear shot with his
swivel guns. And then, hurtling into
the battle, came three fighters!

Trent laughed. "Sorry, old bean, but I have to keep brushing up. If we go broke, I may have to return the stage as a magician. But don't worry, I won't forget you. You can be my assistant and help pull rabbits out of the hat."

Crabb snorted. Trent hid a grin, lazily moved his hand. The coin appeared to vanish in thin air. He snapped his fingers, produced a lighted cigarette from nowhere, inhaled contentedly.

"By the way, Mort, remember Rene Cheval?"

Crabb's adam's-apple jerked up and down angrily. "That dirty traitor! As if I could ever forget—"

"Cheval," Trent said pleasantly, "is the man who was murdered."

"Cheval—murdered? How? Where?"

"New York. They found him last night, but they think he was killed the night before. He had a pent-house apartment, so it's obvious he made off with some money when he escaped from Belgium. He'd been living under an assumed name."

"Who killed him?" grated Crabb.

"No clues. The pent-house doors were locked on the inside, and the police had to break them down to get in. Somebody got alarmed when Cheval didn't answer his phone today. He'd gone up in his private elevator, and they found it at his floor with the doors open, so the killer didn't get out that way. There's no fire escape, and the pent-house is twenty floors above the nearest roof."

"Must have been suicide—the rat," Crabb said in a sepulchral voice.

"It's a bit difficult to shoot yourself three times in the back," Trent said whimsically.

"Well, whoever did it, it's good riddance. I'll never forget the night the Nazis caught us in that secret Belgian radio station, after Cheval tipped them off to save his hide. And Smythe grabbing at that Nazi's Bren gun to save the rest of us."

Trent's face sobered a moment. "Poor old Smythe. He saved us, and Luttre, the Belgian major— Say, I just remembered! Luttre's been a refugee here for months. I wonder if he caught up with Cheval."

"I hope he did," Crabb said grimly. He switched on a lathe, started to buff the valve-seat. Trent finished his cigarette, stood up.

"If I can't persuade you to join me for dinner over in town, I'll run along. I've already got the car out, so switch over the gate control."

CRABB SHUT off the lathe, turned to a switchboard, from which he controlled most of his working-models, including a fog-piercing light, a dive-bomber siren and two scream-sirens for bombs, a new talking-beacon, and several other devices. Above each knife-blade switch was a neat label. Crabb threw a two-way lever labeled "Gate," closing a radio-relay circuit by which the gate could be opened by a button on the dash of the car. Trent looked at the switchboard and grinned.

"Mort, you need a special engineer.—" he stopped short, as the radio music abruptly ended. An announcer's crisp voice followed:

"We interrupt to bring you a special bulletin. A second mysterious murder, paralleling the unsolved case of Rene Cheval, French refugee, has just been discovered in Philadelphia. Major Paul Luttre, refugee from Belgium, was found dead at 5:10 this afternoon. Apparently he had been killed last night. Three bullets had been fired into his back by the unknown murderer."

As the bulletin ended, Crabb stared at Trent.

"Luttre! Why would anyone want to get rid of him?"

"I've a queer feeling it's connected with that Brussels—"

There was a crash, and splintering glass fell from a barred basement window. As Trent spun around the snout of a Tommy-gun poked between the bars.

"Raise your hands—both of you!" commanded the man behind the gun. His face was shrouded in the darkness, but his voice sent an electric tingling down Trent's spine. That thick, guttural note was unmistakable. It was the Nazi Gestapo agent who had killed Smythe in the raid on that secret station at Brussels!

"Stand where you are, Mr. Trent," the Nazi ordered hoarsely. "Mr. Crabb, you will unlock the basement door. And remember, I can see you if you try any trick."

Trent remained motionless where he had halted in front of the switchboard, but he flicked a side glance at Crabb.

"Do what he says, Mort. Don't try anything—he's got the drop on us."

Swearing under his breath, the inventor unbarred the door. A swarthy man with a leather jacket and helmet sprang inside, gun in hand.

"Turn your back!" he snarled.

"Not yet, *Dumkopf!*" the Nazi at the window broke in hastily. "The orders were first to make them open the safe—Crabb is working on Army inventions, and we are to take any plans we find."

The words were in German. Trent gave no sign that he understood, but from the corner of his eye he watched as the swarthy German approached, marching Crabb ahead of him. There was an instant when the man's eyes shifted toward the safe. In a lightning movement, Trent threw himself backward against the switchboard.

With a deafening screech, the dive-bomber siren went on just as the blinding rays of the fog-piercing light stabbed at the wall with the windows. Trent hurled himself to one side, lashed out at the German's right forearm. The pistol blazed as the man's finger contracted, but the bullet went into the floor. Before he could fire another shot, a mighty blow from Crabb's fist sent him thudding against the switchboard, knocking the siren switch open.

Flame jetted from the muzzle of the Tommy-gun and Trent saw the man behind it, his face taut with rage as he fired blindly toward the fog-light. A strangled cry rose above the snarl of the machine gun, and the swarthy Nazi toppled to the floor. Trent snatched up his pistol, pumped two shots at the window. There was a clanging sound and the whine of a ricochet, and then through the broken window Trent heard the thud of running feet.

"Come on!" he told Crabb, and they ran for the basement door. The rays of the fog-light were streaming out into the dark and Trent saw the Tommy-gun on the ground. The magazine was empty. The Nazi agent was running toward an autogyro which stood fifty feet inside the wall. Half-way to the ship he flung a look over his shoulder and saw Trent and Crabb. At the same moment Trent realized that the gyro's engine was dead, was not turning over.

"Look out, Mort—the car!" he shouted. But even as he gave the warning, the German sprinted desperately toward the machine. Trent pitched a shot after him as he leaped under the wheel.

THE MOTOR roared and the car plunged down the drive. Screaming in second gear, it smashed headlong into the gate. There was a crashing of broken headlights, fenders, and bumper as the gate went down. Then the car lurched drunkenly out onto the road and turned toward Washington. Trent wheeled to his partner.

"Get that gyro's engine started! I'll be right back."

He raced to the basement, hastily searched the dead German. In one pocket was a hotel key, in another a wallet and a Washington guidebook. The other pockets yielded nothing of importance. The sputter of the gyro engine was settling into a steady drone when he reached the ship. Crabb hurriedly relinquished the pilot's seat.

"You take it! I don't know how to fly these things."

Trent snapped his safety belt. "Hang onto your hat, Mort. Here we go!"

The engine revved up and the motor suddenly whirled to top speed. With a breathtaking upward leap, the gyro jumped twenty feet in the air and then swung ahead under Trent's skillful touch.

"You crazy idiot!" grated Crabb. "You're supposed to take at least a little run with these things."

"Not this baby," said Trent. "Our friends have presented us with a 'Leaping Lena'—one of the new jump-gyros. They're made for operating off British freighters in convoys."

He had slid the cockpit enclosure shut. Now he swooped down over the road, trying to spot the fleeing Nazi.

"There are a hundred cars down there," howled Crabb. "You'll never pick him out—and what could you do, anyway?"

"Unless the Brownings they've got hidden under this cowl are made out of wood, I can do plenty. What's that sliding hatch behind you?"

Crabb twisted around. "The devils have got another gun

hidden there! But we can't go blasting at him—we might hit the wrong man. Besides, that's a brand-new car!"

"Fine time to be thinking about money, when the Gestapo is on our neck," said Trent. "That blood-thirsty lad down there is the bird who killed Smythe. He and his confederate were probably the ones who murdered Cheval and Luttre. The gyro would explain how they got at Cheval. They could have easily landed on the pent-house's terrace and jumped off again after killing him."

"But why?" demanded Crabb. "Why should the Nazis want to wipe out Luttre and Cheval?"

"And us," said Trent. "We're in on it, too. For some reason, they evidently want to get rid of everybody who was in that cellar at Brussels. We were third on their murder schedule."

Crabb shivered. "Well, thanks to you they missed connections. Hey—look out!"

Trent had nosed the gyro down steeply. They skimmed over a line of cars at the approach to the Highway Bridge. Trent pulled up as astonished motorists gaped at them, disgustedly shook his head.

"Wrong car. He gave us the slip, all right. Take over while I see if this stuff will help us any."

The inventor gingerly took the controls, climbed out of the Memorial Highway lights. The ceiling was low, with only an occasional break, and he held the ship at six-hundred feet. Trent inspected the German's wallet and hotel-key under the instrument-board light.

"Hotel Plaza-Grand, Room 817... H-m-m, plenty of folding money here, but no identifications. From this guide-book it looks as though he's been putting on a tourist act. Several places here are marked. 'Be sure to see this.'"

Trent was holding the guide-book closer to the light when Crabb gave an ejaculation. The next instant, landing-lights flared through the gloom, focussing on the gyro.

"Grab it, Eric!" Crabb yelled. "Get us out of here—I can't see!"

Trent seized the controls, banked swiftly. One of the lights angled after them, brightly flooding the ship. Trent pulled up in a full-throttle climb. He had barely hauled the stick back when four glowing streaks of tracer shot past the nose of the ship. With a crescendo screech that rose above the drone of the gyro's engine, a Curtiss P-40 hurtled down through the glare of light.

CHAPTER II
Fugitive Flight

TRENT THREW the gyro into another hasty turn. He shook off the dazzling light-beam for a moment and the P-40 roared past. As the fighter twisted back, he had a brief glimpse of the passenger plane. It was a four-engined Consolidated bomber with the regulation running-lights.

The Consolidated banked sharply as the P-40 charged again at the gyro. One of its lights flashed across the tail of the gyro, but Trent zoomed out of the rays before they could blind him.

"Give that P-40 a burst!" he shouted back at Crabb.

"Are you crazy?" Crabb howled. "That's an Army ship!"

"Army or not, I don't like bullets!" Trent snapped the gun-circuit switch, tripped the hidden Brownings on his cowl. The fighter twisted aside, its tracers just missing the rotor. Trent heard a muffled yell above the din of engines and he saw Crabb jerk the concealed rear-cockpit gun up into firing position.

"Hold it—I'll give you a dead shot!" he ordered. The Curtiss job was curling back from the top of a swift chandelle. Trent banked hastily, threw in the rotor switch. The gyro gave a wild leap, and the P-40's tracers blazed into empty space. In a furious attempt to down the gyro before he overshot, the fighter pilot ruddered into a brief skid. Trent yanked the throttle shut and the P-40 catapulted on past, its tracers lancing over the Consolidated. The big bomber nosed down, plunged across the Potomac toward Bolling Field.

The gyro had come almost to a complete stop in mid-air. Just as it started to settle, Mortimer Crabb snapped a fiery blast from the .30-.30. The P-40 gave a crazy lurch, then zoomed frantically. Searchlights from Bolling Field and the Naval Air Station were pawing at the sky, and Trent saw the fighter's insignia just before it disappeared in the lowering clouds.

It was a Royal Canadian Air Force plane!

He opened the throttle, climbed the gyro after the fighter. There was a small break in the clouds, but when he climbed through it was too dark to see anything. He cruised away from the glowing spots where searchlights probed at the overcast, then let down a few miles West of the Potomac.

"Drop that gun back out of sight," he directed Crabb. "We're going to pay a little visit to Bolling, and I don't want them to get off on the wrong foot."

"I never knew it to fail," Crabb said dismally. "Just when everything's nice and calm, you drag me into some mess and I nearly get killed."

Trent looked back in mock indignation.

"I suppose I hired those Nazis to start the ball rolling. A lot of gratitude I get, saving your neck."

"Why the devil did that Army pilot jump us, anyway?" grated Crabb.

"He wasn't an Army pilot—not our army, at least. That was a Canadian job. I'm wondering about that Boeing pilot, too. Maybe it was just to keep clear of us that he spotted us with his lights, but that P-40 pilot certainly had a good target."

"I was a fool to get into this ship," Crabb said sourly. "If I had any brains I'd never get within a thousand miles of you."

"Think of the excitement you'd miss," grinned Trent. He headed the gyro across the river, letting it settle slowly as they approached Bolling Field. The floodlights were on, and he saw the Consolidated in front of a hangar, with a crowd of men around it. Several cars were parked nearby. The gyro was four hundred feet from the ground when some one saw it. A guard detail came running as Trent landed, and four rifles instantly covered them.

"Well, well, the reception committee," said Trent. He cut the engine, climbed out.

"That's the plane that attacked us!" a voice said fiercely,

and a big, raw-boned RCAF squadron-leader pushed his way through the crowd of Air Corps officers and mechanics. Back in the glare of the floodlights Trent saw thirty or forty other men in RCAF uniform.

"You're under arrest—both of you!" barked an Air Corps major who had followed the squadron-leader. He turned to a pompous, middle-aged man in civilian clothes. "It's all right, General. We've nabbed them."

"Now that you've all spoken your little pieces," Trent said amiably, "suppose you listen to mine."

"Eric Trent!" sputtered the general. "What the—have you lost your—"

"Now, now, General, think of your high blood pressure. Mort, you remember General Busby, assistant chief of G-2. We gave him some slight help in the Red Devil affair."

Crabb nodded gloomily, and the Canadian squadron-leader looked blankly at the general.

"But they fired on us, sir! It was obviously a plot to block our plans."

"There must be some mistake, Woring," muttered Busby. "These two men have helped the Government several times on special jobs. As a matter of fact, Mr. Crabb is right now working on a device for the Army."

He turned to the Air Corps major. "Get that crowd back, Major Kendall. I want to talk with these men privately."

KENDALL ORDERED the guard detail to release Trent and Crabb, and in a few moments only General Busby and Woring remained with them.

"Now, Trent," Busby said huffily, "suppose you explain—"

"I still think you're making a grave mistake, General," Woring broke in. His cold blue eyes rested on Trent. "I've heard this man's name before. He was mixed-up in some affair in France—"

"He's always mixed up in some crazy business," growled Busby. "But he's no traitor, or he wouldn't have exposed that Nazi Red Devil scheme."

"Thanks for the kind words, General," chuckled Trent. "Here's what happened." He described the murder-attempt at the mansion and what had followed. Woring had a stare of plain disbelief and even Busby looked dubious when he finished.

"Don't take my word for it," said Trent. "You can find the German's body in the basement. By the way, what about that P-40?" he added, turning to the squadron-leader.

"Just what I was about to ask you," Woring said caustically. "The pilot appeared to be working with you."

"Are you blind?" snorted Mortimer Crabb. "He was doing his best to kill us."

"All I know, you both fired on us," Woring retorted.

"Stop this wrangling," snapped Busby. "Trent's story is a little fantastic at first thought, but after remembering other things done by the Purple Legion it's not so hard to believe."

"Purple Legion, eh?" said Trent. "Apparently I haven't been keeping up with my reading."

Busby hesitated, with a quick glance at Woring. The squadron-leader shrugged.

"We've kept it quiet," the general said, "but since you've been dragged into this you may as well know about it. England's bought twenty-six Consolidated B-24 bombers—they're calling the ship the Liberator."

Trent nodded. "I know. Range 3,500, top speed 340, power-driven .50-calibre turrets, four tons of bombs, ceiling 36,000 and other highly secret details that everybody knows. By the way, just what happened to the Liberator that left La Guardia Field and never reached England?"

Both Woring and Busby gave a start.

"How'd you know that?" demanded the general.

"Private Intelligence service. Was that your Purple Legion?"

"It was," growled Busby. "Five minutes after it took off, we received an anonymous message signed 'The Purple Legion,' saying the bomber was doomed. We tried to contact it by radio, but they never answered. Nobody ever saw it again."

Trent glanced past him, at the open door of a hangar.

"So now you're sending them off from here, under Air Corps auspices?"

"The RCAF is taking them over after factory pilots fly them to Bolling," admitted Busby. "But there's more than just an Atlantic ferrying job to it. The Nazis have two surface raiders in the North Atlantic. British Intelligence thinks it's learned their approximate area of operations. These bombers are going over, with, a full load of eggs, hoping to spot the raiders. They're going to spread out and cover a 180-mile lane. If they don't find the Nazi warships, then they'll unload their eggs on the French and Belgian invasion-ports before making a landing in England."

"A neat scheme," said Trent. "And the Purple Legion is threatening to spoil the party?"

"You're a good guesser, Mr. Trent," Woring said stiffly. "Almost too good."

"Oh, it's really nothing. Anyone can do it with a little practice." Trent winked at Mortimer Crabb, looked back at the general. "When do the Liberators take-off?"

"Pretty soon. The ships will be ready in an hour, but we're waiting for a British Embassy attache. He has to take the senior pilots to the Embassy for special orders. All the RCAF men were flown down here from Canada."

Woring looked at his wrist-watch. "The attache should be here by now." His eyes shifted back to Trent. "You have no clue to the identity of the men whom you say attacked you?"

"Eric, you've forgotten about the key!" broke in Crabb. "That ought to—"

"How stupid of me," said Trent. "I completely forgot. When I searched the man who was killed I found a hotel key—but I was in such a hurry to get to the gyro I didn't even notice what hotel it was. I left it back there on a workbench."

"And you call yourself smart!" fumed Busby. He spun around, shouted for an orderly. "Get my car!"

"No need for that," said Trent. "We can fly back in the gyro and land there before you could even reach the bridge. I'll phone you the name and room number, and anything else we find."

"All right, I'll be at Operations," said the general.

Trent turned to Crabb, who was looking at him goggle-eyed. "Hop in, Mort. Leaping Lena awaits."

CRABB CLIMBED in, and Trent was halfway into the front cockpit when a long black car halted at the edge of the line. A heavy-set man with a briefcase jumped out, hurried toward Woring and Busby. Woring raised his hand in a hasty gesture.

"Ah, there's Captain Smythe now," exclaimed Busby.

Trent stood motionless, staring at the newcomer's grim, blocky features. Mortimer Crabb's jaw had dropped in sudden amazement.

"Smythe!" Trent said incredulously. "I thought you were dead!" Smythe jerked to a stop, glaring up at him and Crabb.

"You butchers! So it was you who killed Luttre and Cheval to hide what you did to me!"

General Busby gaped at him. "What's this? I don't underst—"

"They're traitors!" Smythe broke in savagely. "They sold out to Hitler—betrayed me to the Gestapo and left me for dead one night in Brussels."

Busby wheeled toward the gyro, a stunned look on his face. "Trent, in the name of Heaven—"

"I tell you they're killers!" rasped Smythe. "Trent's the secret head of the Purple Legion! We just learned how they killed Rene Cheval, landed that gyro on his pent-house—"

The guard detail was running toward the scene, with the crowd at their heels. Trent flung himself down at the controls, snapped ignition and starter switches.

"Stop them!" bawled the general. "Don't let them take-off!"

The roar of the engine drowned the rest and Trent swiftly locked in the rotor. The gyro's vertical leap took them clear just in time. Rifles blazed below. Trent transferred power to the propeller, and the ship thundered away in a steep climb. By the time the searchlights came on, the gyro was in the edge of the clouds.

"Now you've done it," groaned Crabb. "You nincompoop, do you realize we're fugitives from justice?"

"Fugitives from three shots in the back, you mean," amended Trent. "For a second there, Mort, we were almost finished by those boys."

"And what are we now?" Crabb moaned. "It was bad enough, having Smythe come back like that, accusing us—"

"Don't worry your gray matter over Smythe," said Trent. "We've a job to do. How long will it take you to hook that smoke-screen gadget up in this bus?"

"Maybe half an hour, for temporary use. But what's that got to do—"

"A lot—but we can't spare half an hour. You'll have to fix it after we take-off. They'll be after us like hornets."

"Why didn't you stay there and explain to Smythe?" insisted Crabb.

"From the looks of things, you and I would have been reposing in a cell—or on a marble slab—before midnight. And I'm opposed to both as a matter of principle."

"Do you realize Smythe actually thinks we sold him out? He thinks *we* did what we know Cheval did, and that we got rid of Luttre and Cheval to cover up."

"After the bullets that Nazi put through him that night, it's a miracle he's here to think at all," said Trent. "We can straighten out matters with Smythe later. Right now, I'm wondering about that P-40 pilot. If he bailed out, he may have been ordered to go to our place and remove the evidence. They obviously tipped him off by radio from some secret shortwave station near here before he attacked us, and they might do it again."

"Who tipped him off?"

"Whoever engineered that attack on us. Probably the Nazi who escaped in our car got to a phone and called their short-wave station, so they could warn the P-40 guy to be on the look out for us, to keep us from spilling the well-known beans."

"It's getting too deep for me," Crabb said dismally. "You said somebody was trying to get rid of Luttre and Cheval and us to cover up the Brussels business. And now Smythe pops up—"

"Did you notice the mud on that Stratoliner's wheels?" Trent broke in suddenly.

"No. Anyway, what of it?"

"I'm beginning to get a glimmer—but we'd never convince Busby if we went back now. We'll have to go it alone."

Trent warily let down through the overcast, swung back, and began an almost vertical descent toward the mansion. One or two blips of the engine carried them into position for a landing inside the wall.

The shattered gate lay where it had fallen, and there was no sign of anyone in the grounds. Trent left the engine idling, and they made their way to the basement.

"I'll switch off the fog-light," said Trent. "Hook that smoke-screen release tube up to a small tank that we can put in the ship, while I get a couple of automatics." Trent set out in search of the fire-arms.

CRABB QUICKLY set to work. Trent went upstairs, to a huge closet they had converted into a storeroom. Several souvenirs of the European war were piled in one corner. A chest of magician's paraphernalia and props stood in the other, near a locked case. He took two .38s from the case, delved into the magician's chest. Slipping a ring of skeleton keys into his pocket, he took off his coat and fastened on a shoulder harness with a dangling strap and a rubber tube ending in a bulb. Then he bent over a compartment filled with prop pistols, knives, magnetized wands, and other implements.

A few moments later, coat in place, he left the closet. He was starting for the stairway when the phone rang shrilly. He picked up the handset.

"Le Fung Lo, laundlee," he said in a singsong tone. "What you want, pleece?"

"Damn that operator!" came General Busby's infuriated voice. "Gave me some blasted Chinese laundry."

The receiver crackled as he hung up. Trent grinned, went downstairs. Crabb had already carried the smokescreen apparatus out to the gyro, and was at work in the rear pit.

"I've got the tank behind the rear seat," he told Trent. "Poke a hole near the tail and I'll slip the tube back there. I'll connect the valve to the other end after we take-off."

In another minute the tube was in place, and Trent climbed into the pilot's seat.

"Hold on!" the inventor burst out. "Before we start on any more lunatic rides, I want to know what's up. Why'd you want that smoke-tank?"

"I'm going to do a little skywriting, to a blonde over in town," Trent said confidentially.

"Don't be funny! Anyway, that smoke's black—it won't show at night."

"That's all right. She's so dumb she won't know the difference."

"If you think I'm going with you without even knowing what—" Crabb's angry protest ended with a gulp as Leaping Lena jumped into mid-air and started across the wall.

"As you were saying?" queried Trent.

"Go ahead," Crabb said bitterly. "Land me in jail. Get me executed for murder and treason. I deserve it for ever tying up with a maniac like you."

"If you insist, we're going to pay a little call, over at the Plaza-Grand."

"You don't mean we're going to land on the roof?" Crabb said in dismay.

"Why not? It's a trifle small, I admit. But I've seen a couple of hundred dancers packed together on it, when the roof-garden was open. Fortunately for our purposes, it's not quite roof-garden weather yet."

"If I had a parachute, I'd leave you flat," Crabb said morosely.

"It'd be a trifle chilly, dropping into the Potomac tonight. Here, take this guide-book and help me spot the Grand-Plaza when we get over Washington," Trent answered.

"What if people see us landing?"

"People never look up that high unless they see lights or hear noise. We're going to omit lights and come in dead-stick."

Crabb groaned, bent lugubriously over the guide-book. They cruised across the Potomac, came in over George-town, and angled South over the city. Trent climbed close to the clouds. He had located the Grand-Plaza and was about to cut off the engine for a silent landing when without the slightest warning the RCAF P-40 charged out of the mists above them. But for his jerk at the throttle, the gyro would have been caught in that first furious burst.

Trent hurriedly swung toward the river, engine now full on. This time, Mortimer Crabb needed no urging. The rear-pit Browning clattered into action as the fighter whipped around in a vertical bank. Trent saw his solitary tracer-stream go wide of the twisting P-40.

"Give him the smoke!" he shouted.

The gyro trembled as solid slugs from the P-40's guns drilled the turtleback. Tracers scorched over Trent's head for an instant, then they suddenly veered off. Trent saw the black smoke spurting from the gyro's tail and he swiftly nosed down as though the ship were hit. The P-40's guns went dark. With a violent zoom, Trent jerked the gyro's nose up at the fighter, and his thumb rammed the stick-button.

Streams of hot lead followed by phosphorescent tracer slugs streaked Steadily at the bull's-eye markings on the Canadian craft.

CHAPTER III
The Purple Legion

THE RIGHT wing of the P-40 crumpled under a direct hit, and the wrecked fighter pitched onto its side, went plummeting down toward the river. Trent pulled the gyro up to the very edge of the clouds, swinging in a wide circle. Mortimer Crabb had shut off the chemical smoke.

"Well, I hope you're satisfied," he said gloomily. "Now we've got another crime chalked up against us."

"Don't let your conscience bother you," Trent told him. "I could knock off a dozen killers like that and still eat a hearty dinner. And speaking of dinner, it's just dawned on me that I'm starved."

"How can you talk of eating at a time like this?" Crabb shook his head. "I suppose you had this all figured out, to use the smoke like that."

"Well, it was the general idea—sort of a cuttlefish trick to protect ourselves if we met somebody we couldn't handle. But I didn't expect anyone to believe we were on fire. Can't think how I overlooked the possibility."

"Your brain must be slipping," Crabb said sarcastically. "That is, if it still has anywhere to slip to."

"I'm afraid you're right, Mort," Trent said in a contrite tone. "I've handled this pretty badly."

"What are you up to?" Crabb said with suspicion. "First time I ever heard you admit you'd made a mistake."

"Just thinking maybe I'd better land somewhere else and drop you off, before I head for the Plaza-Grand. You can wait and see—"

"Are you intimating I'm scared to go through with this?" roared Crabb.

"Not a bit, old bean. But I'll admit it's a cockeyed notion.

All I've got to go on is a hunch. If we're caught this time, well—"

"We're not caught yet," snapped Crabb. "After what I've been through in the last two years, I guess I can stand another night of it."

Trent smiled to himself. He had known that the inventor would stay on the job with him.

"Mort, your bark's worse than your bite."

"Never mind my bark. Go ahead and spot that hotel again. If my figuring is anywhere near right, we'll only have about five minutes before a car could reach there from Bolling Field."

"Two minds with one thought. Well, here we go."

Trent let the gyro hover a few moments to get the wind drift. Then he started down toward the hotel roof. Washington was a maze of lights, with the Capitol dome and the Washington Monument standing out prominently.

Engine silent, the ship settled perpendicularly the last hundred feet. Trent brought the nose up in a last-second stall, and the gyro dropped lightly onto the roof. He set the parking-brake and took a quick look around. There was no one in sight.

"Seems to be okey this far," he whispered to Crabb. "Here, take this .38. If we get in a jam, use the butt unless it's necessary to shoot."

The inventor followed as Trent tiptoed across the roof for a hurried glance down into the street, ten floors below. No one was looking up as far as could be seen.

"Come on, we'll have to move fast." Trent led the way to the service rooms which were used when the roof-garden was open. The door was locked, but it yielded to the second master-key he tried. He left it slightly ajar, and they crept down the service stairs.

"Two floors below," Trent said in an undertone.

WHEN THEY reached the eighth floor, he peered out cautiously into the hall. A bellhop was coming down the corridor with a telegram. Trent waited until the boy had delivered it and left, then motioned Crabb to follow.

A light showed over the transom of Room 817, and a muffled voice was faintly audible from within. Trent put his ear to the door.

"It's our killer friend—the one who got away," he whispered to Crabb. "I think he's telephoning someone, but I can't hear what he's saying."

He tried again, then tiptoed to the room adjoining 817 and took out his keyring. An adjustable master-key slid noiselessly into the lock, and a moment later the door swung open.

"Lock it, while I try that connecting-door," he told Crabb in an undertone.

The connecting-door was locked on the other side, but the voice of the Nazi killer was louder now. Trent heard a guttural "Thanks," then a brief silence. It was followed almost at once by the jangle of the telephone bell. There was a brief interval.

"Hello," the unseen Nazi said. "Yes—this is Schill. Where are you?"

Another brief interval, then:

"Don't worry about those two. I just called one of the newspaper offices, after I heard about that air fight. They caught on fire and fell in the river.... *Ja*, the fighter did, too. But maybe it is a good thing. We don't need him any more.... Yes, I tell you it is safe up here. No police have come, or anyone.... Yes, I can look in the lobby before you come up."

The phone clattered onto its cradle, and Trent heard the door of 817 open and shut.

"Come on, here's our chance," he whispered to Crabb. They waited a few seconds, then went into the hall. Trent unlocked the door of 817, made a quick survey of the room. The light was still on and a packed bag stood at one side. There was a flat leather packet beside it.

"Listen for the elevator," Trent told the inventor; then he hurriedly opened the packet. A carefully drawn sketch lay on top of a folded map. He recognized at a glance that it was a chart showing the location of their Virginia retreat. He opened the map, saw that it covered Washington and its suburbs. Replacing both papers, he quickly opened the traveling bag. A gun with a Maxim silencer met his eyes first. Between the wadded up shirts beneath it were several Tommy-gun magazines, loaded.

"Look out—someone's coming!" Crabb said hoarsely.

Trent snapped the bag shut, sprang to the door. He had barely time to lock it and follow Crabb to a fire-escape alcove diagonally across the hall when the footsteps of three or four men sounded.

"If you hadn't bungled your job, this wouldn't have happened," he heard Woring's surly voice. The man was speaking German.

"Keep quiet," another muttered. Crabb grasped Trent's arm.

"Isn't that Smythe?" he whispered. Trent nodded, risked a swift glance as he heard the door of 817 open. Schill, the Gestapo agent, stood at one side, with a smaller man whose beak nose and close-set eyes gave him a hawklike appearance. Woring and Smythe were halfway into the room.

As the door closed, Trent and Crabb silently re-entered the adjoining room. Trent leaned against the connecting-door, heard Schill's protesting voice.

"It wasn't my fault. How was I to know they had a lot of trick lights and sirens down there? They all went off at once and I thought a Stuka had hit the place. The light blinded me—"

"It's done now," Smythe said coldly. "Thanks to good luck—and my quick thinking—it didn't ruin us. I managed to scare Trent and that sour-faced partner of his into running for it, so Busby and the rest of them don't suspect anything."

"What if Trent called Busby and gave him a warning before they crashed?" Woring asked in an uneasy tone. "Trent must have begun to see through it."

"Busby tried to call him, at the place in Virginia," Smythe answered. "He couldn't get any answer. It must have worked out just as I expected. Trent went back and found the key that Weiman had, and then he and Crabb started for here in the autogyro. We could probably have caught them before they asked the management too many questions, but Martz saved us the trouble—even if we did lose him."

"We'd better call Hans, at the field," Woring said anxiously. "I told him to be at that booth telephone in the canteen, so he could warn our men if anything went wrong."

"Go down and dial him from a lobby booth," Smythe ordered. "It was dangerous enough calling Schill on this line. Don't take any more chance that a hotel operator might listen in."

"I'm glad they sent you to handle this, Mannrich," Woring said nervously. "Creating that Purple Legion scheme was a masterpiece, and tonight I'd have been sunk if you hadn't turned the tables on those snooping fools."

"I've been a year training for this," Smythe answered, with a touch of complacency. "It naturally shows results. Go make the call. Tell Hans all is well, that the plan is unchanged. Tell him to have the crews ready to take-off the instant we return to Bolling Field. Then wait in the lobby. I'll phone Busby from here to have the engines warmed up and ready and then we'll join you."

TRENT STEPPED back from the connecting-door, felt his way through the darkened room to where Crabb was guarding the hall entrance.

"Woring's going downstairs. We'll give him a few seconds and then drop in on our friends next door. Have that gun ready—they're tough customers."

The hall was deserted when they stole out. Trent tried the knob of 817, turning it with infinite care. The door was unlocked. Pistol in hand, he flung the door open and sprang inside.

"Up with them, *mein Herren!*"

Smythe spun around, went rigid as he saw Trent's face. Schill and the hawk-faced little man stood paralyzed, their hands in the air.

"Sorry to startle you, gentlemen," Trent said pleasantly. "Mort, put the bead on *Herr* Schill. If he bats an eye, let him have it."

"You *Teufel!*" croaked the man called Smythe. "Will you never stay dead?"

Trent grinned. "I've an aversion to rigor mortis. Now suppose you three boys scrutinize the wall for a minute. Mort, go through Mannrich's pockets and see what you can find."

"Which one's Mannrich?"

"That rat in the middle—the chap who's been posing as Smythe. A clever act, Mannrich, but you made a mistake trying to remove the four of us who were in that cellar. Probably none of us would have heard of you and wondered about 'Smythe's' coming back to life."

The German glared at him, but did not speak.

"Lord help me, I'd have sworn he was Smythe!" Crabb ejaculated.

"The Gestapo must have stumbled on a double of his," said Trent. "Smythe was on a lone-wolf assignment, and the British wouldn't think it was strange if he didn't show up for some time. I heard this fellow tell Woring—who's another Nazi, obviously—that he'd trained a year for this job. He probably worked to get the attache job here so he wouldn't be running into too many of Smythe's friends, as he would in London."

Crabb maneuvered around the impostor so as to search him without interfering with Trent's aim. After taking out the spy's personal effects, he laid a manila envelope and a folded tracing on the desk.

"Open the envelope," directed Trent.

"Here's a confidential report on British convoy positions," Crabb said after a moment. "And a typewritten message signed 'The Purple Legion'—something about the end of aid to Britain. You think this guy's the real head of the Purple Legion?"

"This guy *is* the Purple Legion—hide, hair, and toenails. He made it up to cover their scheme for making off with American bombers. It's a hundred to one shot that they substituted Nazis for the crew of the Liberator that took-off from La Guardia Field. Probably that ship is over in Hitler's air force right now, raiding England."

Crabb's adam's-apple gave a convulsive jerk. "Then all those crews in Canadian uniform are Nazis! They're going to grab all six of the Liberators at Bolling!"

"They *were* going to, until we horned in," Trent said affably. "And unless I miss my guess, they had a lot more in mind. Let's see that tracing."

Crabb unfolded the transparent sheet, and in a quick side glance Trent saw half a dozen red circles connected by a broken red line. Each of the circles was marked with a name, in German. The first circle was lettered "Bolling Field," but in that hasty look he had no time to read the other labels. Smythe's double had cautiously turned his head, was looking back over his shoulder. Trent flipped the .38 muzzle toward him.

"As you were, *mein Freund.* Mort, get on the phone and call Operations at Bolling Field. When Busby hears about this, his toupee will hit the ceiling."

"Don't forget he's got a dragnet out for us," Crabb said dismally.

"We'll be the little tin heroes when we turn in this mob," answered Trent.

Crabb stepped toward the phone. Just as he picked it up, there was a sound of running feet in the hall. Trent whirled, took a hasty step back, but it was too late. The door burst open, slamming his gun-hand against the wall. Before he could recover, Woring charged into the room, a pistol in his hand!

CHAPTER IV
Death on the Dotted Line

"**DON'T MOVE!**" Woring snarled. He jammed the gun against Trent's head, snatched the .38. Mannrich had leaped at Crabb, knocking the phone from his hand, and Schill seized the inventor's gun from the desk where Crabb had laid it.

"Let it go, operator," Mannrich said hastily into the mouthpiece. He cradled the handset, closed the door. *"Gott sie Dank!* If you hadn't come back—"

"The crash report was a mistake," Woring said tensely. "I heard a radio flash after I phoned, downstairs. It said only the fighter crashed. I came back as fast as I could. Then I heard Trent in here—"

Mannrich stuffed the convoy reports and the tracing into his pocket, wheeled toward the door.

"We've got to get out of here! If they landed that gyro on the roof someone may have seen it. The police might surround the hotel and we'd be trapped."

The hawk-faced German turned pale. Mannrich flung a taut look at Schill.

"You and Kurt take care of these two—use the gun with the silencer. Then get out as fast as you can, and report to the New York office later."

Before Schill could answer, Mannrich and Woring were gone. Kurt kept Mortimer Crabb covered, but the fear in his eyes grew swiftly.

"Did you hear?" he said huskily to Schill. "If the police come we can't get out—they've left us in a trap!"

"Stop your sniveling," the Gestapo man rasped. He covered Trent, felt behind him for the handbag. "We'll get this done and be out of here in two minutes."

"What if it's too late?" Kurt said in a shaking voice. "If we kill them and the police come before we get away, we'll be caught and electrocuted. They'd find we were in on what's going to happen tonight—we'd never have a chance with that added to a murder charge."

"We'll shoot them out in the hall. There'll be nothing to hook it up with this room," snapped Schill. "Even if the police did hold everyone in the hotel, they couldn't connect us—"

"Have you forgotten the powder tests? They can tell from your hands if you have fired a gun—even a silenced one—"

"You're right," Schill muttered. "We'd be in a trap. Get on downstairs—see if there's any sign of police. I'll wait—and don't try to run out without me, or I'll find you and slit your throat!"

Kurt scuttled into the ball and Schill braced himself against the connecting-door, where he could cover both men. From across the room, Crabb looked desperately at Trent.

"Don't try it, Mort," Trent said hopelessly. "He'll shoot if we try to rush him. Our only chance is the police—"

"Shut up!" rasped the Gestapo agent. His finger twitched on the trigger of his automatic. "And keep your hands up!"

Three minutes dragged by. Perspiration stood out on Schill's forehead, but his unblinking eyes did not leave the two captives. In another minute or two Trent's arms began to sag.

"Hold your hands up!" Schill repeated savagely.

"I can't keep them up," Trent mumbled. "Try it yourself sometime."

Crabb's arms were also shaking from the effort to force his weary muscles. Schill glowered at the two men.

"All right, but make one move and you're through."

Trent let his arms drop slowly. He could feel the rubber bulb in his left sleeve compress slightly as his elbow touched his side. If only Schill would relax for a second....

Ten more minutes passed. Schill swore under his breath, then a sudden look of decision came into his eyes. He reached out toward the traveling-bag with his left hand, fumbled with the catch.

The bag came open, and Trent's fascinated eyes saw the German's hand close on the silencer gun. Schill was about to lift it from the bag when with a hasty rap at the door Kurt reappeared.

"I couldn't help it," he whined, meeting Schill's angry gaze. "The hotel detective got suspicious of me and I had to wait."

"What of the police?" snarled the killer.

"No sign of them—"

"*Gut!* We'll march these two into that rear hall." Schill lifted the gun with the silencer. "Lift your hands!"

Trent pressed his left elbow tight against his side and swiftly raised his hands. There was a flash, a hiss of steel, and the dagger he had hurled buried itself in Schill's throat. With a terrible gasping sound, the Gestapo man slid to the floor.

FOR ONE fateful second, Kurt stood paralyzed with horror. Trent swung a jolting left to the man's jaw, Kurt's head snapped back, and he crumpled in a grotesque heap.

"Good Heaven!" Crabb said in an awed voice. "That knife—where did it come from?"

"Out of my sleeve," Trent told him. He looked down coolly at the dying Nazi. "I was afraid he'd see the hilt drop into my hand—the release-bulb on the harness worked a trifle too fast."

Crabb shivered, took his eyes away from Schill's body. "I'd already said my prayers. I still can't believe I'm alive."

"You can pinch yourself on the way to the roof. We've a tough job if we're to head off Mannrich and those phoney Canadians!"

"Wait! Why not phone General Busby?" Crabb said as they reached the hall.

"At the rate Mannrich and Woring are probably driving, they could be clear to Anacostia, and it's not much farther to Bolling Field. I just remembered that Mannrich would have a diplomatic license-tag and the cops can't stop him for speeding. Busby would probably be out on the field, and even if we got him he wouldn't believe us. One of those Nazi devils might intercept the message and they'd race off without even waiting for Mannrich and Woring."

Crabb panted after him up the service stairs.

"You're right, Eric, it's up to us! If Hitler gets those bombers, he can raid convoys halfway across the Atlantic."

"That's only a small part of it. Remember that tracing? Those red circles are bomb-targets *in Washington!*"

"What?" groaned Crabb.

"I'll tell you the rest in a minute." They had come out on the roof, near the waiting gyro. They climbed in and Trent quickly switched on the starter. The warm engine caught, backfired with a loud report. A window in an office building across the street slid up and a man looked out. As he saw the gyro, he ran back into the office.

"As if we didn't have enough trouble," Trent said ironically. "There he goes, calling the cops—I suppose the story of the 'gyro killers' is on every radio station."

The engine sputtered, changed to a smooth roar. Trent jumped the ship clear of the roof, swung it straight across the city.

"Are you sure—about their bombing Washington?" Crabb said anxiously.

"Not much doubt. I should have guessed it before—that story about their carrying bombs in hopes of seeing German raiders was undoubtedly framed up by Mannrich. Busby would never question it since it came from the British Embassy."

"Lord help the capital if those bombers get off," Crabb said grimly. "They could tie up Washington for weeks, until the buildings were rebuilt."

"It's worse than that, Mort. They're planning to paralyze the Government. That first red circle was for Bolling Field, but it's only a starter. They'd drop one or two eggs there and maybe a couple on Naval Air, then go on to the Navy Yard. From there that dotted red line led to the Capitol."

"Congress!" exclaimed Crabb. "They're having night sessions! I just remembered!"

"The Nazis must have figured on that." Trent stared over the side of the gyro. "If I've got that red courseline straight in my mind, the White House is one of their main targets. They could come straight down Pennsylvania Avenue, with all those lights, and pick off whatever they wanted—Department of Justice, with all its spy-records, Treasury, State-War-Navy, and a dozen others. With Naval Air and Bolling crippled, they'd never get enough fighters in the air to do any good, even if they had time. And when those butchers got through, they'd simply make a dash for the Atlantic and get away."

"Look—they're turning on the floods at Bolling!" interjected Crabb.

Trent peered out over the cowl. "That's a P-40 hangar. Mort, those babies are coming after us!"

He sent the gyro up steeply into the clouds, until he could hardly see the ground through the mists. Then he headed at top speed across Anacostia Hill and the asylum at the top. As the gyro descended toward Bolling, its engine idling, he spied a car racing around the side of a hangar toward the first of the six Consolidated bombers.

"Mort, they've made it! That's Mannrich and Woring!"

THE LIBERATOR crews were gathered in a group near the leading ship. They swarmed around the car, then turned and hurried toward the big bombers. Trent threw the gyro into as steep a dive as it would take. Abruptly, a searchlight blazed on, lifted toward them. He plunged the gyro down through the beam, leveled off a hundred feet above the staring crowd of Air Corps men.

"Busby!" he shouted. "Grab those Canadians. They're Nazi spies—they're going to bomb hell out Washington!"

"You madman!" howled Busby. "Land and give yourself up, or I'll have you shot down!"

"Search Smythe!" Trent yelled back. "He's got the targets marked on—"

A roar from one of the first bomber's engines drowned the rest of his warning. Busby whirled, and in the glare of the floodlights Trent could see the alarm on his pompous face. He ran toward the first Liberator, just as Mannrich and Woring scrambled in behind the crew. Mannrich twisted around, fired a hastily-aimed shot, and Busby's hat flopped from his head. Two more of the Liberator's engines roared and the huge ship lunged out from the line, scattering the crowd.

Army men were rushing toward the other Liberators, and as Trent gunned the gyro after the first bomber he saw the prop of a P-40 whirl into life. He swooped over the fleeing ship, pitched a quick burst at the pilots' compartment. The front-gunner frantically spun his mount and hurled a fiery blast at the gyro. Trent flung his ship toward the ground.

"Get ready with the smoke Mort!" he shouted. "Give 'em all you've got!"

The Liberator's fourth motor was now revving up, and the bomber surged ahead under full power. Trent lifted the gyro in a dizzy climb, then charged down straight into the big ship's path. The Liberator was off, climbing fast, as the gyro dropped in front of it. Black smoke suddenly eddied from the gyro's tail, a split-second before the nose-gunner opened fire. Tracers flamed through the smoke-screen and the Nazi's bullets clipped the top of Trent's enclosure.

Crabb's swiveled .30-.30 hammered out three short bursts, as he aimed in the general direction of the Liberator's nose. The big bomber skidded in a wild turn. Trent dropped the gyro underneath, came up in a crazy zoom on the other side. Another cloud of dense black smoke spread back and hid the bomber's nose. Beyond, Trent could see five or six P-40's streaking in.

One more desperate fusillade from the blinded nose-gunner probed wildly through the smoke. A rotor-blade gave a dull zing as a bullet nicked it, and the remains of the cockpit enclosure collapsed. The black smoke was starting to thin out when the P-40's closed in, above and behind the bomber. Trent hoisted the gyro out of the way with a neat climbing turn, watched the red fangs of the fighters' guns crisscross in front of the stolen ship. The Liberator's lights flashed on and off frantically in token of surrender.

Trent drew a deep breath, clawed pieces of Plexiglas out of his hair. "Mort, I never thought I'd see the day when I'd deliberately get in front off somebody's guns. What do you say we go back and make old Busby eat humble pie?"

"NOW, TRENT," General Busby said pleadingly, "you won't give this story to the newspapers, will you? No need to make a fool of the Army—undermine public confidence."

"Tell you what," said Trent amiably, "you let us keep Leaping Lena and we'll call it square. That is, providing you call off the cops you put on our trail."

Busby mopped his forehead. "Take the gyro—we don't want it, and it's a cinch the Germans won't claim it. I've already explained to the police. The whole thing was a diabolical plot. This Mannrich has been impersonating Smythe for two months, but he didn't know the full circumstances about that Brussels thing. When he found that there were four people who'd swear that Smythe was dead, he got the jitters. On top of that, some news photographer snapped a picture of him at a British Embassy function, and it was due to come out in next Sunday's rotogravure. So he got his Gestapo unit into action, to wipe out the four of you. He'd intended to stay on in Washington when the original plan was merely to steal the ships. Then, when they switched to the bombing plot, he decided to fly back to Germany with them.

"He squealed on Woring, too. Woring faked a forced landing with the Liberator that was bringing the real Canadian pilots, and dropped in at an isolated field in New York State.

Nazis with machine guns captured the Canadians, took their uniforms—and you know the rest. We've flashed word to the New York police to arrest the Germans they left on guard and turn the pilots loose."

"Let's hope they give them some clothes first," Trent observed. "Unless you're trying to add insult to injury."

Busby let out a bellowing laugh. "It wasn't that funny," Mortimer Crabb said gloomily. "In fact, it wasn't funny at all."

"He's just trying to keep me happy," said Trent. "It's all right, General. I won't expose you. But don't forget about that smoke-screen gadget of Mort's. If that wasn't a perfect demonstration, I never saw one."

"He'll get the contract, don't worry," Busby assured him.

"Well, I guess we'll be jumping off," said Trent. "Now that we've got Leaping Lena, though, we'll drop in on you one of these days."

"Wait a second," interrupted Busby. "How can I get in touch with you?"

"Sorry," said Trent, with a chuckle, "I keep my telephone number confidential."

Mortimer Crabb snorted.

"Confidential my eye! Just ask the nearest blonde."

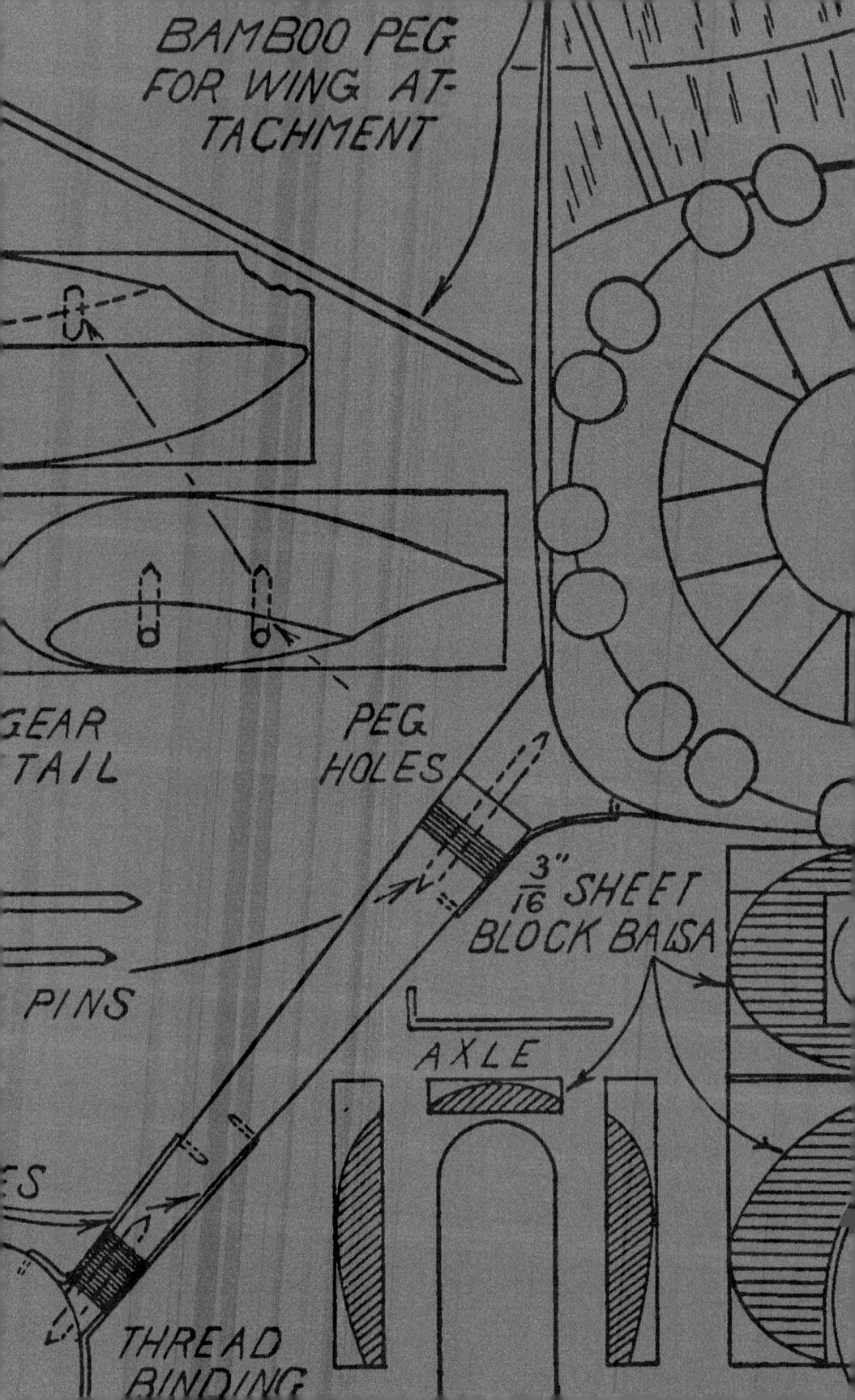

BAMBOO PEG
FOR WING AT-
TACHMENT

GEAR
TAIL

PEG
HOLES

PINS

$\frac{3"}{16}$ SHEET
BLOCK BALSA

AXLE

ES

THREAD
BINDING

Death Dives the Douglas

CHAPTER I
The Man on the Roof

ENGINE IDLING, the autogyro settled slowly through the fog that shrouded Washington. Eric Trent grinned back at his sour-faced partner, Mortimer Crabb.

"Sorry to drag you away from your beloved lab, old top. But from the quiver in General Busby's voice he's either in another jam, or he's lost his toupee."

"You lame-brain!" croaked the inventor. "A foggy night, and we go barging off in this crazy contraption. It's only half an hour's drive from our place."

"My dear Mort, where's your adventurous spirit? Think of the millions who never get the chance to flit down onto people's roofs."

Crabb snorted. "Some time you're going to pick a weak roof and land in somebody's lap."

"Not a bad idea. Boy meets girl. Make a note under 'future research.'"

"That reminds me," snapped Crabb. "What happened to those miniature tear-gas pencils I was working on? If you're up to another one of your smart-aleck magician tricks—" he broke off in a howl as a blurred red light showed just below.

"Oops!" said Trent. He flipped the gyro to one side, and the lighted tip of the Washington Monument slid away into the fog. Crabb dropped back heavily into his seat. Trent chuckled.

"It's all right, Mort. Just one of those embarrassing moments."

He let down through the thinning mists, found the ceiling at three hundred feet. The lights of the city sprang into quick focus, and he turned, following the Mall. To the right of the reflecting pool that led to the Lincoln Memorial the multi-winged Navy and Munitions Building showed.

"Watch out, you idiot," Crabb said hoarsely. "Remember they've got antennae strung in five or six places."

"Not on the wing where Busby hangs out. H'm'm, must be quite a pow-wow, from the offices they've got lighted."

The gyro was less than sixty feet from the roof and was settling vertically. Trent switched on the landing-lights, tilted them downward.

Instantly, a figure became visible in the glare—a man stretched full-length at the edge of the roof. From a box beside him a cable dangled over the gutter, with a microphone at the end.

Then another jet-black Corsair hurtled from behind blasting away at the autogyro's empennage!

As the lights fell on him, the man leaped to his feet and snatched a gun from under his coat. Flame jetted from the muzzle, and a bullet drilled the Plexiglas enclosure beside Trent. He ducked, and a second bullet zinged from the dural rim of the cockpit.

"Pull up out of here!" howled Crabb.

But the gyro was almost to the roof. Trent snapped off the switch, backsticked. There was a thud, a muffled cry, as the ship crunched to a dead stop. Trent hurriedly opened the cockpit enclosure, climbed out.

"Look out, he'll kill you!" Crabb warned him.

"I hardly think so," Trent said. "It seems he didn't duck quite fast enough."

THE MAN lay in a crumpled heap beside the left wheel. An ugly gash in his head showed where the landing gear had hit him. Trent made a brief examination.

"Job for the coroner. Too bad, I'd like to have had a little talk with that unfortunate chap."

Crabb had followed Trent out of the ship. "Somebody's coming!" he said suddenly.

A door that led to the third-floor stairs opened abruptly and several men scrambled up onto the roof. The gyro's lights fell on the fat, pompous face of General Rufus Busby, assistant chief of G-2—more generally known as "Old Fuss-Buzz."

"It's a plane!" Busby ejaculated. He stopped, blinking in the glare, then recoiled as he saw the dead man.

"Don't get upset, General," Trent said amiably. "He's quite defunct."

"Eric Trent!" spluttered Busby. "What the devil—who's this person?"

"Sorry, I never had the honor of his acquaintance." Trent gestured toward the pistol in the dead man's hand. "He dispensed with the formalities—seemed somewhat annoyed at our dropping in on him."

The rest of the group stared at the corpse. Trent recognized bald, gimlet-eyed Admiral Sharp, new chief of Naval Intelligence. Two younger officers and a uniformed building-guard stood by the admiral, gaping at the dead man.

"Why, it's Blackston!" the guard exclaimed. "He was a civilian code clerk in the Signal Corps."

"Signal Corps?" said Busby. He looked across at the box on the edge of the roof, from which an electric cord ran to a light-socket near the stairs. "The poor wretch must have been trying some radio experiment. Trent, you've killed an innocent man—he thought you were up to something crooked and—"

"Before you call in the law," Trent interrupted pleasantly, "suppose you haul in that cable dangling over the gutter."

Admiral Sharp wheeled, pulled up the cable. "A microphone! Busby, this man was listening in on our conference! It was dropped right by that open window."

Mortimer Crabb bent over the box. He peered at the dial setting a moment and then flicked off a switch.

"Well, it's done now," he said gloomily, "but I suppose they'd have got wise anyway."

"What do you mean?" barked Admiral Sharp.

"This thing's a short-wave transmitter. It was still on when you pulled the mike up, so they know we've grabbed their man."

Busby's jaw sagged. "Then our whole conference—everything—went out on the air?"

Crabb nodded mournfully. "No doubt about it. Anybody tuned in on that setting could hear it. But it's way up in the experimental frequencies."

Sharp turned a cold eye on General Busby. "A fine Intelligence service you've got! In the Navy we check every man in a responsible job."

"Like that Naval Reserve lieutenant who had charge of blueprinting the new fire-control plan?" Trent put in. "By the way, Admiral, did they ever catch him?"

Sharp's face purpled. "That was before I took over Naval Intelligence. Busby, are you sure of these men? It looks mighty suspicious to me, dropping in here with a gyro."

"They're the two I told you about—Eric Trent and Mortimer Crabb," said old Fuss-Buzz. "Trent is—er—a little unconventional in some of his ideas, but he's helped us out two or three times. You must have heard of some of Crabb's inventions."

Sharp grunted. Eric Trent took out his cigarette case, put it back in his pocket apparently without touching its contents. An idle flick of his hand, and a lighted cigarette appeared in his fingers.

"That's *not* one of my inventions," Crabb said sourly. "He used to be a professional magician."

"Don't worry, Admiral," said Trent. "I promise not to pull any rabbits out of your hat."

"Your humor is ill-timed," Sharp said stiffly.

TRENT LAZILY exhaled. "Referring to the deceased? Surely you don't expect me to shed crocodile tears. Aside from being a traitor, he was most unpleasantly quick on the trigger."

He turned to Busby. "If I may suggest it, a search of Blackston's pockets might prove of value."

The guard went through the dead man's clothes, but the only thing of importance was a driver's license with his name and address.

"I'll call the F.B.I. and have them send a couple of men out there," said Busby. "They can help cover up this death, too. We don't want the public to know—that is, it would look a trifle odd—"

"Yes, you'd get a nice panning from the papers," Trent agreed, as Busby floundered. " 'Spy in code job listens in on Brass Hats' secrets.'… By the way, just what caused that hurry call tonight?"

Busby hesitated, looking at the guard. "I'll explain down in my office. Watchman, you stay here and don't let anybody come up on the roof until the F.B.I. agents arrive."

"Think I'll take this set down and have a look at it," Crabb said, as Busby led the way toward the stairs.

When they reached Busby's office, the general called the F.B.I. and had two agents sent to Blackston's address. Then he hung up, looked glumly at a report on his desk, marked "Confidential."

"I'll give you the plain facts. We've had a series of peculiar crashes. At first we thought they were the result of the speed-up in training. Then last night there were two cases nobody can explain. A Navy patrol bomber flying from Puerto Rico to Norfolk cracked up in the Florida Everglades, a hundred miles off its course up the Atlantic. The other ship was a Flying Fortress. It left Bolling Field at nine-thirty, but it never got to Langley. A Neutrality Patrol destroyer found the wreckage out in the Atlantic Ocean, a hundred-and-twenty miles southeast of Langley."

"No survivors in either case?" asked Trent.

"One—from the Navy plane. Seminole Indians brought him to a 'Glades ranch where there was a phone. He swears they were on their course, out at sea. They'd hit bad weather and had dropped down low to see if they could get under it. That's when they crashed into the Everglades."

"No radio report from the Flying Fortress after it left Bolling?"

"One, saying they'd be at Langley in an estimated fifteen minutes. They were above the clouds and asked the ceiling. That's the last word Langley heard. The ship had been fueled for that short run, with the usual safety margin. Apparently they ran out of gas—but why in Heaven were they way out in the Atlantic?"

"The other crashes you mentioned—were the ships off course, too?"

"Yes, but nothing like this. These two planes carried expert navigators, men who'd handled jobs ten times harder." Busby looked searchingly at Trent. "You haven't any idea what could have caused those crashes?"

Trent looked astonished for a second, then he smiled whimsically. "My dear General, I assure you I'm as innocent as a new-born babe."

"I didn't mean anything like that," Busby said peevishly. "But you were in Europe during '39 and '40, and you learned a lot of their tricks. I thought maybe you might have heard something—or some of your undercover contacts here—"

"I'm afraid you've drawn a blank this time," said Trent. "But I'll admit it has an ugly look. Navy flying boat cracks up a hundred miles from the ocean. Army bomber pulls the same trick in reverse. Too much to be coincidence in one night."

"They were both going to take part in tomorrow night's maneuvers," interposed Admiral Sharp. "That's another angle of similarity."

"Maneuvers?" said Trent. "This must be something special. I haven't heard a word of it."

"We've clamped on a tight censorship," explained Sharp. He gave Trent a thin-lipped smile. "Likewise on these two crashes. What you learn here is strictly confidential."

Trent nodded. The admiral looked at Mortimer Crabb.

"You needn't worry about me," Crabb said in a gloomy voice. "I've got enough trouble without spilling Navy secrets."

"It's a joint Army-Navy problem," said Sharp. "Tomorrow night a Navy 'invader' force is going to try to take Hampton Roads, Langley, and Norfolk. Another Navy unit will try to block them—with Air Corps backing. We're putting everything into it—submarines, destroyers, cruisers, dreadnaughts, and aircraft carriers. We set tomorrow night because there's no moon, and from the weather reports the visibility will be low—the kind of soup a real invader would choose."

Trent looked at him oddly. "You're still going ahead with the plan?"

"Certainly. What difference could two crashes—" Sharp stopped as the phone rang. Busby answered, listened a few moments, banged down the handset.

"Too late! When the F.B.I. men got to Blackston's apartment, it had been ransacked."

"Fast work," Trent said, with a trace of admiration. "They must have gone into action the second they heard Admiral Sharp's voice coming through the mike."

"Then you think Blackston was relaying our conference to some point in Washington?" Sharp demanded of Trent.

Before Trent could answer, some one knocked hastily at the anteroom door. One of Busby's junior officers opened it, and a man in shirt sleeves hurried in.

"What's the matter, Briggs?" asked the officer.

"A queer radio message just came in for General Busby," Briggs said breathlessly. "It wasn't signed. We tried to get a bearing on the station but they went off too fast."

Busby took the message, then spread it on the desk for the rest to see. They bent over the message eagerly, strained to read its message in the dimly lighted office.

> Brig. Gen. Rufus Busby, G-2.
> Tune in on 985 kilocycles at ten tonight. Perhaps you will hear something of interest.

"It's almost ten now!" exclaimed Sharp. "Mr. Crabb, is that set a receiver, too?"

"No, only a transmitter. And a strange one at that."

"There's a set in the next room, for news broadcasts," said Busby. The others followed as he went in and turned it on.

"That's just above WRC," muttered Crabb. "I wonder what idea—"

"This is Station WRC, Washington. The time, ten o'clock," came the smooth voice of an announcer. There was a brief pause, then the signature song of a well-known orchestra began. Almost immediately, the loud hiss of a powerful carrier-wave was audible and WRC faded into the background.

"To the news correspondents of Washington," a sibilant voice abruptly spoke. "Ask General Busby, of Army Intelligence, why he has hushed up the story of last night's Flying Fortress crash… Nine men were killed when the bomber fell into the Atlantic…. Ask Admiral Sharp, of Naval Intelligence, why he has kept secret the crash of a Navy patrol bomber in the Everglades last night… Six men were killed…. In the last two weeks there have been nine other Army and Navy crashes, none fully explained. Why?… Ask General Busby!… Ask Admiral Sharp!"

CHAPTER II
Mystery Ship

*T*HE VOICE ended, and a moment later the carrier-wave went off the air. As the group in the office stared at the radio set, the orchestra music of WRC was interrupted by the announcer's crisp accents:

"Ladies and gentlemen, we interrupt to bring you a special bulletin.... A speaker from an unknown station has just accused the Army and Navy of keeping two disastrous crashes secret.... The officials named were—"

"Cut that thing off!" rasped Busby. One of the officers switched off the set. Admiral Sharp glowered at the G-2 brigadier.

"A fine mess! It'll be all over the country in an hour."

The telephone jangled again. One of Busby's aides answered it.

"It's the Associated Press, General. They want to know—"

"Tell them I'm out of town! Tell them you don't know anything about the crash story."

"What are we going to do?" demanded Sharp, as they went back into Busby's office.

"Why not call Federal Communications?" Trent asked indolently. "Ever hear of monitor stations? You know, chaps listening in and taking bearings."

"Never mind the sarcasm," said Busby. He went over to his desk, put in the call. Trent produced another cigarette, absently juggled a paper-weight and two erasers until Busby hung up.

"Impossible!" muttered the general. "They say they spotted it right in the middle of Dismal Swamp. Nobody could get any power lines in there, and that was a big station."

"Did you get the exact position?" asked Trent.

"Yes. It's seven miles northeast of Drummond Lake."

"There are several waterways leading in there," observed Trent. "It wouldn't be impossible to ferry in broadcasting equipment and hide it. If the swamp growth and trees weren't enough, they could use camouflage."

"I'll have planes over that spot first thing in the morning," said Busby. "With this fog, the ceiling's too low for any search tonight."

"Unless somebody used a gyro," put in Trent.

"You mean you'll do it?" demanded Busby.

"We might take a little jaunt down there, drop a flare, and have a look-see. How about it, Mort?"

"Well, maybe," Crabb said grudgingly. "I'm sticking my neck out, but this radio business has got me curious."

"Good!" exclaimed Busby. "I'd send an Air Corps gyro, but they've turned theirs over to Britain for convoy duty."

He went up on the roof with Trent and Crabb. The guard moved Blackston's body, and Trent started the engine.

"Something tells me I'm going to regret this," Crabb said gloomily as he climbed in.

Trent engaged the rotor, gunned the motor. "Leaping Lena" jumped twenty feet into the air, forged ahead under propeller power. Trent looked back at his partner.

"Tune in 985 and see if our hissing friend comes on the air again."

Crabb switched on the radio. Trent climbed up into the fog, headed south.

"One thing, we won't have to worry about airliners tonight," he told Crabb. "All schedules have been canceled."

"Some people have brains," Crabb said.

IT WAS one-hundred-and-sixty miles to Dismal Swamp, by a direct course. Trent laid a more easterly bearing for Norfolk. Once over the city, it would take only a short time to reach the Swamp. By eleven o'clock, according to his reckoning, they had passed over Yorktown. The unknown station had not come back on the air, although Crabb had traversed the dial regularly. By now, the fog had thinned. Stars could be seen occasionally, though the ground was still hidden.

Suddenly, the lights of another ship became visible, ahead and slightly lower. The plane was banking into a turn, and from the lighted cabin windows Trent could tell it was a DC-3.

"Thought you said no airliners were flying tonight," Crabb shouted from the rear cockpit.

"That's what Washington Airport—" Trent stopped, peered blankly over the side. An odd, shapeless figure could be seen at one of the DC-3's windows. There was something about it that made his flesh creep. He edged the gyro in as close as he dared, keeping inside the big plane's turn.

An astounding scene met his eyes. One window had been shattered, as if by gunfire. Sprawled back in the adjacent seat was a headless man!

"Good glory!" Crabb said hoarsely. "He's been decapitated!"

Trent stared at the other windows. Incredibly, none of the other passengers seemed to know or care what had happened. The ship was a club-plane, and he saw one man lounging in a swivel-chair, smoking, reading a paper. A blonde woman near him calmly gazed out into the night. Up forward, a uniformed steward was bending over a woman passenger, holding a tray laden with food.

As Trent eased the gyro a few feet closer, a light flickered briefly in the DC-3's cockpit. He had a glimpse of a goggled face, a heavy jaw, as the pilot stared across from the left-hand seat. The cockpit light went out, and after a moment the ship's running lights flashed the code-letter "F."

Trent reached for the gyro's running-lights switch, flipped it three or four times. But his attempt at faking an answer failed. Instantly, the DC-3's cabin went dark, and with a swift climbing turn the ship started to hoik away into the night.

"Not so fast, my friend," said Trent. He pulled the gyro up steeply, turned on the right-wing landing-light. The beam bored through the faint mist, spotted the tail of the Douglas. Trent slanted it forward, across the cabin windows. The headless figure was still there—the rest of the passengers still calmly unconcerned. There was something uncanny about the scene, as more vividly revealed by the gyro's powerful light. But Trent had no time for a second look.

Two cherry-red streaks flashed over the top of his cockpit, lanced above the cowl. He threw the gyro into a hasty turn, and a black Vought Corsair plunged by, guns flaming. Trent had to zoom at full climb to miss the DC-3 as the cabin ship twisted back. The Corsair hurtled into a split-"S," charged back at the gyro. Trent had swiftly cut in the Brownings hidden under the gyro's cowl. His tracers gouged at the black ship's prop, but the pilot kicked out of the burst.

Trent switched off the landing-light, stabbed another blast at the dark blur of the Corsair. The Vought's guns had stopped flaming as the light went off, but with Trent's tracers to guide him the unknown pilot again opened up. The gyro jumped and quivered from a fusillade that grazed the cowling. Mortimer Crabb had brought the hidden rear-pit gun up from its recess. A quick burst drove the Corsair into a turn, and momentarily the gyro was alone in the murky night.

ALMOST IMMEDIATELY, lights probed beneath the ship, twisting hastily to spot them. Trent saw the huge wing of the DC-3 behind the lights. He banked to get away from the glow, but too late. The black Corsair, its prey again revealed, came roaring in furiously. Trent let the gyro drop beside the Douglas, to blanket the Vought's fire. But before he could gain its protection, another stream of tracers blazed through the darkness.

A second black Corsair was on their tail!

"Hold off that second devil, Mort!" Trent flung back at his partner. "It's curfew, and I'm going to put out the lights!"

Crabb's Browning .50 was already chattering viciously. Trent pitched a blast at the DC-3's lights, and one beam went out. The first Corsair tried frantically to cut between the gyro and the Douglas. Trent flipped the gyro into a sudden bank, raked the black wing that swam before him. The Corsair staggered, its rear guns abruptly silenced, and the pilot whipped off into the mists.

Trent flung the gyro back toward the DC-3, but the remaining light went out before he could fire. The other Corsair let go a final, ill-aimed burst in the darkness, and vanished. Trent peered around, above and below, but could see nothing of the Douglas.

"You can put away your pop-gun, Mort. Our friends seem to have remembered another engagement."

"I've had enough!" Crabb said hollowly. "When planes with headless bodies start coming at me, I'm through!"

"A headless body won't hurt you," said Trent. "It's the lads with heads still on them you have to worry about. Besides, all I saw was one decapitated gentleman."

"One's enough," grated Crabb. "And those black Corsairs! What kind of deviltry's going on around here?"

"There you have me. We'd better drop in at Langley and pass the word along the airways about that trio. I'd call in and tell them now, but it might bring back our uninvited guests."

"You think this business has got anything to do with the crashes Busby told us about?"

"It wouldn't surprise me. One of those black Corsairs could slip in and shoot down a bomber without, warning. But that doesn't explain why the Army and Navy ships were so far off course."

"And it doesn't cover that body in the DC-3," Crabb said grimly. "How on earth could those other people sit in there like that, not giving a hang about the poor fellow"

"There's something phony about that," said Trent. "It looked as though they were putting on an act."

"An act?" snorted the inventor. "Why in tarnation would they stage an act in an airplane on a foggy night, with one chance in ten thousand that anybody'd see it?"

"I'll admit it's all quite cockeyed," Trent said amiably.

"In fact, I'm not sure it isn't the lobster Newburg I had for dinner."

"Well, I didn't have any lobster, and I saw it, too," growled Crabb.

"Even the blonde?" asked Trent.

"Certainly," snapped his partner.

"Pretty little trick, wasn't she?"

"You make me sick!" exploded Crabb. "Here we run into murder and Lord knows what else, and you start mooning about some yellow-haired skirt."

"Merely a professional interest, old bean. She'd have to explain her criminal connections before I'd consider adding her to my little red book."

"Since when have you been so particular?" retorted Crabb.

"Not particular—just careful. I'm a bit wary of young ladies who go in for headless associates. It might be a habit."

The gyro had been slowly descending, and in a few moments it broke through under the ceiling. A dark expanse showed below, with not a single light. Trent looked at the compass, cranked back the bullet-torn enclosure, and gazed down into the blackness. The altimeter showed five hundred feet when he switched on the landing lights. White-capped waves shone in the glare.

"A swell navigator you are!" yelled Crabb. "That's the Atlantic!"

"Chesapeake or Atlantic, I don't like it," returned Trent. "I'd have staked my bottom dollar we were over Langley."

Crabb switched on the radio direction finder, tuned in a Norfolk station, and Trent offset his course for the Air Corps field. The lights of Norfolk finally appeared, off to the left.

"We must have been twenty miles out from Hampton Roads," Crabb erupted. "You were almost forty miles off your course, headed straight for Africa."

"Just what happened to that Flying Fortress," Trent said, puzzled. "Something has a piscatorial odor and it isn't in Denmark."

TWELVE MINUTES later the gyro came in for a landing at Langley Field. A lanky Air Corps officer met them at the line, and Trent recognized Captain Hal Pearson, G-2 man for the field.

"What are you doing here?" demanded Pearson.

"Is that any way to greet a couple of old friends?" Trent said reproachfully. "Especially when they've just escaped a watery grave."

"But General Busby said you—hey, what in Hades happened to your ship?"

"If I tell you, you'll think I'm drunk," grinned Trent.

"Maybe not," grunted Pearson. "There's been some mighty queer goings-on lately. Cough up—where'd you get the bullet holes?"

Trent told him. Pearson's jaw was sagging when he finished.

"Then Rogers was telling the truth!"

"You mean you'd already heard about that ship?" asked Trent.

"Not fifteen minutes ago. One of our pursuit pilots landed with a wild yarn about shooting a man's head off. He said he'd been attacked by a black ship without lights—said it was escorting a DC-3, and in the fight he hit the Douglas. He even saw the blonde dame—but we naturally rought he'd gone nuts, they hauled him off to the hospital for observation."

"Good thing he got here first," Crabb said dryly.

"How come you had a ship up tonight?" queried Trent.

"Several squadrons have been practicing dead reckoning hops, getting ready for tomorrow night's 'invasion.' Queer thing, too—Rogers' squadron and one bomber outfit got lost and had to ask for the radio-beacon to be turned on so they could get back. The bomber C.O. said they'd been thirty miles beyond the Capes when they figured they were ready to land—but it's probably a rush of the jitters, after those crashes last night."

"You think so?" said Trent. He described their descent over the ocean.

"This calls for a drink," muttered Pearson. "Come on over to my quarters."

"Before we follow that excellent suggestion," said Trent, "suppose you have Operations check with Civil Aeronautics and find out what DC-3 club-planes are in the air."

Pearson stopped at Operations, put in the request. Half an hour later, as he was filling the glasses a second time, an orderly brought a message to his quarters.

"No luck on that angle," Pearson said, after reading the message. "According to Civil Aeronautics, there isn't an airline club-plane flying tonight east of the Mississippi. There are ten or fifteen private-owned DC-3's on this list, but no telling where they are since they don't have to report like the airliners."

"Let's see that list," said Trent. "Standard Oil, General Motors, Allan Sales Company, J.T. Dayne—is he the Dayne that owns part of Universal Aluminum?"

"That's the one," nodded Pearson. "You've probably read about him recently. He exposed a Nazi scheme to cut down aluminum production in America, got a German attache kicked out of the country."

"Yes, I read about it," said Trent. He went on down the list, halted at another name. "Vaughn Doering—Chairman, Keep America at Peace Committee. I've always wondered about that lad."

"Here's another I'm dubious about," observed the Air Corps captain. "Alfred Grude, New Orleans. He does a lot of flying in Mexico and Latin America. Nobody seems to know what his business is. G-2's been checking on him, but he's close-mouthed."

"Well, Old Fuzz-Buzz should be able to get a quick check on all these private ships, sometime tomorrow. He told you why we were heading this way, I gather?"

"He phoned me about the mystery-station. But you won't

be flying over Dismal Swamp tonight. Operations had a man check over your gyro, and one rotor is badly shot up."

"It brought us in here all right," said Trent, unperturbed. "We'll risk it."

"Maybe *you'll* risk it, but count *me* out," interjected Mortimer Crabb.

"Anyway, Operations won't let you off the field until the ship's fixed," added Pearson.

"Thank Heaven somebody in this flying game has a little sense," growled Crabb.

Trent sighed. "Fate seems against me, Mort. I suppose we may as well go rustle up a night's lodging—"

"I've plenty of room here," said Pearson.

"Not that I was hinting," Trent chuckled. He lit a cigarette, counted the number remaining in his case. "Have one, Hal? Take one up at that end—not getting tight, but the others are trick stuff."

"Yeah, so he can pull lighted cigarettes out of the air," said Crabb morosely. "Some day I'm going to fix it so that stunt will backfire and—"

The telephone rang and Pearson went to answer it. In a few minutes he returned, a strange expression on his face.

"Your mystery-station just came on the air again. They called Communications here, with a message for you."

"Well, well," said Trent. "Our sibilant friend does keep track of his adversaries. What was on his mind this time?"

"Here's the message." Pearson handed him the sheet and Trent read it with uplifted brows.

"To Eric Trent, care of Langley Field G-2 officer. Stay away from Dismal Swamp, if you want to keep your head on your shoulders!"

CHAPTER III
At the Hide-Out

DARKNESS WAS settling over the gloomy expanse of Dismal Swamp, as the gyro droned along above the edge of Drummond Lake.

"Why waste any more time?" Mortimer Crabb wanted to know. "There's no hidden station in the Swamp. Those F.C.C. men got their bearings mixed."

"I'm afraid you're right, Mort," Trent agreed reluctantly. "That warning last night was obviously intended to keep us hunting in the wrong direction."

He put the ship into a climb, headed toward Langley Field.

"Maybe Pearson will have some word about those private DC-3's," he added, "although it's possible that ship was foreign-owned. There have been at least thirty DC-3's sold abroad in the last—"

"Hey! That station's come on the air again!" Crabb broke in excitedly. "Cut in your phones!"

Trent hurriedly switched from the intercom to the radio. The sibilant voice rasped into his ears:

"— and these crashes are only a hint of the weaknesses in our armed services! Demand the truth, America! Force General Busby and Admiral Sharp to give you the answer.... Clean out the ill-trained men of the Army and Navy before it is too late!"

Trent jerked around in his seat. "What's the bearing?"

"Almost due south," exclaimed Crabb. "Head east five miles and I'll get a cross-bearing on it."

Engine full out, the gyro swung back across Dismal Swamp. The mysterious voice was still talking.

"— these helpless mechanics and pilots, being sent to their death, men unfit for their duties because of poor training, Government politics—"

"The dirty liar!" roared Crabb. "We've got the best-trained air force in the world, and the best ships."

"Don't let the propaganda get you, Mort," said Trent. "What's the fix?"

Crabb took another bearing just as the station went off the air. "Why, it's right in the middle of Drummond Lake!"

Trent peered down at the shadowy pool.

"Not a thing there. But I think I've got the answer now."

He sent the gyro climbing at top speed. Broken clouds drifted at two thousand feet and it was darker as they went up through them, but a circling plane was visible half a mile distant. The ship was heading in their general direction as it banked. Trent swerved to come in closer. The other machine started to level out, then tightened its bank. Abruptly, its cabin and running-lights came on.

"It's the same DC-3!" ejaculated Crabb.

Trent gazed in at the cabin. It was the same as the night before—except for the headless figure. Now the man had a head—a queer, stary face, with a blur around it. The blonde still looked calmly out into the gloom. The man with the newspaper was still reading, smoking. The steward was still bending over the other woman passenger, holding his tray.

"Swing your gun out of the niche!" Trent said swiftly. "We've got to force that ship down."

He switched on the hidden Brownings under the cowl and Crabb turned to lever the rear-pit gun out of its recess. Just as the weapon lifted into sight, the formerly headless figure gave an odd jerk. The stary face twitched sidewise, disappeared, leaving a black spot like a hole clear through the cabin. The next instant the snout of a machine-gun poked through the dark space, and tracers flamed across at the gyro.

A lightning premonition had seized Trent as the man's head flipped side-wise. He yanked the gyro up in a corkscrew turn over the top of the DC-3, and the first blast of tracers missed them by inches. Crabb gaped down at the Douglas.

"Did you see that?" he cried hoarsely. "That gun came right out through his head!"

"Cut loose with that fifty, or it'll be your head!" Trent shouted back.

"But the women?" yelled Crabb.

"There aren't any women in—" Trent hastily banked as a dark outline materialized from the clouds. Another shape charged down from the other side, and the two black Corsairs hurtled in at the gyro. Crabb frantically poured a burst into the path of the first ship and the pilot kicked away to save his prop. A hail of cupro-nickel slugs thudded into the gyro's tail. Trent pitched a blast at the second Corsair, dived for the clouds. Tracers blazed after them, curved away to the left as he made a quick right turn.

"Call Langley! Tell them those ships are over Dismal Swamp!" he tossed back at Crabb. I'll hover in this cloud."

CRABB SNATCHED up the microphone. He was halfway through the message when another fusillade of tracers sparkled through the cloud-mists. Trent gunned the motor, sent the ship ahead for two- or three-hundred yards. Then he grabbed at the front-pit mike.

"Langley! We've been hit—will try to stay in clouds. Get back to—"

He let the words die in a groan. Then he cut off the transmitter.

"Where are you hit, Eric?" Crabb asked anxiously.

Trent looked back, chuckled. "Right in my self-esteem, old top. I should have guessed that trick last night."

"What's the idea acting as though you were dying?" snorted his partner.

"So the DC-3 mob and their friends in the Corsairs won't be watching too closely for us. Keep your eyes peeled. I'm going to ease up for a quick look."

"You're stark crazy!" moaned Crabb. "They'll see this windmill and plug us sure."

"It's getting too dark for that." Trent warily lifted the gyro until they were in the top of the cloud layer. For a moment he thought they had lost the three ships, then he saw the DC-3 angling northeast, with the Corsairs barely visible above it.

"Don't be a fool, Eric," pleaded Crabb, as Trent shoved the throttle wide open. "We just got away by the skin of our teeth. Now you want to go back, begging for more!"

"Not this time," said Trent. "We'll play it safe. I just want to see where they squat down. One of those Corsairs seems to be crippled, so we ought to be able to keep up with it."

The DC-3 forged ahead, was quickly lost in the darkness. Despite the low cruising speed of the crippled Corsair, it slowly drew away from the gyro. Trent was about to give up, as the exhaust flares of the black ship faded, when the Corsair suddenly nosed down. He followed in a fast glide, leveled out in the bottom edge of the clouds as lights became visible below.

Against an almost unbroken expanse of dark ground, the red, green and white lights of a landing field stood out sharply. The DC-3 was taxiing toward a hanger at one side and the other Corsair was just landing. Trent held the gyro to a course directly over the field, hovering upwind as the second Corsair spiraled down.

"What are you going to do?" demanded Crabb.

"We're going to hike back to Langley and tip them off about this field. If we try to warn them by radio, those lads will hear it. Langley can rush some parachutists to take over the place in jigtime while a few fighters cover them."

"Fine idea," Crabb said gloomily, "only how do we find Langley—or anywhere else? Look at the compass."

Trent stared. The compass was spinning like a top!

"Mort, we stumbled onto the answer! But we can't leave here now—we'll never be able to find the place again in time."

"We can climb on up till we see the stars—"

"That second layer of overcast goes up past twelve thousand feet," Trent interrupted. "I saw the report before we took-off. We've got to sneak a landing and find that field. I've a hunch it'll be too late tomorrow."

Crabb groaned. "Go ahead. I guess I've lived long enough, anyway."

"Spoken like a true patriot," grinned Trent. He watched the second Corsair taxi slowly toward the other ships. The lights went out just as he switched off the engine.

"With a little luck they'll never hear us. Just so we don't land on the hangar—"

"Or one of those jagged pines," Crabb said dismally.

THE GYRO settled with hardly a sound. Trent tilted the ship to one side as a brief glow on the ground marked the opening of a door.

"Must be a house back under the trees," he told Crabb. "Open the greenhouse and be ready with that gun if we drop into the frying pan."

Crabb slid back the rear enclosure. Trent's cockpit was already opened. He leaned out, brought the gyro down a hundred feet behind the darkened hangar. The machine settled into thick grass without even a bounce. He waited, hand on starter and ignition switch, but there was no alarm.

"Come on, Mort," Trent whispered. He reached for his holstered .38, climbed down, and tiptoed to the rear of the hangar. The muffled sound of voices became louder. With Crabb at his heels, Trent stole to the end of the hangar, cautiously looked around the corner. Two mechanics were examining the crippled Corsair with the aid of a flashlight. In the glow three other men were visible. One was short, heavy, middle-aged, with a plump and perspiring face. Trent instantly recognized him as J.T. Dayne, co-owner of Universal Aluminum. Next to him was the Corsair pilot, a taller man, with a square, hard-set face. A third man, about thirty years old, with a dark, sardonic countenance, stood between them. He was dressed in the uniform of a Navy chief petty officer.

"But what if their message to Langley Field did get through?" Dayne said in a frightened voice.

"*Dummer Ochs!*" said the man in Navy uniform. "Do you take me for a fool? I jammed it with artificial static before he said five words. Pull yourself together."

"It's all right for you to talk, Blaummer," Dayne said sullenly. "If things go wrong, you can slip out of the country and nothing lost. Everything I own is here, and if this thing fails I'm ruined."

"What are your petty affairs compared with the *Fuehrer's* plans?" snarled the pilot. "We are nothing—none of us—"

"We've no time to waste squabbling," Blaummer cut in. "Zotta, go check over the Douglas. Make sure the rudder is safe where that last burst raked us."

The pilot glowered at Dayne, strode toward the DC-3 where two other mechanics were working. Blaummer turned abruptly to Dayne.

"You had better not try to back out now, *mein Freund*. You are in too deep."

"I'm not backing out," blustered Dayne. "But Zotta makes me sick with his incessant yammering. If he's so determined to sacrifice himself for *der Feuhrer* why didn't he get that gyro tonight or last night?"

"Those are tricky ships, especially in the dark," retorted Blaummer. "And Zotta had orders not to attack any one until we signaled that our little 'camouflage' had failed."

Dayne looked nervously at his wrist watch. "We'd better take a final look at those maneuver plans. It's only thirty minutes till we take-off."

"Time enough," replied Blaummer. "There's only one important change in the 'invasion' plan. I was lucky to get that through Schmidt, in Naval Communications at Norfolk. Come inside, and I'll show it to you."

"Are you sure it's safe to stay here?" asked Dayne. "If that rudder is all right we can take-off now and circle until we're ready. Don't forget this old plantation is in my name. Civil

Aeronautics is checking up on the owners of all private DC-3's, and if they trace—"

"I've covered that," snapped Blaummer. "I had our man in New York report you on a trip in Mexico."

He led the way toward a rambling colonial house just visible back in the shadows, and Dayne reluctantly followed. Trent turned and put his lips close to Crabb's ear.

"Dayne—the aluminum chap—is a Nazi stooge. That DC-3 is his ship. Come on, we've got to get into the house and find what they're up to."

Keeping close to the hangar, they tiptoed behind it and on toward the old plantation house. Zotta was inspecting the tail of the DC-3 with a flashlight. As he turned, the beam crossed the cabin windows. Crabb caught Trent's arm.

"Look!" he whispered. "There's that headless guy—and the woman."

"That's a painted screen just inside the windows," Trent said in an undertone. "There's one on each side, with lights shining on it so it looks like a real cabin. That spot where the man's head was must be a hinged piece they can open for a gun-port. That Air Corps pilot didn't hit the ship last night. They broke the window to fire at him."

"I get it," muttered Crabb. "The painted screens are to hide their radio transmitter. It must be a huge set, from the power it had last night when it blanked out WRC."

"It's a smart trick, disguising the ship like that," said Trent. "They could fly anywhere, and nobody'd suspect the plane unless he got right on top of it the way we did."

"I'd like to have a look at that set," the inventor said in a curious tone. "I figure their carrier-wave is what threw our compass off and caused those crashes. They must have some special coils and tubes to—"

"Sh-h!" whispered Trent. A faint red spot had appeared from the gloom ahead, and in a moment the figure of a man with a cigarette became visible near the house. They drew back into the deeper shadows, went around to the side. Trent stared back toward the hangar as another flashlight went on. The pilot of the second Corsair was going over his ship.

"We've got to work fast," he told Crabb. "They'll be set to take-off in a few minutes."

"What are you going to do?"

"We've got to find what they're up to. I've a strong hunch it's tied up with the Navy's 'invasion' force. Blaummer mentioned a plan—he's going to show it to Dayne. They must be upstairs—a light just went on. Maybe I can get close enough to hear something."

THEY STOPPED beside a trellis, above which a second-story balcony showed dimly. Trent took out his silver case.

"You can't smoke here!" Crabb said frantically. "Somebody will see the glow."

Trent laughed softly. "I'm not lighting up, old top—just something to steady my nerves."

He put the cigarette between his lips, holstered his automatic. "Stay down here and keep guard. I hope that trellis will hold my weight."

He tried it gingerly, then went up, careful not to make a sound. As he swung onto the balcony he saw Blaummer spread a map on a table in the lighted bedroom. Dayne bent over it, while the spy traced a line with his finger. Trent crept nearer to the window and the voices became audible.

"All radio stations, including airways beacons, have been cut off in this area during the maneuvers," Blaummer was saying. In his hasty, clipped accents Trent suddenly recognized the sibilant mystery-voice. "Norfolk and everything for thirty miles up and down the coast will be blacked-out. The ships will have only faint blue guide-lights at their sterns, for the next in line. Force 'A' is coming in ten minutes earlier than Force 'B'—that's the change I mentioned. If I hadn't learned about it, everything would have been ruined."

Both men turned as Zotta came in from the hall. The Nazi pilot had a fierce, eager gleam in his eyes.

"All three ships are ready! Why do we wait?"

"Have the engines started," said Blaummer. "We'll be there in a few minutes."

"Heil Hitler!" exclaimed Zotta. He pivoted, went out swiftly.

"Well, it will soon be over," Blaummer said with a grimly exultant note. "Everything has gone as I planned."

"You planned?" said Dayne, ruffled. "What about my getting this hideout—smuggling in your special radio equipment—giving you my ship and getting those Corsairs? How far do you think you'd have got if I hadn't paved the way? Faking that expose about the aluminum shortage was as smart as anything you've done—they'd never suspect me now, and the story was about to come out, anyway."

Blaummer smiled sardonically. "No one will rob you of the credit, *Herr* Dayne. If America falls to us later, you will be rewarded. Your mistakes will be forgotten."

"I'm not the only one who made mistakes," Dayne said in a sullen voice. "Having Blackston pull that trick on the roof last night—when we already knew what the conference was about. What if he'd been caught instead of killed? He might have betrayed us."

"Not he—Blackston was another Zotta. And since you must know, I was afraid they had learned something important when I heard about their sending for Eric Trent and Crabb. Those two have spelled bad luck too many times."

"Well, their luck went into reverse tonight," Dayne said with an ugly satisfaction. "It sounded as though Trent was about finished, from that call he—"

The engines of the DC-3 rumbled to life, drowning the rest. Trent edged closer to the window as Blaummer bent for a final look at the map. The old-fashioned latch was unfastened. He cautiously tried the window, and it gave readily for an inch or so. Taking out his .38, he crouched by the ledge, gave the window a sudden upward shove.

CHAPTER IV
The Fleet in Danger!

WITH A screech, the window went up halfway—and jammed. Prepared for a quick jump into the room, Trent had to dive underneath. He landed on one knee, and before he could swing his gun Blaummer kicked the weapon out of his hand. Dayne snatched it up with shaking fingers, covered him.

"Blaummer—it's Eric Trent!" he said tensely.

The first alarm had faded from Blaummer's dark face.

"So I see," he said coolly. "Very clever, *Herr* Trent, that dying-groan act."

Trent got to his feet. "Glad you liked it, *Herr* Blaummer. A bit hammy, but I didn't have time to rehearse."

"He knows you!" exclaimed Dayne. "He probably knows the whole plan. What if he radioed Langley or Norfolk—"

"Our operator here would have heard it," the spy said, unworried. "It's obvious he and Crabb followed and landed to learn what they could."

"That means Crabb is running loose outside!" intoned Dayne.

"He can't do much harm alone," said Blaummer. He took the pistol from Dayne. "He's probably down below that balcony, waiting. Go down and take a couple of men and round him up. Shoot him if he resists."

Dayne hurried to the door. Blaummer looked at Trent with mock regret.

"If we weren't pressed for time, I'd enjoy a little conversation with you, *Herr* Trent. Unfortunately, there is something more important at hand."

"So I gathered," Trent said calmly. "Do you mind if I have a last smoke?"

Ironic amusement showed in Blaummer's eyes. "Play-acting to the last, *hein?*"

Trent smiled, shifted the dangling cigarette to the corner of his mouth. There was a sharp plop as he bit down on the end. A stream of tear-gas shot from the tip, squarely into Blaummer's face.

With a strangled oath, the spy tumbled back against the wall. Trent threw himself down as the gun roared. Blaummer fired again, blindly, then the weapon fell from his hand and he clawed at his eyes. Trent seized the gun, scooped up the map, and leaped out onto the balcony. His swift jump almost bowled over Mortimer Crabb, who was climbing over the rail.

"Over you go, Mort!" Trent said hastily. "We've got to grab one of those ships!"

Crabb scrambled back down the trellis. Trent swung over the rail, dropped to the ground just as Dayne and another man plunged into the bedroom.

"Stop them, you fools—I'm blinded!" cried Blaummer.

Three men were running toward the house as Trent and Crabb reached the clump of trees. Back at the hangar, two or three others remained by the idling planes.

"No time for the gyro!" said Trent. "Make for that first Corsair!"

They were sixty feet from it when one of the men saw them.

"Halt!" he shouted. A pistol blazed—fell from his hand as Trent triggered a shot from the .38. The two other men dashed for cover and Trent vaulted into the Corsair's front pit. Crabb jerked the chocks, tumbled in after him. The door to the house burst open as Trent reached for the throttle and Zotta charged after them, Dayne and Blaummer behind him. A bullet creased the cowl, then the Corsair went roaring down the dark field and up into the night.

A floodlight went on, tilted up to spot them, and Trent saw the other Corsair taking off. Behind it, the DC-3 began to roll. He flung a hurried look at the compass, then headed northeast. It was in the nick of time, for three seconds later the compass began to swing wildly.

"They're at it again!" yelled Crabb.

"I've got the approximate course," Trent shouted back. "Hold Zotta off if he gets close: I can't turn or we'll get lost again."

CRABB ROTATED the rear-pit gun, pitched a burst at the zooming two-seater. Zotta's gunner answered with a hasty blast, but the range was too great. Trent climbed into the clouds, leveled out, eyes fixed on the bank-and-turn indicator. Without a compass, he was bound to deviate somewhat from his course, but it would be only a few minutes to the ocean or Chesapeake Bay.

"What in Hades happened up there?" Crabb said breathlessly through the intercom.

Trent told him in a few quick sentences.

"Tear gas? So that's where my pencils went!"

"Couldn't have served in a better cause, Mort." He grinned as he remembered Blaummer's face. "You never saw a more surprised Nazi in your life."

"But this map you grabbed—what is it?"

"The plan for tonight's 'invader' maneuvers. Take over while I have a look at—"

"There's a light below—I saw it through a cloud break," Crabb interrupted.

Trent nosed down, came through into clear air. A few scattered pinpoints of light showed in the darkness beneath.

"Norfolk!" he said, in quick relief. "Thank Heaven the black-out isn't perfect."

The compass had stopped spinning. He looked at it sharply, peering down at the solid blackness of Hampton Roads.

"That power-wave in the DC-3 is offsetting the compass to the north," he told Crabb. "Can't tell how much, but it must be at least twenty degrees."

"I've been figuring on that," Crabb answered. "It must be a narrow beam they can swing. They couldn't get enough power otherwise."

"Take over and hold her on 75." Trent turned on the cockpit light, held the crumpled map under it. Positions of the 'invader' fleet units were drawn at three places, with courses and the time marked beside each. Force "B," coming in past Cape Charles, was to divide, one half going up the Chesapeake, the other to discharge a landing-force against Langley Field. Force "A," coming in past Cape Henry, was to attempt capture of Norfolk, after a theoretical shelling. Surprise was the keynote, and the air forces from Langley and Norfolk were not to go into defensive action until the "invaders" were inside the Capes.

"Good Lord!" he exclaimed suddenly.

"What is it?" demanded Crabb.

"They're almost to the Capes, if that clock's right. Blaummer's trying to make the two forces collide in the dark! We've got to signal them—no, not the radio! They jammed our other call and they'll be listening for that."

Trent snapped on the Corsair's landing-lights, dived at full throttle. The altimeter showed 1,500 feet when tracers abruptly flamed out of the darkness above them. He had a flitting glimpse of the DC-3 off to the left, then Zotta's Corsair was on them. He whipped into a vertical turn. Off against the black expanse of water he thought he saw the sleek hull of a speeding cruiser. The wing-lights blinked out before he could look at it the second time.

"I cut 'em off!" howled Crabb. "He'd have had us in another second."

"Flares!" shouted Trent. He back-sticked, engine full out. The flare-pulls gave at his fierce jerk, but only one magnesium torch blossomed underneath. Beyond it he saw a wide fan of destroyers, cruisers, and dreadnaughts. Force "A" was Tunneling into a column to enter the Roads. But instead of a westerly course, Force "A" was steaming northwest—

straight into the path of "B," which was dimly visible south of Cape Charles!

The flare had barely lit up when Zotta's Corsair whirled in a furious renversement. In the same instant the DC-3 swerved as Trent hastily opened fire. At terrific speed, Zotta hurtled in to blot out the flare, before the Navy men below could see the trap.

Too late, Zotta saw the DC-3 twisting into his path. The Corsair skidded madly, hooking the flare with its wing. Then with a deafening crash it struck the Douglas head-on!

A great blast of flame spurted out from the interlocked wreckage. In that lurid glow, Hampton Roads and the Capes were brightly lit up. Trent let out his breath as he saw the speeding battleships curve away, water foaming aft of the dreadnaughts and cruisers as their turbines went astern. Seconds later, as the blazing ruins of the two planes twisted down the sky, searchlights came on from every direction.

"Whew!" expostulated Crabb. "Think how the Fleet would have looked in another minute or two, if you hadn't dropped that flare."

"I'd rather not think," said Trent. "Let's mosey back to Langley Field before some Navy lad gets an idea we were in on the scheme and starts shooting."

IT WAS five minutes to midnight. Eric Trent reached for the cocktail shaker, looked up at Captain Pearson.

"Guess you're stuck with us one more night, Hal. They probably won't find that field and Leaping Lena until daylight."

Pearson shook his head. "I still can't get over it. The thought of what could have happened to the Fleet—"

"You're just like Mort," said Trent. "He worries for fear something's going to happen. And when it doesn't, he worries about how bad it could have been. You two ought to team up."

"It'd be a better team than one I could mention," Crabb

said acidly. "Pearson, you'd never believe the things I go through with this—"

Some one knocked, and the door came open to admit General Busby. Half a dozen newspapermen were at his heels.

"Wait a minute, General," said one reporter. "Let's have the details. You say you suspected a scheme to wreck the Navy, and you planned that trap to capture the spies who caused all those crashes—"

"Er—ah—you'll have to wait, gentlemen," stuttered Busby, as he met Trent's eye. "The details are—ah—confidential."

He pushed the reporters out, closed the door.

"Now, Trent, I wasn't to blame—don't know how they got that story."

"But since they've got it, of course it's a bit difficult to contradict it," Trent said smoothly.

"Well—um—it's only that the public might lose confidence in the General Staff if—"

"We understand, don't we, Mort?" said Trent. "After all, publicity sometimes backfires. If we were public heroes we'd never have a quiet evening out. People would be gaping at us, asking for autographs."

"You said it," Crabb grunted. "None of that stuff for me."

Busby looked relieved. "Then you don't really mind, Trent?"

"Not a bit. Here, have a cigarette on it," Trent added as Busby started to leave.

"Thanks, Trent. You're sure, now, you don't mind?"

"It's really a pleasure." Trent held a match to the tip of the cigarette. "Now go out and give the boys the works."

Busby went out beaming. Trent sat down, with a covert grin at Crabb. A moment later there was a sharp plop from outside, followed by the sound of a commotion. Pearson hurried to the door. When he returned he had a blank look.

"Something wrong?" queried Trent innocently.

"General Busby's out there crying," said Pearson. And the

reporters are about a hundred feet up the road, cussing him out for a fare-you-well."

"Tsk, tsk!" said Trent. "You know, I had the strangest premonition this publicity was going to backfire. I wonder what could have happened."

"Yeah," said Crabb. "I wonder."

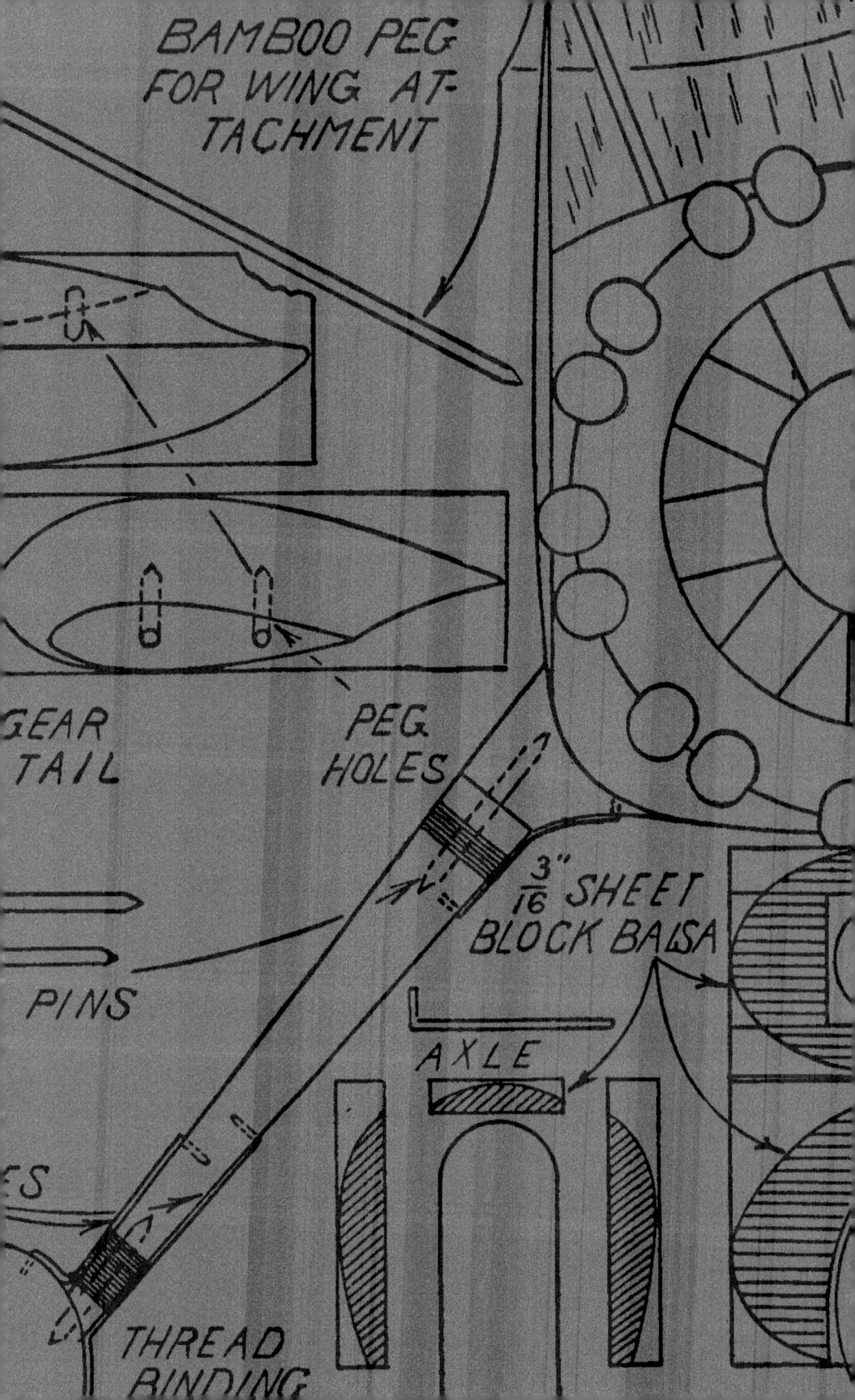

BAMBOO PEG
FOR WING AT-
TACHMENT

GEAR
TAIL

PEG.
HOLES

PINS

$\frac{3"}{16}$ SHEET
BLOCK BALSA

AXLE

ES

THREAD
BINDING

Ryan Retribution

CHAPTER I

The Man with Two Faces

ERIC TRENT took another quick look at the rearview mirror. The other car was still following, back in the fog that shrouded the Mount Vernon boulevard. He could see the amber ditch-lights, yellow blurs in the mist, keep pace as he speeded up and slowed down.

Trent smiled to himself, patted his silk hat over at a jaunty angle. Then he looked across at his mournful-faced partner, Mortimer Crabb.

"What are you so happy about?" grated Crabb.

"You know, Mort, people shouldn't try tricks on an old hand like me. They're just asking for trouble—and I'm an obliging soul."

Crabb eyed him with deep suspicion. "There's something queer going on around here. When a guy like you stands up a blonde for a brass hat—"

"Business before blondes, that's my motto."

"Since when?" snorted Crabb.

"Tonight."

Crabb, dressed in a rumpled, sack suit, with an oversize derby pulled down on his ears, stopped chewing his gum to look sourly at Trent.

"What's the idea of getting duded up just to meet that fat-head Busby?"

"Tsk! Tsk!" said Trent. "Is that any way to talk about a general—and the Chief of G-2, at that?"

Crabb said in a huffy voice, "You're holding out on that telephone message. I want to know—"

" A n d beside," Trent said amiably, "this isn't the usual white-tie-and-tails. Remember that magician suit I showed you— the one I used on

A hail of hot lead came from the captured B-25, but Mort Crabb held fast and continued to pour Tommy gun venom at the bomber! Then, suddenly, the nose gunner crumpled!

the stage back in my professional days?"

Crabb jumped. "Not the one with all those magic props clipped inside?"

Trent looked at the mirror. The amber ditch-lights still showed, back in the fog. "That's the one. Unfortunately, I had to dispense with the rabbit. But I've a few other items tucked away. If things get dull I can be the life of the party."

"The last time you used that suit we landed in jail," Crabb said bitterly.

"We got out, didn't we?" Trent's dark, restless eyes probed ahead as the highway curved. He recognized the turn. They were about a mile from the interesting clover-leaf that led up to the Fourteenth Street bridge into Washington. The new airport lay behind them, hidden in the mists.

"I want to know what Busby said," Crabb repeated stubbornly. "Just why are we chasing over there on a night like this?"

"It-wasn't the general—bless his stupid soul."

"What?" howled Crabb. "You told me—"

"It was somebody imitating his voice. Good job, too, but he didn't get quite that wheedling note when old Fuss-Buzz wants something."

"Then somebody's trying to trap us!" Crabb said, dismayed. "I told you this would happen, with you always poking your nose into the Gestapo's affairs."

THE SUDDEN drone of a low horse power airplane engine became audible from up in the murky night. The unseen ship seemed to be making an erratic power-approach to the airport.

"Sounds like some poor devil's in a tight spot," said Trent.

"Never mind him," snapped Crabb. "What about the spot we're in? In a fog like this, we could easily be murdered!"

"You get the nicest ideas," said Trent. "Here, hold my hat."

"What's this for?" demanded Crabb, as Trent handed him the silk topper.

"We're going to play merry-go-round." Trent grinned, took a swift look at the mirror as the coupé neared the clover-leaf. He bore down on the gas and the car behind speeded up. He sent the coupé racing up the inclined approach to the bridge. Halfway up, the lights fell on a "Do Not Enter" sign marking the nearest road leading down from the upper level.

Trent spun the wheel, plunged into the one-way road, horn blasting. The pursuing car skidded with screeching tires, then followed. A truck rumbled by in front of Trent. He swerved behind it, missed a bus by less than two feet, and charged across into the opposite lane of traffic. Behind, there was a crash of fenders.

"Have you gone crazy?" Crabb said hoarsely as the coupé cut off to the right amid a clamor of horns.

"Just shaking off—" Trent stopped as he heard a muffled pounding, up in the fog. He pulled the car to a quick halt near the old airport, now dark and deserted. From up in the gloom came another brief clatter—the staccato pound of a machine gun. It ended, and the motor of the unseen plane went on again.

"Don't tell me you knew about *this?*" Crabb grated.

"I didn't. We were being followed, and I had to get rid of that car. But this is something else." Trent jerked the coupé into gear as a faint glow appeared in the mists. Something tumbled past the blurred light, then it was dark again.

"What was it?" exclaimed Crabb.

Trent had cut off the car lights. He sent the coupé bouncing over the abandoned road, stopped near the fence which had barred sightseers from the embarkation area.

"Somebody bailed out, I think," he said as he put on his hat. "He didn't have far to fall."

The roar of the plane's engine abruptly increased. Its landing lights again stabbed out, trying to penetrate the murk. Trent had a glimpse of a figure swaying under a chute, then the plane dived at the spread of silk. For an instant Trent thought the pilot meant to plunge headlong into it. But the ship zoomed at the last second, its tail whipping across the billowing chute.

The silk ripped, but the man beneath it was already on the ground. He lay in a heap, just beyond the fence, and the chute collapsed limply over him. Trent flung open the gate, ran to the spot. The plane was circling back, landing.

"Help me get the chute off of him," Trent said rapidly. They jerked the massed silk aside and Trent produced a pencil-flashlight from his magician's coat. The man had evidently been half-stunned by his fall. He lay on his back, eyes closed, breathing heavily. He was fairly tall, with hair prematurely white and bristling black eyebrows in sharp contrast. His face, bronzed, rugged in outline, appeared to be that of a man about thirty-five. But there was something odd about it. Two diagonal streaks, pinkish-white, ran across one cheek, as though he had been clawed. And from one heavy black eyebrow a darkish smudge trailed down his temple.

Trent whistled softly, drew a gloved finger across the unmarked cheek. The bronze surface smeared and normal flesh-color showed beneath.

"Why, he's disguised!" exclaimed Crabb.

"Make-up, and an excellent job," said Trent. "Must be a professional."

He hurriedly unfastened the man's harness. But before he and Crabb could lift the man to his feet the plane moaned down to a quick landing. The lights flipped over the three of them and the ship swung with brakes swiftly set. Trent's right hand made a quick motion. The pencil-flashlight disappeared and a small automatic seemed to materialize from thin air.

THE PILOT of the plane jumped down, something gleaming in the reflected light. Trent saw that the ship was a Ryan three-place SC cabin job, devoid of markings. In the same flashing glance he saw the Tommy gun in the pilot's hand. Apparently there was no one else in the Ryan.

"Get him over here!" the pilot snarled. Then he saw Trent's pistol and swerved the Tommy gun. Trent fired. The Tommy thudded to the ground and the pilot stumbled back, clutching at his arm. With an oath, he suddenly whirled and dodged back of the Ryan. Trent sprang after him, thinking he was trying to climb into the cockpit. But the pilot fled into the fog, was almost instantly lost from view.

"Take that Tommy gun and keep an eye out for him," Trent told his partner. "He may try to sneak back."

Crabb picked up the weapon. "Let's get out of here! The men in that car will be looking for us. If they heard that shot—"

"Wait a second," Trent interrupted. "This chap's trying to tell us something."

He bent over, and the man with the made-up face caught at his arm. "Army field... Bolling... hurry or it'll be too late...."

"Give me a hand, Mort," Trent said quickly. "No, not the car—the Ryan."

"You can't steal that plane—even if the pilot did try to shoot you," protested Crabb.

"Who's stealing? Here, take his other arm."

The stranger tumbled into the cockpit, crawled into the rear seat.

"Take the car—meet me at Bolling," Trent began. Then he changed his mind. "No, that pilot might jump you in the dark. Pile in."

"Not me! I've had enough for one night."

Trent gave him an unceremonious boost, and Crabb's awkward figure toppled into the ship. Just as Trent climbed up with the Tommy gun, a siren wailed from the highway. A police car with a red light careened to a stop by the fence. Trent jumped into the cockpit, gunned the 145-h.p. Warner. The report of a revolver came faintly through the engine's thunder as the ship charged into the fog.

"Now, you've done it," groaned Crabb as Trent pulled the Plexiglas hatch shut. "They'll find our car, and there'll be a dragnet out for us in no time."

"Nobody will complain about our stealing this ship," Trent said, unperturbed. "The registration number was painted over with aluminum paint. This is a crook's job."

"What if he stole it from somebody else?" Crabb said dismally.

Trent grinned. "You worry too much, Mort. Switch on that overhead light. I want to check on our friend."

Under the brighter light, Trent saw that the man had been struck on the temple; he now seemed to have slipped back into a daze. Trent climbed up to a thousand feet, set a blind course for Bolling Field.

"Switch on the radio, Mort. It might help if Bolling gave us a localizer-beam."

He took off the topper and donned a head-set as Crabb threw the switch. Setting the selector, he started to call the field, then stopped as he heard the Bolling operator say:

"Bolling to Mitchel.... Still no report on missing B-25. G-2 requests full details on the dead man found in Stewart's apartment, also further details on the B-25 pilot supposed to be Stewart... Telephone G-2, Bolling, immediately, by Army direct wire... Acknowledge."

There was a brief silence, then:

"Mitchel to Bolling... Okay."

Trent looked around at Crabb.

"What's the matter?" asked Mort. "Why don't you ask for the beam?"

"Just cut in on a peculiar report," said Trent. "Seems the Army lost a B-25, and somebody's been found dead in the pilot's apartment. G-2's hot on it—and I'm wondering if that first call by Busby had anything to do with it."

"But you said it wasn't Busby."

"He called first—but somebody cut him off almost at once and pretended to be old Fuss-Buzz. Maybe it was—" Trent stopped, watching the man with the made-up face. The stranger's eyes were wide open, with a look of consternation.

Trent snapped the throttle closed. "So that worries you, Mister? What do you know about all this?"

The man's lips moved shakily and Trent barely heard his words. "Please—I'll tell them—get me to the Army field!"

"Coming right up," said Trent. "But don't try that possum act any more. I had a hunch you were faking."

He flipped the transmitter switch, lifted the mike, and called Bolling. The operator answered immediately.

"Stewart to Bolling," said Trent. "Give me a beam or landing lights." The operator's excited voice rattled into the phone: "What is this, a gag? Stewart's dead!"

"All right, then I'm a ghost! Give me a beam, anyway— even a spook can't fly blind on a night like this."

"Listen, wise guy, you can't land on an Army field."

"I'm coming in, sonny boy. I'm following that sweet little voice of yours right down to the ground! And if I crack into your nice new tower I'll sue you."

LANDING-LIGHTS CAME on below, blurred in the fog. Trent chuckled, cut off the radio and let the Ryan settle. The lights gave him the general direction of the field and he chose the long runway, landing slightly crosswind. As the ship touched and began to slow, he saw a green light wink hastily from the tower. He taxied in, switched off the engine in front of Operations. Half a dozen men ran toward them through the misty glare of the floodlights. Back of the men who seized the Ryan's wings, Trent saw several officers hurrying from Operations. A tall, thin, sandy-haired major shoved his way to the side of the ship.

"What do you mean landing—" His jaw dropped as he saw Trent's tailcoat and silk topper. "What the devil is this?"

"Evening dress," said Trent. "More or less common in civilized communities. Really, Major, you ought to get around more."

"You insolent pup!" roared the major. "Sergeant, hold this man for investigation in the murder of—"

A guard-sergeant gripped Trent's arm, but a heavy-set colonel with shrewd gray eyes motioned him aside.

"You're the one who radioed for a beam, gave Stewart's name?"

"Could be," said Trent.

"I'm Colonel Hilton, C.O. here. You'd better explain fast— if you can."

Trent gave him a flippant salute. "Mort, see if you can persuade our passenger to show himself. He seems to have got bashful all of a sudden." As Crabb turned around in the cockpit the floodlights went off.

"Orderly, have those lights turned on again!" barked the skinny major. In the interval following, Trent heard some one say in a lowered voice, "Colonel, did you notice the number had been painted out? Do you suppose this is the Ryan that was stolen from my investigator in Baltimore?"

"We'll soon know, Mr. Snell," came Hilton's crisp answer. The floodlights came on again and Trent stole a sidelong glance at the man named Snell. That swift glance turned suddenly into a stare of amazement, as he saw Snell's deep-tanned face, prematurely white hair, and bristling black eyebrows.

Instinctively, he turned to look at the man with the made-up face. Feature for feature, the two faces were identical.

CHAPTER II
Actor's Alibi

FOR A moment, there was stark silence. The impostor had stepped to the ground, with Mortimer Crabb behind him. As he saw Snell, a look of terror came into his eyes. He whirled blindly to run, but the major snatched the guard-sergeant's .45 and leaped after him.

"Halt, you!"

The masquerader turned, raised his trembling hands.

"Don't shoot… they made me do it!"

"Keep him covered, Green!" Colonel Hilton ordered.

Snell was staring at his double with a look of blank astonishment. "Incredible!" he muttered. "He looks enough like me to be my twin."

"It's theatrical make-up," said Major Green, after a close look at the streaks on the impostor's face. He glanced significantly at Snell. "That list you gave us—I'll bet it's back of this."

The man watched the look that went between Snell and the G-2 major. His eyes narrowed and he looked from Trent to Colonel Hilton.

"Could I talk with you—alone?" he asked Hilton huskily.

Hilton's face hardened. "You'll talk in the presence of witnesses. Whatever trick you're up to, it won't work, Mister." He nodded toward Trent and Crabb. "Sergeant, have these men brought into Operations."

"I knew it," Crabb said dismally. "Talk your way out of this, Mr. Smart-aleck Trent."

"Trent?" said the C.O. "Not Eric Trent, the one who—"

"Yeah, the one who sticks his nose into everybody else's business," Crabb said gloomily.

"I've heard Major Green mention you two men—I suppose you're Mortimer Crabb, the inventor?"

Crabb nodded morosely. Major Green broke in, with an ugly look at Trent. "Colonel, I've heard plenty about these two from General Busby. They've been mixed up in some pretty shady business. Even if they have helped out G-2 a couple of times, the Chief says he wouldn't trust them as far as he could see them. Especially Trent."

Trent ironically tipped his hat.

"Dear Fuss-Buzz," he said pleasantly. "Give my compliments to the old hypocrite next time you see him."

"You can't talk that way about the general!" snarled Green.

"That's funny, I thought I did. Mort, remind me to have my ears examined."

"Get inside!" fumed the G-2 major. Colonel Hilton led the way to an inner office, Major Green and Snell followed behind. When they reached the office, Hilton motioned for the guard squad to withdraw, then closed the door.

"All right, Mister," he told the impostor. "Talk fast. Why are you disguised as Mr. Snell?"

The man's eyes flicked from Snell to the .45 in Major Green's hand.

"Speak up!" snapped Green.

"And it had better be a good explanation," Snell said coldly. His eyes, frosty blue and startling against his bronzed face, bored into the other man.

"I—I'm an actor," the masquerader said hoarsely. "My name's Peter Ellicott—I used to be a quick-change artist, a make-up expert, back in the days of vaudeville—"

"Never mind all that," Green cut in hoarsely. "Why are you made up like Snell? And what do you know about that B-25 and Lieutenant Stewart's murder?"

Ellicott's eyes widened. Trent, watching him, would have sworn his surprise was genuine if he had not known otherwise.

"I don't know about any murder—and I don't know what you mean by B-25. These two men kidnapped me, forced me to make up from a large picture they had—I didn't know it was Mr. Snell."

"That's a lie!" roared Mortimer Crabb, his mournful face a picture of indignation.

"Shut up!" barked Green. "So they kidnapped you? Why did they want you to impersonate Snell?"

Ellicott shook his head uncertainly. "I'm not sure. Trent told Crabb something about getting a list. They first offered me a thousand dollars if I'd—"

"The Gestapo suspect list!" Colonel Hilton interrupted. "Snell, they were after that secret roster you secured for us! These men must be Hitler agents!"

"Eric, for Heaven's sake, tell them the truth!" moaned Crabb.

Trent grinned. "It's his act. Let him hog the spotlight."

THE ACTOR shot a nervous look at Trent. "I was living at a little rooming-house in Baltimore. One night this man Trent came to see me. He said he was going to produce a big musical on Broadway and he wanted a quick-change comedy sketch. I went out to his car, and that other fellow, Crabb, pulled a gun. They blindfolded me, drove to some place— a farm, I think—and kept me in the cellar. I heard a plane several times. That was ten days ago."

"Get to what happened tonight," Green said curtly.

"They had me practice making up like Mr. Snell. Tonight they took me out to that plane. I heard Trent say they'd make me get the list. I'd turned down the thousand dollars because it sounded crooked."

"Hold on," Snell interrupted. "How much did they know about me? Did they coach you about impersonating me?"

Ellicott quailed under Snell's cold eyes. "They started to tonight—and then something went wrong. He and Crabb decided to land here. I couldn't hear what they said, but I guess they were going to make me pretend to be you all the way through."

Green turned a gloating smile on Trent. "Let's see you talk yourself out of that!"

Trent yawned. "Why bother? Frisk him and you'll find proof he's lying—unless he's thrown it away."

The G-2 major glowered at him, wheeled to search Ellicott's pockets. The actor started as Green brought out a small automatic.

Green plunged his hand into Ellicott's left coat-pocket, produced an aluminum cylinder the size of a fountain-pen, with a small hook at one end.

"What's that?" said Colonel Hilton.

"It's one of our new miniature tear-gas grenades," muttered Green. "They're specially made for G-2."

"I tell you I don't know anything about it," protested Ellicott.

In grim silence, Green brought out a loaded cartridge clip, a wallet, and two folded sheets of paper. As he smoothed out the first paper his eyebrows went up in astonishment.

"It's a duplicate of that Nazi agent roster!" he told Snell.

"That proves he was lying," Hilton interposed. "He said they wanted him to get the list. What's the other paper?"

Green handed it to Snell, with a puzzled look. "Aren't those the names of your corporation's confidential investigators?"

"You're right." Snell glared at the actor. "Where'd you get this?"

Ellicott's streaked face set in sullen lines. He did not answer.

"That's my wallet," said Trent as Green opened it. "He took that when he held us up tonight, to make sure who I was."

"Held *you* up?" said Colonel Hilton. "Let's get this straight."

"Somebody called me tonight, said he was General Busby and asked me to meet him at the old airport. He said he had a lead on a spy-case and wanted some 'outside' help. We drove over there, and this chap Ellicott jumped us with a Tommy gun. You'll find it in the Ryan. He knew I was a pilot, and he evidently needed one badly. He made me start the engine, and he kept Mort covered so I had to fly the crate. When we got inside, he started to shift to that pistol—the Tommy gun took too much room. Mort socked him. He fired one shot and then I knocked him cold. After that I tuned in to call you for a landing. I heard your operator reporting on the Stewart business, and figured the quickest way to get action was to use his name."

THERE WAS a long silence as Trent finished. Snell motioned to Green, whispered, something. The G-2 major looked sidewise at the table on which he had put the objects taken from Ellicott and studied them.

"Good idea," he said. He handed his .45 to the C.O., went into an adjoining office and closed the door. Colonel Hilton looked sharply at Trent.

"Your story is as strange as Ellicott's. You mean to say you've no knowledge of the B-25 or Lieutenant Stewart?"

"Only what your operator kindly spilled," said Trent.

Hilton said slowly, "Lieutenant Stewart was found dead in his Long Island apartment some hours ago, when a time-fuse burned out before reaching a room drenched with gasoline. But a dozen Mitchel Field men saw Stewart take off in a B-25 this afternoon. The B-25 is missing. Any ideas?"

"Ask Ellicott," said Trent. "Somebody must have doubled for Stewart—obviously another make-up job." Before Hilton could question the actor, Major Green came back with a triumphant grin on his face.

"You were right, Snell. I found it in the files. Colonel Hilton, that tear-gas pencil was designed by Mortimer Crabb under a War Department contract. I just remembered something else. General Busby said Trent used to be a professional magician. I figure he planted all that stuff on Ellicott while they were marching in here. He and Crabb are about the only ones who could have access to those tear-gas pencils beside G-2."

"That settles it," said Hilton. "Call the F.B.I. to come get—"

Some one knocked, and Green opened the door. A middle-aged chauffeur, a thin-faced, tired-looking man, came in apologetically.

"Beg pardon, Mr. Snell, but you said to tell you in time for that meeting in Washington."

"Be there in a minute," said Snell. As the chauffeur went out, Trent thought he heard a faint drone of engines, but the phone rang before he could be sure. Green answered. After a minute he put the phone down.

"Well, Mr. Trent, I think that just about sews you up. The Virginia police have broadcast a warning to all airports in this area to be on the look out for that Ryan. *And* they described you—silk hat and all—as the guy who had the Tommy gun just before the ship took-off. Also, they've got your car."

"What's the charge?" Trent said amiably.

"How do I know? Probably carrying weapons without a license."

"I have a license. *Even* for a Tommy gun—special permission, through Naval Intelligence."

"I've no time to waste here," Snell cut in brusquely. "Colonel, I'll telephone you tomorrow—or Major Green. Obviously my investigators will have to be changed, after all this."

"Before you leave," said Trent, "wouldn't you like to see what your double looks like, underneath?"

Snell's cold blue eyes flicked to the actor. "I'll have plenty of time to see him, behind the bars. I suppose, Colonel, you'll hold these men in the guard-house until the G-Men arrive?"

Hilton nodded. "Might as well march them out now, Major Green, and have the guard detail take charge. Have Trent and Crabb searched before they're locked up."

Snell went into the hall and Green gestured with the .45 for the prisoners to follow.

Just as they emerged from the building the floodlights

went on. A big plane had landed, was rolling swiftly toward the line, only its running lights turned on.

"It's a B-25!" exclaimed Hilton. The ship pivoted with a roar and stopped, its twin rudders pointing almost straight back at Operations. "Why, that's the number of Stewart's ship—the one that's missing!"

The access-door of the bomber opened and four men sprang down. At the same moment the tail turret .50's, whipped around to cover the assembled mechanics and the guard-squad. Then the engines went dead.

"**DON'T MOVE,** anybody!" rasped the first of the four men. A sub-machine gun glinted in his hands and Trent saw Garand rifles in the hands of the three who spread out beside him. Handkerchiefs covered the lower part of the gunmen's faces.

Ellicott gave a muffled cry as the leader strode toward him. He whirled, but Colonel Hilton seized his arm. The scuffle knocked the .45 from Hilton's grasp.

"Don't try to get it, Colonel!" the masked leader said grimly. "Look out for that sergeant!"

The guard-sergeant had clawed suddenly at his holstered gun. One of the Garand rifles caught him a vicious blow above the ear, and he went down with a stifled groan.

"Get Ellicott and put him inside," snapped the leader. "Hold on—which is Ellicott?"

He stalked over to the group, and two of the masked gunmen followed, their Garands leveled. The tail turret guns swiveled to cover the huddled mechanics and guards. Ellicott shrank back, recoiled as he saw Snell beside him. The leader hesitated, turned to Trent and spoke in a hurried undertone.

"Chief, hadn't we better take both of them?"

"Trent, you traitor!" raged Colonel Hilton. "So you were back of this all the time!"

Trent saw the mocking glint in the eyes above the handkerchief. The man was expecting an angry protest—a protest that would make no impression on Hilton.

Trent scowled. "What kept you so long? You're fifteen minutes late."

The gunman blinked. Trent could almost see his jaw sagging behind the tightly drawn handkerchief.

"Never mind," he said tartly, before the man could answer. "Tell Joe to get the engines going, before somebody turns on the alarm."

"Eric, you idiot!" groaned Mortimer Crabb. "You'll never get out of this now. They'll all think you're guilty."

One of the masked gunmen seized Snell's arm, shoved him toward the bomber. Snell made a frantic lunge toward the Garand, but the gunman's fist connected with his jaw and his resistance ended. Ellicott was being herded toward the bomber by one of the other men. The leader motioned angrily to Trent and Crabb.

"What're you waiting for? By Heaven, if you've framed up some double-cross—"

"Come on, Mort," Trent said cheerfully. "You know how Hank is when he's crossed."

The leader moved carefully backward, the Tommy gun cradled in his arms. Trent followed him a few steps, turned, and ironically lifted his silk topper to Hilton and Green.

"Good night, gentlemen. Thanks for the party."

What followed seemed only a blur of motion, as his hand snatched a coil of silk ribbon clipped inside the hat.

The coil whirled straight for the masked leader's face, unwinding as it flew, and the man jumped back with an oath. Trent gave a swift pull and the coil looped, spun around the gunman's neck. Two or three wild shots drilled into the ground as Trent jerked him off balance.

Trent was on him before he could recover. The bomber's tail-turret guns rotated toward him, but the gunner held his fire as Trent lunged against the leader. The shriek of the alarm-siren cut through the abrupt rumble of the B-25's starboard engine. Trent snatched the Tommy gun, drove a stiff uppercut to the masked man's chin. Major Green and four or five men were running toward the B-25 as the remaining gunmen scrambled aboard.

The tail turret .50's whipped toward the Army men. Trent triggered a burst from the Tommy gun, and the man in the bomber's tail slumped in a heap.

The port-motor of the B-25 roared, speeding up as the big ship hastily pivoted into the wind. Trent sprinted for the Ryan. He set the switch, was jumping back to pull the prop when Mortimer Crabb lumbered out of the mist.

"I'll twist her!" howled Crabb. "We've got to stop those devils or our goose is cooked."

The bark of a .45 came faintly above the din of the bomber's motors. Trent caught the engine on the first spin of the prop, hauled Crabb aboard.

"I saw another clip for this gun back there," he shouted. "Get it loaded!"

Shadowy figures were running through the fog as he kicked the Ryan around into the wind. One materialized into Colonel Hilton's broad figure, with the misty glare of the floodlights yellow on his face. The C.O. had recovered the .45. Flame jetted through the mist and two more shots blazed after the Ryan as Trent brought up the tail.

"He must be loco!" Trent flung at his partner. "Didn't he see me drill that tail gunner?"

"Nobody could see except Snell's chauffeur and me," moaned Crabb. "The slipstream blew the rest of them back—those that hadn't started to run. And in that fog you couldn't tell much, anyway. Hilton thought you were firing at his men."

The Ryan bounced across a runway, took-off. Ahead, the B-25 was lifting into the murky night, at an angle to their course. Trent cut in sharply, closing the gap.

Tracers flamed suddenly from the nose-turret of the bomber, and Trent felt the rudder jump as bullets nicked the tail. Then Crabb leaped up, thrust the Tommy gun through the opened hatch. A quick burst jabbed back at the man in the bomber's nose.

CHAPTER III
Fugitive Flight

"**H**OLD IT, Mort!" Trent shouted. "Try to hit a prop! We've got to force them down!"

The B-25 lurched into a turn and the huge wing almost hooked the Tommy gun from Crabb's hands as it swung. Crabb ducked back into the cockpit and Trent dived clear. The bomber was twisting out over the river, barely a blur in the fog when he zoomed back after it.

"This is the last clip, Eric!" Crabb yelled down from the open hatch.

"Make it good!" Trent flung back. "Wait until you see the whites of their eyes, old bean!"

A light came on momentarily in the nose of the bomber. Two figures were struggling, one the gunner, the other—

"It's Snell!" bawled Crabb. "He's knocked down the gunner!"

"Now's your chance!" Trent flipped the Ryan up under the massive wing and Crabb triggered a blast at the starboard prop. But the B-25 slued away hurriedly just as he fired and the tracers missed the flashing disc by inches. A furious burst blazed from the tail-turret and Trent had to dive to save them from disaster. With a last barrage, from both tail and nose guns, the bomber lifted into the mists and was gone.

"I'm sorry, Eric," Crabb said in a hollow tone as he closed the hatch. "I guess I'm not much of a shot."

"Maybe it's just as well. We might have made them crash, though that ship's supposed to maneuver on one engine."

"Well, what do we do now?"

Trent switched on the radio. It was still set at the Bolling Field frequency. The tense voice of the Army operator rattled into the phones:

"—and relay to all Army, Navy and civil airports! Keep

watch for the Ryan and the B-25, and if they land, detain the crews by force if necessary... Use caution, as crews of both ships are armed and desperate... Both planes without numbers... Men in Ryan—one tall, dark eyes, small black mustache, dressed in evening clothes... The other shorter, extremely homely man, long, hollow face and protruding adam's-apple, grating voice, dressed in old tweed suit and derby... Men in B-25—"

Trent shut off the radio. "I'd sue that operator, Mort. He makes you sound like Karloff at his worst."

"What of it? Nothing matters now. We may as well go back and give up."

"And let Busby crow over us?" said Trent. "Not a chance. We've been in tougher spots than this. Remember the time we were on the stage of that German theater, pretending to be Nazi actors?"

"That's just it," mourned Crabb. "We've pushed our luck so far that there's none left."

"Who needs luck? All we have to do is the unexpected." Trent wriggled out of his magician coat, on the inside of which were clipped a small dagger, a cartridge clip, a keyring, and a blackjack, in addition to various magic props such as trick cards, self-lighting cigarettes, and packs of wadded ribbon.

"What, no shotgun?" Crabb said sourly.

"Too bad I couldn't get back that automatic," Trent said regretfully. "But I did manage to retrieve my wallet. The gun has no numbers on it, anyway."

"They don't need that. They've got enough to put us away for a hundred years—if they don't hang us."

"They have an electric chair in the District of Columbia, Nothing vulgar like hanging. Give me your vest and that derby."

"What's the idea?"

Trent ripped off his white vest, collar, and tie. He rolled

up his sleeves, slapped on the derby, and pulled on the vest that Crabb reluctantly handed over.

"Now, where are we?" Trent climbed up until he was on top of the fog layer. "That must be the Avenue, with all the lights. That jog must be Fifteenth Street, at the Treasury. The White House will be about there."

"You lunatic, you're not landing on the White House lawn?" howled Crabb.

"Just an aiming point. Fasten your belt, in case I hook the Treasury by mistake."

The Ryan angled down, wings barely moaning. Trent cut off the engine, eyed the clock. "A minute ought to do it. Yell if you see trees and stuff."

Fifty seconds later something flitted past under the left wing.

"Top of Commerce Building, I hope," said Trent. "If not—"

Trees whisked under the ship, and then there was an open space into which he hastily dropped the three-seater. The Ryan hit, bounced hard, and came back with a wrenching of landing gear.

"Where are we?" gasped Crabb.

"Ellipse—right behind the White House. Flip on the light and be sure we haven't left anything they can trace."

Crabb complied. "Nothing—except that map. It wasn't ours, anyway."

"What?" Trent snatched at the map, gave it a hasty look and rammed it into his pocket. "Take my coat—roll it under your arm and get under the trees over near Commerce. Wait there."

CRABB DISAPPEARED in the fog. Trent kicked at the main fuel valve until gas spurted down into the cockpit. Then he soaked one end of his handkerchief, climbed out on the wing. Lighting the soaked end, he hung the cloth on the edge of the window and jumped to the ground. He had covered two-thirds the distance to the trees when the explosion came. Flames shot through the mists, making an eerie scene, and cars ploughing through the night were abruptly visible north of the Ellipse.

Trent waited under the trees until a score of people were running toward the fire. He dashed across to the nearest car.

"Get the fire-engines!" he yelled. "There are men caught in there—I heard 'em yell right after the plane crashed!"

"Good Lord!" gasped the driver. "Nothing can save them now!"

The passengers of the car behind ran up, and Trent heard the driver repeat the story. He slipped back into the mists, circled under the trees until he found Crabb. In five minutes the Ellipse roadways were jammed. Fire trucks came with screaming sirens, police radio-cruisers howling an accompaniment. Trent led his partner to the edge of the jammed-up traffic. Thirty seconds later they were on their way to the Highway Bridge in a borrowed sedan whose driver had joined the crowd.

"Now it's car-stealing," Crabb said hopelessly.

"Just borrowing it," Trent corrected. "We'll park it a few blocks from our place. The cops will find it later and we'll pay the owner after this is cleared up."

"Don't talk to me," grated Crabb. "All I hope is that they put me on the same rock-pile—with a big hammer."

"Take a look at this map while I drive. There's an X marked 'boat.' Find it?"

"Yeah. It's a map of the Potomac and Anacostia. Shows Bolling Field and Naval Air, part of Haines Point, and the Army War College. Here's the X—it's between Naval Air and the War College. There's a dotted line to Haines Point and another down the river below Bolling Field about two miles."

Trent took a quick glance at the marked spot. He drove for several minutes, thinking back over the events of the evening. Then a sudden gleam came into his eyes.

"What gets me," Crabb said dourly, "is the way that guy

Ellicott double-crossed us. We saved his neck—and then he framed us with that crazy lie."

"He was scared to death, Mort. He didn't dare talk."

"Sure he was scared. He never expected to run into the fellow he was impersonating. He had some big stunt doped out to trick the officers at Bolling, and it backfired."

"I'll give you fifty percent on that. Why do you think those birds in the B-25 kidnapped Snell?"

"From what that colonel said, Snell must've been helping the Army, letting his company investigators check on spy leads."

"All right, why did the pilot of that Ryan try to kill Ellicott? And why did Ellicott bail out?"

"Who are you, Professor Quiz?" snapped Crabb. "If I were smart enough to dope that out, I wouldn't ever have let myself be roped in by a wild-eyed idiot like you."

Trent chuckled. "Mort, I won't say another word until we get home. By then maybe you'll have recovered that sunny disposition of yours."

Half an hour later, Trent stopped the car in a side-road a quarter of a mile from the old Virginia mansion they had rented.

"Wipe off that door-handle, Mort. Don't leave any prints."

"This is a good spot for a murder. Get out of here before I'm tempted too much."

"I'll take that coat now," said Trent. "Getting a bit chilly. Here's your iron hat; sorry I got a dent in it."

"Too bad it wasn't in your skull," grated Crabb.

TRENT LOOKED around warily as they neared the gate, but there were no waiting police cars. A high stone wall, topped with barbed wire and an electrified conductor, surrounded the grounds. The wall and the wire had been erected by the former owner, an eccentric recluse. The charged wire had been Crabb's idea, installed to prevent theft of his various inventions. At various intervals, a small red bulb illuminated a sign, "DANGER! 100,000 volts!" That the amperage was too low to kill, Crabb had thoughtfully left unmentioned.

Trent opened a hinged box built into the wall beside the steel-barred gates. A telephone mouthpiece and small built-in amplifier became visible. He pressed the button—two longs, three shorts, and one long. A bell sounded faintly within the darkened mansion. A light flashed on above the gates and they then silently opened.

"Welcome home!" a voice suddenly said, behind them. "Turn around—slow, now!"

Crabb groaned, lifted his hands, and turned. Trent looked over his shoulder.

"Well, well, what a pleasant surprise. Have we kept you waiting long, General?"

Busby's fat face had a complacent smirk. He kept his pistol pointed at Trent's back.

"None of your tricks. I've got you cold. Turn around and get your hands up."

Trent pivoted. The G-2 chief was dressed in civilian clothes, just now soiled and wrinkled.

"Too bad we weren't home to receive you," Trent said genially. "It must have been cold in that ditch."

"Just back up—both of you," ordered Busby, "And don't think I won't shoot. I heard the broadcast when I was driving out here—and any court would acquit me as doing my duty."

"It seems the game is up, Mort. Our career of crime is ended."

Busby followed closely as they backed through the gate-way.

"Mort," said Trent, "You'd better warn the general about our automatic protection. If he gets hit—"

There was a click just after Busby passed by a concealed electric-eye that operated the gates, and the steel barriers began to grind shut.

Busby whirled frantically. Trent's hand flashed down,

whisked the blackjack from under his coat. The next second the general collapsed with a grunt.

"Now you've done it!" Crabb ejaculated. "Even if we could have got out of those other charges, they'll call this murderous assault."

"I just gave him a light tap. It would take a pile-driver to crack that skull. Pick up his toupée and help lug him inside."

"What are you going to do?" demanded Crabb.

"Stage a little act. It seems to be the fashion tonight. Maybe we'll win a prize."

Busby was still unconscious when they carried him into the big room where Trent kept most of his magician paraphernalia and the various costumes he had assembled in his adventurous career.

"I'll help you undress him," Trent told his partner. "Then get him into the Army uniform they loaned you when we were on that Fort Bragg case. Put brigadier insignia on the straps; there's everything from shavetail bars on up in that box. Stick some campaign ribbons on his chest. If he starts to get tough, tie his hands. But I think he'll be out for a while longer. When he comes to, tell him the gates hit him."

"What are you up to?" said Crabb as Trent slid open the wardrobe doors.

"I'm joining the Army for a couple of hours." He brought out an enlisted man's uniform, a web belt, and holster. He made a quick change, took an Army Colt from his gun cabinet. "When you're through, bring him down to your lab."

"All right," Crabb said gloomily, "I guess nothing makes much difference now."

Trent patted his shoulder. "I knew I could count on you."

"Sure, I might as well be dead, anyway, the life I lead around here."

TRENT GRINNED, went out to the hall and down to the basement laboratory. He turned on a floodlight, glanced out through a barred window at "Leaping Lena," the autogyro they had annexed in a case some months past. Then he turned to the automatic recorder which Crabb had connected to their all-wave receiver. He switched on the receiver, listened for the Washington police broadcast. There was no mention of Crabb and himself. Evidently the burned plane had not cooled enough to permit a search for bodies.

He glanced at the transmitter switch, rummaged through Crabb's supply cabinets until he found a clock with a relay attached. Then he quickly set to work with wire cutters and a soldering iron.

When Crabb and General Busby came down the steps, fifteen minutes later, Busby's toupée was awry from the bump where the blackjack had struck him. The uniform trousers were too long, the blouse a trifle baggy.

"You'll pay for this, Trent. Trying to kill me!" the general wheezed.

"I tried to warn you about those gates. So sorry about your head, but we'll take you right over to a hospital.

"Hospital? Then what's the idea of rigging me up in this uniform?" fumed Busby.

"Just so they'll appreciate your importance, old chap. I'll tell them I'm your orderly and see that you get real service. Take him outside, Mort. I'll be with you in a jiffy."

Trent waited until Crabb had unlocked the door and taken Busby outside. Five minutes later, with a small portable radio under his arm, he went out to where Crabb and Busby waited by "Leaping Lena."

CHAPTER IV
Masks Off!

*T*HE GYRO droned steadily up into the murk, after its leaping takeoff from the walled yard. General Busby was wedged disconsolately into the space between the tandem seats, with Crabb behind him, knees buckled up like a grasshopper about to jump.

"And there's the whole story," said Trent, concluding a swift sketch of what had occurred after the telephone call.

"That's the craziest lie I ever heard," retorted Busby. "And that phone call story—you hung up on me. That's why I decided to come out to your place. You hung up as though you were scared."

"Your wire was tapped," Trent cut in. "When you called me, they had to make sure I didn't barge in and break up things, so somebody impersonated you on the phone and told me to come to your house in two hours. Then they rushed some men out in a car to tail us—probably to grab us when we parked."

"Where are you taking me?" demanded Busby, ignoring Trent.

"I'm heading for St. Elizabeth's."

"But that's the hospital for the insane!"

"They probably won't know the difference," said Trent. "But I'm not sure I can find it in this fog. In case we crack-up and you come out alive, I'll give you a last warning. Something big's popping in Washington tonight—so big that if it comes off you're going to be court-martialed."

"Bah!" said the general.

"They needed a make-up expert to impersonate some high-ranking officers. So they kidnapped Ellicott from his boarding-house. They've had him practicing ever since. They needed a long-range plane for their escape, after pulling this job. They forced Ellicott to make up a double for that B-25 pilot, and murdered Stewart to hide the impersonation. Somewhere along the line, Ellicott saw a chance to escape with papers that would prove the whole scheme and—"

"Bunk!" said the G-2 chief. "You've foxed me for the last time, Trent. Somebody offered you big dough to get those lists. You had Ellicott pose as Snell, after you stole the Ryan. That Ryan belonged to one of Snell's investigators. His insurance company has policies covering hundreds of defense factories. And Snell's job, as you well know, is to guard against sabotage in those plants. Snell turned up plenty of leads. He helped us, and G-2 helped him. You probably heard Snell was giving that list to the C.O. at Bolling and figured you'd get there first, have Ellicott pose as Snell, and give them a fake list. Then you'd waylay Snell—only he got there first and broke up your little scheme."

"Mort, I told you you needn't worry about his skull. It's even thicker than I thought."

The gyro had been settling slowly through the fog. Trent kept an eye on the blurred pattern of lights which showed up through the mist. He cut off the engine, peered over the side. "Leaping Lena" went down silently, its rotor blades swinging overhead. Suddenly the roof of a large building appeared at the left. Trent slipped the gyro to one side, and the next moment the landing gear crunched.

"Good Lord, Mort, we're in a bad spot!" he exclaimed. "We've dropped into the War College by mistake!"

He climbed out hastily, the portable radio tucked under his arm. As Crabb followed, Busby let out a yell.

"Help! Sentries! Corporal-of-the-guard—over this way!"

"That fixes it!" Crabb said hopelessly.

"Keep back in the fog and don't do anything!" Trent tossed at him. "Let the old boy yelp!"

Voices sounded as he turned and felt his way toward the War College. A flashlight went on, and as it spotted the gyro he saw an Army lieutenant with officer-of-the-day belt. At his heels was a tall, rangy figure in civilian clothes—a man whose face Trent instantly recognized.

"It's General Marshall, Chief of Staff!" groaned Crabb. "Busby'll tell him everything!"

"Good Heavens, General Busby!" gasped the O.D. "How did you get into uniform so fast? I thought you were in—"

"Grab him!" roared the tall civilian. "He's an impostor! The real Busby's in the War College!"

The G-2 chief's mouth fell open. "But, General Marshall, surely you recognize me?"

THE O.D. blew a whistle and two sentries came ploughing through the murk. Busby was seized, hustled toward the dark War College. Trent tiptoed after them, halted back in the gloom as faint light showed near the entrance. He cast a look at the luminous hands of his wrist-watch, switched on the portable radio.

"Mort, when this thing—" he jerked around, but Crabb was nowhere to be seen.

"I tell you I'm General Busby!" the G-2 chief's wail rose from a mutter of voices. Trent stole closer. By the glow of the O.D.'s flashlight he saw two men emerge from the War College. Both were in civilian clothes. The first would have been recognized by any newspaper reader, as the Secretary of War. Behind him was a pompous, fat little man who was an exact duplicate of Busby, except for the uniform.

"General Marshall, that man's a fake!" howled Busby. "He's—"

"Keep him quiet!" snapped the man who looked like Stimson.

The O.D. was staring from Busby to his double.

"That gyro belongs to Eric Trent," said the false Chief of Staff. "That means he's loose somewhere on the grounds, probably with Crabb. They are the two men the F.B.I. and police are looking for. Get your men busy and find them!"

The O.D. scurried off toward the gyro. After a few seconds, Trent heard the frightened voice of the fake Stimson.

"We'd better get away while we can! We've got the master war-plans, anyway!"

Busby gave a strangled moan. "You devils! Trent was right!"

The fake Marshall reached out, gripped Busby by the throat. "Another yelp like that and it'll be your last. Toller, you and Schwartz get back inside and finish the photostating. If we can carry it out as we planned, they'll never know the secrets have been stolen."

"But it'll take another half hour. That O.D. is already suspicious, and if they find Trent and he talks—"

"Who'll believe him? He's a fugitive and I'll see that—"

"Car 25, call your station… Car 25, call you station," droned the portable radio.

Trent ducked back into the fog just in time.

"*Zum Teufel!*" exclaimed the false Stimson. "What was that—a police car?"

"Must be the radio in that gyro," muttered the man made up as Marshall.

"Get 'em up!" came a sentry's bark. "General, I've caught one of them. Fits the description of that fellow Crabb."

"All right, you've got me," Crabb said gloomily.

"Now what?" whispered Busby's double. His voice was shaky. "We'd better choke him off quick!"

Trent shot a look at his wrist-watch. A tingle went up his spine. Two minutes, but it might be too late. He put down the radio, now set for full volume at the frequency of the Washington police station. He reached for his Colt, then stiffened. His holster was empty! The gun had evidently fallen out as he climbed from the gyro.

Trent, swiftly unfastened the web belt, tiptoed toward the steps. He was within a few yards of them when a flashlight probed through the fog. It was pointed toward the sentry approaching with Crabb, but the edge of the rays glinted on Trent's gun-belt buckle.

Trent sprang to one side, whirled the buckle at the nearest man's head. It was the pseudo-Stimson, and he staggered back with a muffled oath. Before Trent could swing the belt again, a pistol was jammed into his ribs. Over it he saw the grim eyes of the man posing as Marshall.

"One word and I'll drill you!" the man whispered. "Schwartz, it's Trent, in a uniform. He was set for some trick. Get him back there out of sight!"

Hard steel pressed into Trent's back and the man disguised as Busby herded him into the shadows. The sentry came up, marching Crabb before him.

"All right, I'll take over," the fake Marshall said curtly. "I want to question this man privately."

The sentry hesitated, then saluted and faced about. He halted, a blurred figure in the gloom.

"It's suicide to wait any longer!" Schwartz said hoarsely. "If things begin to blow up—"

"Why should they?" said the false Chief of Staff. "These soldiers believe we're the three top men of the Army. That O.D. thinks it's just what we told him—a highly secret rush job to send a copy of one war plan to England, so they'll be ready to cooperate when things break."

"But these three men?" said Schwartz.

"Our car is right down the drive, if we have to make a getaway. You can have the maps copies in twenty minutes. I've got the key plans in my mind—the main points, anyway. We'll load these three men in the car. I'll order that O.D. to tell nobody about it, even his C.O. I'll tell him they're spies who are going to be secretly jailed, to fool the Nazis. We'll take them to Haines Point, load them into the boat, tie them up, and dump them overboard on the way down the river. The F.B.I. will think Trent and Crabb kidnapped Busby, and all this will be covered."

GENERAL BUSBY made a desperate leap for the tall spy's gun. The fake Chief of Staff raised the pistol for a furious blow, then he went rigid.

"*Calling all cars! Calling all cars!*" blared the hidden radio. "Get to Army War College with all possible speed! Spies impersonating Army officials attempting theft of secret plans! Spies impersonating Army officials! Harbor Police look for boat in channel between—"

"Lieber Gott!" moaned Schwartz. He whirled to dash down the steps. Trent tripped him neatly, pounced to snatch his gun.

"Guard detail—seize all those men!" the O.D. bellowed through the mists.

The psuedo-Marshall snatched something from the man made-up as Stimson, then raced down the steps. Mortimer Crabb swung at him but missed. In the gloom, Trent's clawing fingers missed Schwartz' gun. He jumped up, sprinted after the fleeing spy.

"Halt!" bawled a sentry. A rifle poked into Trent's stomach. The O.D. ran up, pistol in hand.

"You numbskulls!" shrieked General Busby. "You're letting a spy escape with the war plans! He's making for a car."

The O.D.'s befuddled eyes twitched from Busby to Schwartz, his double. Trent bent and swiped his hand across the German's face, showing the streaked make-up.

"Holy cow!" groaned the O.D. He spun around as the engine of a car abruptly roared. Trent jerked the lieutenant's .45 from his grasp, pumped two shots at a khaki-colored War Department car which plunged out of the mists. A front tire blew out, and the car hit the steps. As sentries ran toward the machine, the engine of the gyro came to sputtering life. Trent ran toward the ship, Busby and the O.D. at his heels.

A soldier's flashlight flipped toward the ship, caught the taut face of the false Chief of Staff. The rotor suddenly whirled and "Leaping Lena" jumped twenty feet into the air in a wild take-off.

He's got the war plans!" screamed Busby. "Shoot, you imbecile!"

Instead, Trent raised his hand, pointed up at the lifting gyro. "Abracadabra! Stop!" he said dramatically.

The gyro's engine broke its roar, sputtered a second, and

went dead. Leaping Lena settled helplessly back to the ground and the spy stood up with raised hands as rifles covered him from three sides.

Busby gasped at Trent. "How in the name of Heaven—?"

"Just a little ancient magic," Trent said modestly. "Some time I'll show you what I can do with 'Mysto Sesame.' But you'd better take charge of the situation before that poor O.D. goes nuts."

The disguised spy was climbing down, helpless fury twisting his made-up face. One of the sentries retrieved the war-plans book from the cockpit, handed it to Busby.

"Thank God!" said the G-2 chief. He glared at the spy. "Whoever you are, you'll get plenty for this!"

"You can even hang a murder rap on him," said Trent. "I hope you don't mind, Mr. Snell."

"Snell?" gasped Busby.

Trent reached out, plucked off a wig which, with the help of hairstain, had hidden Snell's white hair.

"A clever job, thanks to Ellicott. He covered up those heavy black eyebrows neatly by soaping them flat and putting crepe hair ones on top. Incidentally, there may be a second murder charge, General, unless Ellicott turns up alive."

"We found him in the back of that car," grunted Mortimer Crabb. "Tied up and gagged."

"Between him and these boys," said Trent, "I guess we'll get the rest of—" the siren of approaching police cars cut him short. Half-dressed Army officers began to appear through the murk that hid the officers' quarters across the War College yard.

"It's your party now, General," said Trent. "The credit's all yours—provided you keep Crabb and me out of durance vile."

"WELL, BETWEEN Ellicott and that Nazi, Toller, we got the whole set-up," said Busby. "Except that radio alarm—"

"That was simple," said Trent. He glanced across the War

College office at Crabb. "Remember that relay-clock of yours, Mort? I hooked it up to your transmitter, after dictating that police call to a record and setting it for a play-back to the mike-circuit. I figured a sudden alarm would throw a scare into Snell, and tip off the War College sentries, even if he had them fooled till then."

"Well, it certainly worked," said Busby. "I—er—have to apologize for my previous remarks. If you hadn't doped it out, they'd have had those Army-Navy cooperation plans, and when we got ready to use them we'd have been blocked at every turn. Even if Snell had got away and we knew the plans were gone, it would have been bad enough. He'd planned it perfectly. As chief investigator for that insurance company, he flew around everywhere, checked up plants, got most of their protection secrets, and nobody gave it a thought. That spy-list he gave us was a fake, designed to get some innocent aliens into trouble and cover his men.

"He kidnapped Ellicott, just as you said. He had his chauffeur, Toller, play the Stimson role," the General went on. "Schwartz was the leader of the masked gunmen in the B-25. They got the B-25 as you figured out. Ellicott was flown back to the farm in Maryland where they were going to hide the B-25 tonight until they got the plans. He saw a chance to make-up like Snell and escaped, and he made off with the investigator list and spy-roster to show to the Army. He even fooled the Ryan pilot until they were in the air. Then the pilot got wise, radioed Snell. He was flying back to the Maryland farm when Ellicott managed to bail out. He'd been trying to force the pilot to fly to Bolling Field, so after you two horned in the pilot guessed that's where he'd tell you to go. He phoned Snell—we got that out of Toller—and Snell rushed to Bolling, after having a message sent out to the farm for the B-25 mob to stage a 'rescue.' It caught them while they were starting to paint on new insignia. Incidentally, we found the real B-25 crew out there, tied up. The man who impersonated Stewart had simply landed there at the farm and Snell's men grabbed the crew.

"It was a neat touch, Schwartz trying to make me out the leader of the gang," said Trent. "You phoned Colonel Hilton and Green?"

"It's all been cleared up. Even if you did—ah—sidestep a few rules and regulations. The police have been called off, and there'll be an item in the papers saying it was a mistake about you two. Of course, we'll have to keep the true story quiet."

"How about the car that trailed us tonight?" queried Trent.

"The police are looking for the men. Toller gave us the names and descriptions. They're German aliens.

"If Ellicott had only talked, there at Bolling, he'd have saved a lot of trouble," Crabb said sourly.

"He was scared to death of Snell," said Busby. "And when Major Green poked that .45 at him, he thought maybe Green was in on it with Snell. So he made up that lie about you two."

"Tell him no hard feelings," said Trent, as he stood up. "I've been lied about by experts—even generals."

"Uh—oh, by the way," Busby stuttered, "I was going to ask you, how did you stop that gyro engine with that 'Abracadabra' business?"

"A little emergency fuel-valve, hidden under the seat. I shut it off when I landed, just in case anybody tried to make off with "Leaping Lena." When Snell hopped off, I knew there wasn't enough gas in the fuel-line to last more than a few seconds. I saw a chance for a little mystification—the old professional urge, you know."

"Ah—just about as I figured it," boomed Busby. "By the way, I used to dabble with magic once myself. Takes a fast hand to fool my eye, if I say so myself."

Trent clapped his hand on Busby's shoulder as the general reached for his cap. "You'll have to show me those tricks sometime. Well, Mysto Sesame."

Busby looked after him, puzzled. "What's that 'Mysto

Sesame' stuff?" Crabb asked suspiciously as he and Trent went down the steps.

Trent chuckled. "So it takes a fast hand, eh? Remind me to mail his toupée back to him in the morning."

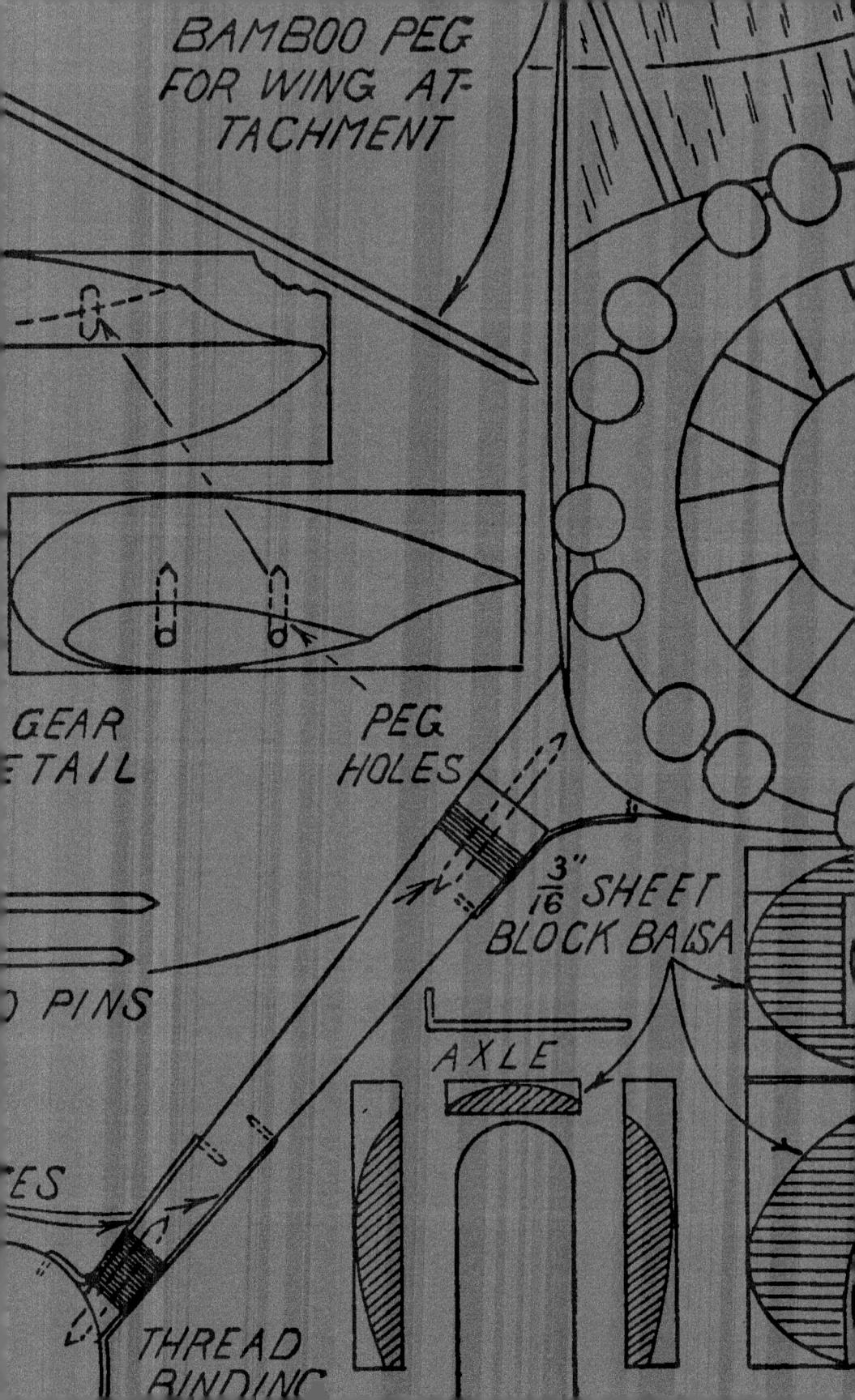

BAMBOO PEG FOR WING AT-TACHMENT

GEAR ETAIL

PEG HOLES

$\frac{3"}{16}$ SHEET BLOCK BALSA

PINS

AXLE

ES

THREAD BINDING

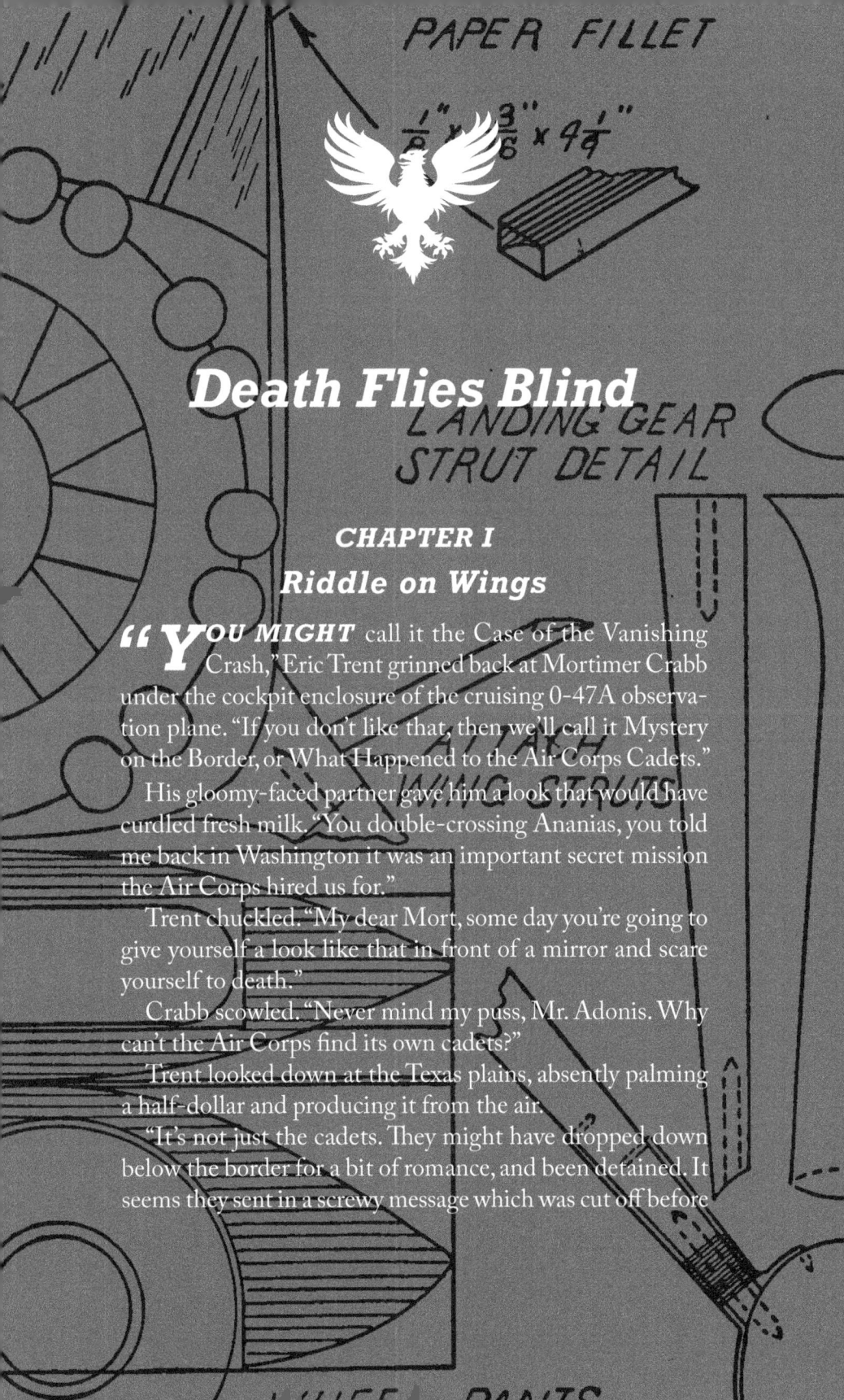

Death Flies Blind

CHAPTER I
Riddle on Wings

"**Y**OU MIGHT call it the Case of the Vanishing Crash," Eric Trent grinned back at Mortimer Crabb under the cockpit enclosure of the cruising 0-47A observation plane. "If you don't like that, then we'll call it Mystery on the Border, or What Happened to the Air Corps Cadets."

His gloomy-faced partner gave him a look that would have curdled fresh milk. "You double-crossing Ananias, you told me back in Washington it was an important secret mission the Air Corps hired us for."

Trent chuckled. "My dear Mort, some day you're going to give yourself a look like that in front of a mirror and scare yourself to death."

Crabb scowled. "Never mind my puss, Mr. Adonis. Why can't the Air Corps find its own cadets?"

Trent looked down at the Texas plains, absently palming a half-dollar and producing it from the air.

"It's not just the cadets. They might have dropped down below the border for a bit of romance, and been detained. It seems they sent in a screwy message which was cut off before

Mort Crabb continued to pour cupronickel at that Caproni, even though its port engine was trailing a long plume of dense black smoke!

anyone could understand what they meant. Randolph Field called them back, but they didn't answer."

"So we have to turn nursemaid," growled Crabb. "I still don't see why the Army can't do its own work."

"Matter of international relations," said Trent. His dark eyes had a sudden gleam. "It's really a peculiar business, Mort. An instructor at Randolph Field took a quick sneak across the border, after hearing the message. He swears he saw the plane cracked up somewhere south of Laredo, in Nuevo Province. He went back and reported it, and the War Department got permission to fly over and spot the wreck so Mexican authorities could get help to the pilots."

"Well, why didn't they?" demanded Crabb.

"The wreck was gone, old bean. They flew around for five hours and never did find it. And that's the last anyone heard

of the cadets. G-2 is in a stew over it, but they can't raise
Cain with Mexico; it's evident the Mexican government
doesn't know anything about it. So they've fixed it up for us
to meander across in a private plane, as aerial tourists, and
do little sleuthing."

"I get it," Crabb said sarcastically. "Mr. Eric Trent, the
great ex-magician, will go down and make a couple of passes
and produce the whole works out of a hat."

"Good old Mort," said Trent. "Never a word of complaint,
always cheerful to the last. Say, am I cockeyed or is that a
Caproni dropping out of the blue?"

CRABB STARED up at the plane, which was angling down in a sharp spiral a few miles to the south.

"It's a Caproni, all right," he exclaimed. "What the devil are they doing here?"

The Caproni straightened into a glide. There was a quick burst from its forward fixed gun, fired apparently into empty space. Trent opened his throttle and the 0-47 raced in, climbing to get above the Italian bomber.

"Watch yourself!" howled Crabb. "That may be a captured ship the Army's trying out. They're not shooting at anything."

"Take another look," Trent tossed back. "There's something just ahead of—"

"I see it now! Well, for the love of Mike. It's only a model plane!"

Trent twisted the 0-47 into a tight bank and the bomber's target came into clear view. The black wings of a model plane showed briefly in the glow of the setting sun. Then another burst smoked from the Caproni's fixed gun.

"Let 'em alone—it's just target practice!" yelled Crabb.

He had barely finished when a blast flamed toward the 0-47 from the rear-compartment guns. Trent kicked the ship into a steep turn.

"Practice, eh?" He tripped his forward guns. The bomber swerved, dived back at its target. A burst grazed the model plane's wings and it skidded wildly. Trent saw half the right wing sheer off as bullets tore through the tiny fuselage.

The rear gunner loosed another blast at the 0-47, Trent plunged under the Caproni, forcing the gunner to drop to his tunnel-gun. He triggered a burst, then whipped back to top position. The gunner was too late. Crabb opened up with his rear guns as Trent raked the bomber's fuselage. Smoke gushed from the starboard engine, then fire mushroomed out.

The bomber reeled, went down in a tightening spin, with a black plume trailing behind it. Crabb plumped into his seat, and mopped his forehead.

"Phew! For a second I thought we were back in Europe."
Trent throttled and nosed the ship down quickly.

"Keep your eye on it, Mort!"

"What are you talking about?" snapped Crabb.

"That model plane. There must have been something pretty important about it, the way they went after it."

"It's the craziest thing I ever saw," declared Crabb. "A bomber chasing a— Say, I just remembered, that Caproni didn't have any insignia."

"I noticed that." Trent looked down at the spot where the blazing bomber had crashed. "And I don't think there'll be any chance to identify it—or the crew."

"Well, it was them or us," Crabb said grimly.

Trent glanced back at the fluttering wing of the model plane. The rest of the battered little ship had plummeted to the ground, near the corral of an isolated ranch. He made a quick survey, saw a level spot clear of cactus not far from the ranch buildings.

"How about putting the wheels down?" grated Crabb.

"I was getting around to it, old chap." Trent motioned down to the ranch. "Seems to be deserted. It would have been convenient to have witnesses to back up our story. Otherwise, we're likely to be packed off to the nearest asylum."

"An asylum would be a nice rest, after two years with you," retorted Crabb. "There goes that wing—it's going to land near the corral."

"I didn't know you were so familiar with—" Trent sat bolt upright. Without the slightest warning, flames had suddenly burst from the windows of the ranch-house. Inside of a minute the entire building was ablaze.

"I've had enough!" said Crabb. "Let's get out of here."

"Not a chance," replied Trent. "This thing begins to smell. I would not miss it for a million dollars."

HE CIRCLED and landed. When they reached the burning ranch-house the heat drove them back. Trent shaded his eyes and peered into the fire. A moment later the blazing roof fell in.

"If anybody was in there, he's a gone gosling now," said Crabb.

Trent waited for the flames to die, but even when the walls fell in the fire showed no signs of abating. He glanced at an overturned gasoline drum near a dilapidated truck.

"That tank was probably emptied in the house," he told Crabb. "See where the fire ran along the ground? It was either set off inside and burned out to where the gas spilled, or it was set off out here and burned into the house."

"Maybe we'd better look over those buildings," muttered Crabb. "They don't look as though they'd been used lately, but somebody might be hiding."

They searched the bunk-house and the ramshackle barn. But the buildings were empty. From the cobwebs and dust, they had not been used for years. Crabb glanced through the open door of a tumble-down henhouse, rubbed his chin, came back to Trent.

"Some chickens in there. They're all dead."

Trent looked in at the dead fowl. They appeared not to have been dead very long. He felt one, and it was still warm.

"Well, what do you make of it?" asked Crabb.

Trent shook his head. "Let's find that model plane, or what's left of it."

They were starting toward the corral when an engine blipped two or three times above them. Trent looked up, saw a light cabin plane. It was a Stinson Voyager. The ship came in for a careful landing, taxied up beside the 0-47. The pilot switched off his engine and climbed out. He was about thirty and was solidly built, with a broad, sun-bronzed face. He wore a big sombrero, riding breeches, and a loose leather jacket.

"So that's the modern cowboy," grunted Crabb. "Why doesn't he put a saddle on the fuselage and ride it that way?"

The pilot strode up, after a look at the burning ranch-house.

"Hello, gents! What happened?"

"We don't know," said Trent. "It's a bit mixed up. Who lives here?"

"Old Jake Overman. Say, where is Jakey? Don't tell me he—"

"He may be in there," said Trent. "I wouldn't be surprised. Was he the kind of man who'd pick that type of suicide?"

"Suicide?" The pilot's jaw dropped. "Say, what're you getting at?"

"Somebody doused the place with gasoline. If anybody's in there, then it was either murder or suicide."

"Who'd want to murder that old coot?" scoffed the pilot. "If you ask me, he set it on fire to collect the insurance. He's probably hiding—or else he fixed it to burn and dug out somewhere to get an alibi."

"You knew Overman pretty well?" queried Trent.

"Enough to know that he was an old miser," said the other man. "My name's Bud Lanigan. I'm up at a dude ranch twenty miles north; I hop the dudes around and do odd inspection jobs on ranches around here. We heard an explosion and I saw the smoke, so I hopped down here to see what was up."

"What you heard was a bomber crashing," said Trent. He pointed across the plains at the plume of smoke. "An Italian bomber, incidentally."

"A *what?*" gasped Lanigan.

"Mort, I think we'd better take Lanigan into our confidence," Trent told his partner. "He knows the setup around here and maybe he can help us."

Omitting reference to their mission, he told Lanigan about the model plane and the Caproni, and how the ranch-house had burst into flame. Lanigan listened, pop-eyed.

"Well, hog-tie me for a— Say, you're not tryin' to kid me?"

"Maybe that model plane will convince you," said Trent.

"Mort, you take the other side of the corral and we'll search over this way."

He found the section of wing a few minutes later. Crabb and Lanigan hurried over, at his shout.

"There's a message of some kind scrawled on it," said Trent. "But I can't make it out. Part of it was on the other end of the wing. Incidentally, it's a metal wing—a bit unusual for a model."

He held out the broken section, and they all three gazed at the letters which had been scratched with obvious haste by a sharp instrument.

OVERMAN
E RANCH
KILLED
DOLPH
IAL TOR
RING 192

LANIGAN PURSED his lips in a soundless whistle. "The old bird's been up to something, after all!"

"Looks like a warning, to me," grunted Crabb. "Somebody knew he was going to be killed."

"Yeah, but how could anybody know that plane was comin' here?" demanded Lanigan. "Hey, hold on—those model planes don't usually fly more than a few minutes. It must have been sent off close to here."

"There's another possibility," cut in Trent. "Overman himself may have sent it, as a message to somebody else. You say he was a hermit?"

"Sure, he lived all alone." Lanigan pulled out a sack of tobacco, started to roll a cigarette. "Now I think of it, though, a big car stopped up by the ranch one day and a foreign-lookin' bird asked how to get here. I'd clean forgot."

"I think we'd better put this whole thing before G-2, at Randolph Field," interrupted Trent, "They can notify the Texas authorities. You'd better fly down there, too, Lanigan. We'll throttle back and cruise with you."

"Why not let me go with you?" said Lanigan. "You've got an extra seat. Somebody can fly me back here to my ship."

"Not afraid of somebody stealing it?" asked Trent.

"If you want to know," said Lanigan, "I ain't crazy about hopping down to Randolph in a ship without any guns—not with things like this going on."

Crabb said sourly, "Mister, if you get into a ship with Eric Trent you'll probably regret it the rest of your life."

"Pay no attention to him, Lanigan," grinned Trent. "He's suffering from ulcers and unrequited love."

"I guess I'll take a chance," Lanigan said.

"First," said Trent, "let's see if we can find the rest of that model plane. I doubt if we'll learn much—the crash must've torn it to pieces. But we might be able to piece out some of those words—let's hope."

They searched for thirty minutes, without success. The ranch-house was still aflame, though the fire was dying.

"We'll have to let somebody else go through the ruins, after they cool," Trent decided. "It's getting late." When they reached the 0-47, he motioned for Crabb to take the pilot's seat. "Take her off, Mort. I want to talk with Lanigan about that fellow Overman. And I think I'll call Randolph, so Captain Mawson will be on hand. He's G-2 at the field."

Crabb climbed into the ship. Trent boosted Lanigan up and handed him the model plane's broken wing.

"I'll help you stow it in a moment. I want to see if we got nicked in that scrap."

Trent stooped and looked under the 0-47's wings and fuselage.

"No damage, fortunately," he reported as he climbed up. Lanigan was in the rear seat. Trent squeezed past the mid-seat, lifted the model's wing. We'd better slide that over farther, out of the way."

Lanigan bent over, and Trent shoved the panel aside with his foot. Crabb looked around disgustedly.

"You'd think you were getting ready for a trip around the world. It's only thirty-five miles to Randolph."

"I like to be comfortable," said Trent. "Go ahead, old chap, wind up the ticker."

"Yeah, let's get goin'," said Lanigan.

Crabb started the engine, taxied carefully into the wind, stopped, and fastened his belt.

"Better fasten yours," Trent advised the cowboy. Lanigan nodded, his eyes on the model plane wing.

" 'E' ranch. I don't get that. Nobody ever called it—" the engine revved up and drowned the rest. Crabb took-off and climbed quickly.

"Hey, Mort, this isn't an interceptor," Trent called to him. "Hold her down a bit."

"Listen, you back-seat driver," snorted Crabb, "you wanted me to fly this bus. You'll take it and like it."

Trent grinned at Lanigan. "He's just showing off for your benefit. Don't look so worried. She comes out of a spin in a couple of hundred feet."

"If you want to know," grated Crabb, "that place gave me the creeps. The sooner it's out of sight—"

"What's the matter?" said Trent, as his partner stopped, open-mouthed.

"Look!" Crabb said blankly. "Now the Stinson's on fire!"

CHAPTER II
Two-Gun Trick

"**W***HAT! MY* ship?" howled Lanigan. He unbuckled his belt, stared down with an expression of consternation.

The Stinson was blazing. The fire seemed to be centered in the cabin, but it was rapidly spreading to the wings. There was no one in sight around the plane.

"Hm-m, never a dull moment," observed Trent. Lanigan gave him an angry look.

"It's all right for you to joke about it. How'll I get another ship? The defense is taking all the new Stinsons."

"What's more important," Crabb said grimly, "is how it got on fire. Maybe we'll get it next!"

He jerked the throttle, nosed down. Trent yawned.

"Never mind, Mort. We won't catch fire. Mr. Lanigan isn't a man to commit suicide just to get rid of us."

Lanigan stiffened, then he whipped his hand back to his hip. It came out from under his leather jacket holding an automatic.

"Nice guesswork, Mr. Trent! Too bad you didn't guess about this."

Trent stopped yawning. "Oh-oh! Mort, I'm afraid I made a slight bust. I'd have sworn he wasn't armed."

"You imbecile!" groaned Crabb. "If you knew he was a phoney, why didn't you—"

"Turn around and keep still," Lanigan ordered. "Head straight south. And don't try anything."

"Do what you please, Mort," interrupted Trent. "He won't plug you—he can't fly a ship like this, anyway."

"For your information," Lanigan said icily, "I have flown ships twice this fast. I would rather take you two alive, but it is not necessary."

"You know, that wasn't a bad act, the cowboy business." Trent eyed him amiably. "I wouldn't have suspected you if you hadn't dropped in so soon. That is, until you pretended you hadn't noticed that burning bomber. Even then, I wasn't sure until you were so anxious to come with us."

Lanigan gave him a contemptuous smile. "You're lying, to cover up being tricked so easily. Not that it would make any difference. I was prepared to shoot both of you down there, but you were taken in completely."

"And you wanted to keep us alive if possible, in case we opened up about the missing cadets," said Trent.

Lanigan's eyes narrowed. "If you don't look out, you're going to talk yourself into a bullet."

"Yes, and me too," moaned Crabb.

"Keep your eyes on that compass," snapped Lanigan. He flicked a side glance at the radio helmet-phones hanging beside his seat. Carefully covering Trent, he put on the helmet, set the wavelength lever, and threw the transmitter switch. Still watching Trent, he picked up the mike.

"K-3 calling. K-3 calling in," he said in a toneless voice. He repeated the call several times, then switched to receiving. Whoever he was calling had obviously answered, for he cut in the transmitter immediately.

"All covered, but had to change plans. Friend Stinson died. Am coming North American, route 47, and I persuaded two guests to come along. May be a little late, as we have to go up over the divide. If it is after dark, have a light ready. Acknowledge."

"What, no 'Heil Hitler?'" said Trent as Lanigan pronged the mike.

"Keep your mouth shut!" snarled Lanigan.

"So you're K-3. I'll bet K-1 and K-2 are lovely boys. All working for dear little Adolf to undermine America."

"You stupid mongrel," rasped the pseudo-cowboy, "you and the rest of your countrymen will soon learn what it means to mock *der Feuhrer.*"

"Lanigan—or whatever your name is," said Trent, "you're a dirty Nazi rat."

The spy turned purple.

"You insolent fool! I'll teach you." He drew back his free hand, whipped it sidewise at Trent's face. Trent jerked back, but the man's fingers raked his cheek.

"I like this way better," Trent said coolly. He clipped the Nazi under the chin, and Lanigan's head rocked back.

"*Schweinhund!*" he screamed. He leveled the pistol at Trent's heart and pulled the trigger. It clicked and that was all. The spy frantically jerked it again.

TRENT REACHED under his coat, and a .38 seemed to leap out into his fingers. Lanigan turned deathly white.

"For God's sake, don't kill me!" he cried. The automatic fell from his hand. Trent eyed him with cold amusement.

"I thought so. Take your gun away and you're yellow, like the rest of your mob of bullies."

Crabb was staring back, wiping perspiration from his face.

"Thank Heaven!" he said hoarsely. "How'd you work it, Eric?"

"I noticed the artillery when he was climbing up on the wing, to get in," explained Trent. "I thought I'd better relieve him of it. That's why I inspected the ship—to empty the gun. I slipped it back in his pocket when he bent over to help move that model plane wing."

The spy looked at him with sullen hatred.

"Yes, you should have bumped us when you had the chance," grinned Trent. "I don't suppose you want to make things easier for yourself and explain that business at the ranch?"

Lanigan clamped his lips tightly shut.

"Well, let's see—" Trent paused. "Mort, pick up the course to Randolph Field. Then call them and ask Captain Dick Mawson to meet us with a car. They'll tell you what operating field to use."

He changed the wavelength, after noting the setting, and Crabb called the Air Corps training, center.

"They'll notify Mawson," he told Trent. "Maybe I should have asked them to have a guard there, too."

"I can handle Adolf's little messenger," replied Trent. "It would be a pleasure to shoot him if he tried to run."

"You've nothing on me," mumbled Lanigan.

"Just attempted murder, setting fire to a man's house, probably murdering him—"

"I landed there after the fire started," retorted the Nazi.

"Also before. You dumped that gasoline, and then left some kind of delayed-action bomb or grenade. The same kind you set off in the Stinson, so nobody could trace it. The question is, why? What were you trying to cover up anyway?"

But Lanigan again was grimly silent. Trent made no further attempt to question him, and the observation ship soon came in sight of Randolph Field. It was nearly dusk when Crabb landed. There were only a few mechanics on the line as he taxied in.

"Must be time for mess," said Trent. "Come to think of it, I could ruin a steak right now. We'll have to look into that, after seeing that *Herr* Lanigan gets his bread and water." Lanigan appeared not to have heard the jibe. He was staring around the darkening base, and his face was taut. Crabb switched off the engine and lifted out the model plane wing, Trent gestured with his .38 for the spy to follow.

"Just to keep this little affair private," he said, "I'm going to put my gun in my pocket. But it'll still be pointed in your general direction."

Captain Mawson was waiting, with a car drawn up near the line. He was a big man, blond and heavy-jawed. He had a briskly efficient manner.

"How are you, Crabb? Hello there, Eric. What's the idea of hauling me away from mess to—" He stopped short as he saw Lanigan. He made a lunge in front of Trent. The spy whirled, leaped for the wing of the 0-47. He was almost into the cockpit when Mawson seized him by one leg and dragged him to the ground.

"Do you know who this is?" Mawson demanded of Trent.

"He says his name's Lanigan," Trent said mildly.

"He's a Nazi spy—a Gestapo agent!" roared Mawson. "It's a wonder he didn't try to kill you."

"He did," said Trent. He got out the .38. "But I had him under control until you started running interference."

"Why didn't you tell me you had him covered?" growled Mawson. He looked a little sheepish.

"I thought maybe you two had a personal fight." Trent glanced at the staring mechanics. "How about talking this over privately. Let a couple of men hold our guest."

MAWSON BECKONED to two husky mechanics. They gripped the spy's arms, held him while the G-2 captain led Trent and Crabb to one side.

"All right, shoot," said Mawson. "Where'd you pick up Krieger?"

"As a matter of fact, he picked us up. But first, suppose you tell me what you know about him."

"He's been run out of three South American countries," Mawson said promptly. "We've got a file on him; I recognized him from secret pictures Brazilian police gave our attaches. He was one of Hitler's secret agents in Poland and Austria. His specials is undermining enemy air forces and stealing aviation secrets. He built up a secret air base in Argentina, but they caught him. He's believed to have murdered an Intelligence office in Bolivia. Mexico ordered him out two months ago, with a lot of Nazi air attaches who were doing espionage. He was supposed to have gone back to Berlin by way of Japan."

"Ever hear of a ranch north of here owned by an old fellow named Jake Overman?" queried Trent.

"I remember the name vaguely. We know most of the places around here."

Trent turned to Crabb. "Show him that wing, Mort."

Mawson gazed blankly at the scrawled letters.

"What's the idea of this?"

"Doesn't mean anything to you?" asked Trent. "Okay, here's the story." He described briefly their encounter with the Caproni and the model plane and what had occurred at the Overman ranch and after their take-off with Krieger. Mawson looked dazed when he finished.

"That's the craziest yarn I've heard outside of the Liars' Club. Why would a Gestapo agent want to murder Overman? And that bomber—you're sure it was Italian?"

"All but insignia. Don't forget Krieger's message. He said everything was covered up. Something was going on at that ranch, and it went wrong. They are desperate enough to risk sending that Caproni up here. It's a pretty good bet it came from some hidden field below the border."

Mawson nodded slowly. "That's possible. The Mexican government is trying to spot them, but we know Nazi agents have fixed up some fields. Even so, that doesn't explain the model plane."

"Forget that a minute," said Trent. "I've a hunch we might trick Krieger if we suddenly mention why Mort and I came down here. If there's any connection—"

Mawson wheeled to a stocky, bald-headed corporal who was gaping at the prisoner.

"Corporal, tell them to bring that man over here."

"Yes, sir." The non-com saluted, and in a moment Krieger was brought over. He had lost some of his sullen defiance; there was a frightened look on his broad face.

"Captain, I demand to be turned over to civil authorities," he blurted out, before anyone else could speak. "Maybe I did try to scare Trent—but we weren't over an Army reservation. It's a case for civil jurisdiction!"

"Very neat," said Trent. "Your friends will put up bail, and you'll skip before—"

From the darkening sky came a low but rapidly increasing rumble. Krieger jerked around, staring off to the south.

The drone of engines grew swiftly into a crescendo howl as two planes dived at Randolph Field. Abruptly, the staccato pound of machine guns came through the roar of engines, and tracers streaked through the twilight.

"It's an AT-6 on the tail of a Vought Corsair!" shouted Mawson. "And it was an advanced trainer those cadets disappeared in!"

A siren shrieked through the din, and a few moments later a searchlight stabbed the sky. The Corsair was down to five hundred feet, twisting frantically to shake off the AT-6. A burst from guns on the trainer's wings raked the Corsair's tail, and the stricken ship lurched into a spin. Its nose came up for an instant, as the pilot cut the engine and tried to pull out. Then it struck with a deafening crash, across the field from where Trent and the others stood.

"Guard this man!" Mawson flung at the mechanics. He sprang toward his car and Trent jumped in after him. The machine raced toward the wreck, just as an ambulance and the crash-truck started out. The AT-6 plunged down past the Administration Building tower, poured a furious burst into the crumpled Corsair. Then it zoomed at top speed away from the probing searchlight.

MAWSON WHIRLED to a skidding stop in front of the Corsair, his lights on the battered cockpit. Trent helped him slide the hatch-cover open. The pilot lay with his head back, an ugly gash above one ear. There was a bullet hole under his right shoulder.

"It's young Dana!" exclaimed Mawson. "He was one of the two cadets."

He helped Trent lift the pilot, and by the time they had him out the ambulance was there. A medical corps man made a hasty examination.

"Probable skull fracture… internal hemorrhage."

Dana was quickly transferred to a stretcher. Mawson looked at the medico.

"Get him in as fast as you can. Have somebody search his clothes after you strip him. Phone my office what you find."

The ambulance rolled swiftly away. Trent stared up at the fleeing AT-6, now almost to the clouds. The searchlights were holding it as three P-39's climbed after it.

"The dirty rats," muttered Mawson. "Strafing him after he had crashed!"

Trent nodded grimly. Then his eyes came back to the wrecked Corsair.

"Did you notice the air force insignia?" he asked.

"Yes, I saw it. But the number's been painted out. The ship was probably stolen from some Mexican squadron, or else that insignia was just painted on for a blind."

Trent bent over, eying the shattered instrument board. "Dana was forced down somewhere, or he and the other cadet landed to check up on something; that's fairly obvious."

"I'd figure it that way," agreed Mawson. "They must have flown over the border just to take a look at Mexico—cadets sometimes do, just for a lark. Or if it was cloudy, they could have drifted over by mistake. But there's one thing certain. There weren't any guns on their AT-6 when it took-off here."

Trent reached down by the rear seat, drew his finger across a dark smear. "Must have been somebody in here before Dana took-off. Looks as though he'd been hit pretty bad. Well, well, what have we here?"

He straightened up with an odd-shaped piece of stone. It was about a foot long, roughly shaped like a club where fragments had been broken off. One side was damp and moldy; the other was carved with curious hieroglyphics. It appeared to have been part of some rectangular section.

"What is it?" asked Mawson.

"It looks like part of an Egyptian frieze, one of those carved inscriptions they had in their temples. Apparently Dana used it for a weapon to get somebody out of the ship."

"But where—there aren't any Egyptian temples in Mexico."

"No. And I don't think it is Egyptian; it just looks like it. I seem to have a hazy recollection about a lost race in Indio-China and traces of them being found recently in Mexico. Let's go back and see if we can pry anything out of Krieger."

CHAPTER III
Secret of the Frieze

TRENT AND Mawson left the crash-truck crew working on the Corsair and drove back to the line. Crabb met them.

"Somebody said it was one of the missing cadets, and he was killed," he told Trent.

"He's in bad shape, but he may pull through," said Trent. "How did Krieger act when he heard about it?"

"He acted petrified until he heard the cadet was dead," Crabb said, with a savage look toward Krieger. "Then he seemed to be relieved. But he still acts scared about something."

"Good," Mawson said curtly. "Maybe we can work on him. We'll get him over to my office."

A guard-sergeant and one of his detail had arrived to take charge of the prisoner. Mawson ordered the Nazi taken to his office, and Krieger was brought in a moment after the G-2 captain led Trent and Crabb inside.

"Wait in the hall," Mawson instructed the guards. He closed the door, turned to the spy. "Krieger, we're going to release you to civil authorities—"

An expression of intense relief showed in the spy's eyes.

"—when you come clean," Mawson finished coldly.

The pallor came back into Krieger's sun-burned cheeks.

"You can't hold me! I demand that you—"

The telephone rang, cutting him short. Mawson answered it.

"Wait a second," he said. He motioned for Trent to take the extension phone. "All right, go ahead."

Trent listened as a crisp voice reported on the wire.

"Somebody just set off a green signal flare, behind Number Five hangar. Nobody knows who did it. That AT-6 was dipping under the clouds, and after the flare went off the ship pulled up into the clouds and disappeared. The P-39's tried to nail it but no luck."

"Could you tell its course?" asked Mawson.

"No, sir. The P-39's are still buzzing around. But we got a bearing on the Corsair and the AT-6 when they came in here. It was about 190—a few degrees one way or the other, maybe."

"Thanks," Mawson put down his phone, looked at Trent.

"Bearing 190," Trent repeated. He turned suddenly to Krieger. "Or maybe bearing 192?"

Krieger started, tried to conceal it with a careless gesture. "I'm afraid I don't know what you're talking about."

"Bearing 192—that's what that line meant on the model plane wing. 'Dolph' might be part of Randolph Field. So we take a bearing of 192 from here. Then we cross it with the south course bearing you had us fly from Overman's ranch. And thus we get a 'fix' where those lines cross."

The Nazi was sitting tensely erect, tiny drops of perspiration on his brow. Trent chuckled.

"I see we've struck pay dirt. You'd better talk, Krieger. It may save your neck."

"I don't know anything," mumbled the spy.

"Maybe you'd be interested in learning about a signal flare one of your buddies just set off? A signal to your butcher friends in the AT-6."

Krieger leaned forward, gripping the arms of his chair.

"So you do know!" roared Mawson. "One of your spies set off that green flare!"

The Nazi sank back, a twisted grin on his face. Trent sighed.

"Did you have to tell him it was green? I was going to say it was red. That green signal evidently was to let the AT-6 pilot know that Dana was dead."

"I'm sorry," Mawson said. "It was thinking about Dana

that made me blow up. Wait—we could broadcast something about his being injured, but not seriously—"

TRENT WAS watching Krieger. "I think we'd better exclude our rat friend from the rest of this. We've learned about all we can from him, unless you want to try thumbscrews."

"I almost wish I could," Mawson said vindictively. He opened the door. "Sergeant, take charge of the prisoner. Lock him up under double guard. He's to see no one without my permission."

The spy was led away and Mawson came back into the office. "What have you got up your sleeve, Eric?"

"No rabbits this time. Just a little trick that should give us the answer. Mort and I will take that 0-47 and fly to where those bearing lines intersect. I'll call in and pretend to be Krieger; we know his code signal and the wavelength. When they show a light I'll bail out, with one of those portable transmitters and maybe a tommy gun. I'll see what's up, tip Mort off by radio, and he can fly back and give you the set-up."

"What about you?" demanded Mawson.

"I'm an old hand at finding my way home. Maybe I'll detour and drop in on a senorita I used to know down in Mexico City."

"I think you're nuts," said Mawson. "But I'll okay it if I go along in the 0-47."

"You're on. Incidentally, while you're getting the equipment ordered out, how about having some sandwiches and coffee sent over? I always like to bail out on a full stomach."

"I'll have them sent to the ship, and I'll get a report about Dana before we shove off."

Thirty minutes later, the 0-47, refueled and guns reloaded, was idling on the line. Trent climbed in, a pack-transmitter fastened across his chest. Mawson was at the controls. Mortimer Crabb handed up a tommy gun and climbed into the rear seat.

"Anything about Dana?" asked Trent.

"Still unconscious," reported Mawson, sliding the enclosure shut. "They think he'll live, but he won't be in shape to talk much before tomorrow. There wasn't anything in his clothes to help us."

"Well, I'm glad he wasn't finished. Let's roll."

"All set," said Mawson, reaching for the throttle. "I didn't tell Operations where we're flying. I said to Overman's ranch, as you suggested, since we're crossing the border without permission."

He got the signal as a P-39 landed and taxied clear, and the observation ship roared out for a quick take-off.

"Better climb to 10,000 and approach that 'fix' from another angle," said Trent. "They'll be suspicious of any ship coming on a bearing from Randolph."

Mawson kept the 0-47 climbing. They went over the Rio Grande at 9,000. The G-2 captain turned around after a minute.

"Eric, you said something about that frieze. Did you remember what it reminded you of?"

"Yes, it was the lost Khmer race. They vanished centuries ago in the jungles of Indo-China, leaving a deserted city named Anghor Wat. They had certain hieroglyphics similar to the Egyptian friezes, and some years ago an archeologist in Mexico found similar characters in a tunnel, one of those military tunnels built a long time ago to connect certain provinces. Some people now think the Khmers were driven out of Indo-China and came eastward across what was then a continent connecting Asia and America, and that they settled in Mexico and were absorbed."

Mawson looked at his map, started a glide. "You mean that piece of stone in the Corsair came from a tunnel?"

"I'm just guessing. Maybe it's something else. But the item I read mentioned the Sierra Madre Oriental range. And that runs through Nuevo Province."

"I'm beginning not to like this." Mawson sounded genuinely worried. "Back there, the way you said it, the thing seemed simple enough. But you're liable to drop into a hornets' nest."

"Maybe I can do a little stinging myself." Trent patted the tommy gun, then reached for the last sandwich and the thermos bottle.

"The condemned man ate a hearty dinner," Crabb said gloomily.

Trent laughed. "I'll give you two to one I'm back at Randolph inside of twenty-four hours."

"We're down to six thousand," said Mawson. "And about ten miles from that spot. I don't think I'd better go any lower until you make that fake call."

Trent switched on the ship's transmitter, set the wavelength. "K-3 calling in. K-3 calling in," he said in a guttural imitation of Krieger's voice. "Delayed but got away. Make a light when you hear me pull the throttle three times."

He switched to receiving, although he had not asked for an answer. "K-3," said a metallic voice, "what route and what guests?"

"Route, North American, number 47. Two guests, same as before," replied Trent. "I am coming in."

There was a long pause, then the metallic voice spoke briefly. "Use west approach."

ERIC TRENT shoved the enclosure open, tested the straps holding his radio, then fastened on the tommy gun. At five thousand feet, Mawson blipped the engine three times. The blackness below remained unbroken. He repeated the signal, and then a tiny blue light flickered rapidly ahead and to the left.

"Spiral down slowly to two thousand, after I jump," Trent called to Mawson. "I'm going to aim for a spot about a quarter of a mile north of that light. You circle over the light and keep them busy."

"Right. Good luck," shouted Mawson.

"Be careful, you idiot," Crabb said gruffly, and then Trent

went over the side as Mawson pulled up. He let himself fall an estimated thousand feet, then jerked the ring. The chute opened almost at once and he pulled the shrouds to stop the pendulum motion.

The blue light was still blinking steadily, and as he settled lower he saw another one beyond it, evidently a range for lining up an approach. He slipped the chute to land away from the nearer light. The ragged outline of mountains showed vaguely to the southwest, against clouds and stars.

Suddenly both lights went out. At the same moment he heard a sharp, ominous drone above the faint moan of the gliding 0-47—the drone of another plane diving out of the night.

Trent stared up, trying to pierce the gloom. His feet abruptly scraped through brush and he hit with a jolt, tumbling down a steep slope before he could stop. His tommy gun broke loose, rolled on down out of sight. He sat up, untangled the shrouds from his radio-pack, then took off his harness. A spotlight beam poked up from somewhere behind a ridge about three hundred yards away. He could dimly see clumps of cactus and a slight hummock on his right.

The 0-47 was visible for a moment in the improvised searchlight. Trent saw the plane bank sharply, then an Air Corps P-39 shot past, guns flaming for an instant. The 0-47 chandelled away from the light beam and the rear guns flung tracers into the darkness, toward the now zooming fighter.

"Let him have it, Mort!" exclaimed Trent. He scrambled along the ridge as well as he could with the radiopack and the recovered tommy gun. The two planes roared overhead, barely discernible in the darkness, with the spotlight trying to follow them. He came to the end of the ridge and then he saw he was above the flat stretch of a dry lake bed. The spotlight had been dragged out from under a canopy of what appeared to be heavy burlap, reinforced with canvas strips. It was held up about twenty-five feet from the ground by several poles. Apparently the entire canopy could be quickly lowered and drawn back against the rocky wall to which one end was secured.

Against the spotlight, Trent could see several men and the outline of an AT-6. Something that looked like a steel girder showed faintly back in the shadows. Men with blue working lanterns were moving around beyond it, and Trent knew that his guess had been right. This was the entrance—or exit—of one of the old military tunnels. It was evident that the Nazis had found it and had widened the opening enough to create room for a secret hideout. The lake bed was long enough for an emergency landing field, and when the canopy was dropped against the tunnel entrance it would undoubtedly blend with the rock wall and hide all traces of an opening. He stopped, switched on the transmitter to warn Randolph Field in case he was captured later. But the circuit was dead, from that tumble he had taken.

As he crawled nearer, keeping close to the rocky slope, he heard a shrill voice above the din overhead. The words were in German.

"*Leutnant* Guden! The observation plane is crippled! The *Amerikaner* in the fighter will get away!"

"Train the Bofors gun on him!" came the sharp retort. "Better that we hit *Herr Krieger* than let the American escape with our secret."

Then Trent saw that a section of the tarpaulin had been dropped, uncovering an anti-aircraft gun. The gun swung around, training on the P-39.

"Halt!" said Guden. Trent had a glimpse of a bony face with a close-cropped head near the light. "Hold your fire; the fighter is landing! It must be crippled, too."

"But it may be a trick, *Herr Leutnant*," exclaimed one of the Nazis.

"If so, it will be his last," Guden said harshly.

Trent edged behind the folds of burlap that dangled nearby. The 0-47 was leveling off, its engine dead. Mawson landed, braked hard, and swung to bring the Bofors gun crew under his .30's. But a blast from the gliding P-39 forced him back to a straight course. The 0-47 stopped and the fighter whipped into a vertical.

"He's escaping!" shouted Guden. "Fire! Bring him down!"

The crew whirled the Bofors gun to catch the fighter, but the pilot closed his throttle and put his wheels down before they could fire. With the gun crew waiting tensely for a trick, the fighter rumbled to a stop directly behind the 0-47. Its engine switched off abruptly.

Crabb's rear pit guns tilted around, but Trent heard Mawson shout for him to stop. "Don't try it! He'll cut us to pieces!"

"*Herr* Krieger!" exclaimed Guden, running toward the P-39. "*Got im Himmel,* we thought you were in the other ship."

Krieger had rammed open the hatch-cover. He jumped down, his face dark with rage.

"Get them out of there—the three Americans!"

Guden barked a command, and two Nazis with sub machine guns covered the 0-47.

"*Handen hoch!*" snapped the German lieutenant. Then he added in English, "Come out, at once, or we fire!"

CHAPTER IV
Blackbirds of Death

"WELL, MAWSON,** they don't leave us much choice," Mortimer Crabb said mournfully. He climbed out, lanky arms raised, and Mawson followed.

"Come out of there, Trent!" snarled Krieger.

"He's not in there," Crabb said dismally. "He stayed up on top in another ship and let us do the dirty work."

"You lie!" Krieger sprang to the wing of the 0-47. He stared incredulously into the empty ship, then jumped down with an oath.

"Guden, get these prisoners inside! I'll soon find out the truth."

"But, *Herr* Krieger," exclaimed the *Leutnant*, "if there is another plane, it might be making a silent approach—to drop bombs on us!"

Two or three Nazis started to edge into the protection of the tunnel. Krieger swore.

"We'd at least hear its wings whining. If that pig Trent was up there in another plane, he must have turned back when he saw he was up against an Airacobra."

"Then he'll send a squadron from Randolph Field!" cried Guden. "They'll never wait for Mexico's permission, once they know what's here."

"You fool," blazed Krieger, "how can they know? All Trent could see was some kind of a base, if that much. This big ox here is the Intelligence officer with whom Trent was working; no one else back there will give any immediate orders on Trent's story."

"Don't be too sure of that, Krieger," Mawson said coldly.

"Take them inside," rapped the spy. He waited until four armed Nazis had searched Crabb and Mawson and led them back under the canopy. Then he motioned Guden to one side. Trent crept as close as he dared.

"There's a chance Trent may have made some special arrangement before Mawson left," Krieger said in an undertone. "Now don't get alarmed. We'll start action at once. But to be on the safe side, have the men roll the Corsair and the AT-6 out from under cover and tell them to warm the engines. We'll carry out the mission—but if a raiding force does come over, we'll have a chance to escape. The men can go back through the tunnel."

"It's blocked, back at the first outlet," said Guden. "It fell in after they tried bringing supplies that way."

"Never mind that, do what I tell you. And put out that light."

Krieger went into the shadowy space beyond the canopy. Guden switched off the spotlight and called several men. Trent stole closer to the entrance, shielded by the folds of burlap. Peeping through, he saw a large opening, apparently natural, narrowing some hundred feet farther in, where a tunnel ten feet wide and as high was visible. Boxes of supplies and ammunition were piled on one side. On the other side, and extending back into the tunnel, were rows of black model planes. Up at the front of the cave-like space was the thing which had looked like a girder.

At his first real look in the eerie glow of the blue lanterns Trent recognized it as a catapult for launching aerial torpedoes. The innocent looking model planes, he suddenly knew, were blackbirds of death. The memory of the dead chickens at Overman's ranch flashed back into his mind. But he had no time to dwell on the meaning of that scene.

"Captain Mawson!" a voice cried out, from back in the bluish shadows. A gaunt, bearded youth in torn cadet uniform tried to lunge to his feet, then dropped back. Trent saw that his hands were held behind him, evidently by ropes also tied around his ankles.

"Captain Mawson—it's me, Cadet Webster! You've got to stop them."

"Shut that fool's mouth!" Krieger turned to the G-2 officer. "I take it you'd like to live. Give me the exact truth about Trent, and you will."

THE P-39'S engine started, and Trent lost Mawson's answer. Krieger glared at the G-2 captain, motioned to the Nazis holding the two prisoners. Crabb and Mawson were marched over to where the cadet was secured. The spy beckoned to the chief of the catapult crew. The roar of the P-39 subsided as the engine fell to idling, and Trent caught the words.

"—and we'll fire one after another, as fast as we can. Lock the first torpedo on for launching and set your elevation. Follow the pattern we mapped out."

Guden pushed his way through the group of Nazis.

"We've set the catapult for latest weather reports at Laredo and Randolph Field," he told Krieger. "If it was as accurate as you reported on the ranch test today—"

"It was dead on," Krieger said with a gloating satisfaction. "I was circling, up at two kilometers, watching. The torpedo hit within one hundred meters of the house and the gas spread in less than three seconds to its full limit."

"Gas?" cried Mawson. "You fiends! What are you—"

"I told you, captain!" shouted Webster. "They're going to shoot cyanide-gas torpedoes at Randolph to wipe out the whole station! I sent a warning—"

"So he was the one!" Krieger said furiously. "Guden, if that warning had been successful we would have probably been wiped out.

"It was not my fault," the *Leutnant* retorted. "He tricked the man who fed him. And it was you who reported the other cadet was killed when he broke away, or we would have been watching for him tonight."

"Well, it makes no difference now," Krieger said gruffly. "Dana accidentally helped me escape. The routine was so upset by his crash that Schaefer, the bald-headed Bundist I got into their service, was able to blackjack the guard sergeant who had me under arrest. I took care of the other guard and Schaefer helped me get the fighter."

Trent looked past Krieger at the black torpedo now secured on the catapult. Something cold went through him as he thought of those black messengers of death speeding through the night to the training center. By a pattern barrage, enough cyanide gas could be laid down to kill every man at Randolph Field.

"You damned ghouls!" Mawson flung himself suddenly at Krieger.

"Only a savage would think of a thing like this!"

Krieger struck him a savage blow, knocked him against the frieze-covered wall. Mortimer Crabb lunged toward the spy, but two hulking agents hauled him back.

"Tie them up!" snarled Krieger. "When we're through here we'll put them in the tunnel and give them a dose of the gas."

"Over my dead body," muttered Trent. He tiptoed around the dark spotlight. He was barehanded, except for a parachutist's belt-knife; he had discarded his .38 in favor of the tommy gun. He loosened the knife, stole toward the Bofors gun, where a Nazi in dungarees had stopped; watching Krieger and the prisoners.

The catapult crew chief shouted something above the rumble of idling engines. Trent ducked behind the gun mount as the man in dungarees turned. The Nazi went across to a cleated rope, loosened it. The tarpaulin above rolled down to leave a clear space for launching the torpedoes. Trent straightened as the catapult-tender started to elevate the girderlike track for the shot. His hands were like ice as he seized the Bofors gun joystick control.

"Mort! Dick!" he shouted. "Hit the ground!"

Krieger and the Nazis whirled. When they saw the anti-aircraft cannon pointing straight into the cavern, the men nearest the tunnel fell over each other in panicky escape.

"Drop your gun, Krieger!" Trent said swiftly. "Stand still, or I'll splatter you all over the place."

Mortimer Crabb was on his knees. He snatched Krieger's gun. Trent jiggled the Bofors' joystick, let the cannon swing toward the catapult crew.

"Keep your paws up, you rats! Dick, get that cadet loose! Step on it, before one of those mechs at the planes comes in here."

He flung his knife at Mawson's feet and the G-2 captain quickly cut Webster's bonds. The cadet jumped to his feet, stumbled. Mawson steadied him, picked up a gun one of the Nazis had dropped.

"Make for the Corsair," Trent told Mawson and the cadet. "Mort, take Krieger and use him for a shield. When you get to the AT-6, give him the old go-to-sleep routine. Get on the ship's rear guns and stall off these mechs."

"What about you?" cried Mawson.

"I'll herd this gang into the rathole with the rest of the rodents and then join Mort. Step on it!"

Mawson and Webster went past, into the gloom, and Krieger started by, with Crabb behind him. Suddenly, one of the catapult crew dived behind the steel beam. Trent flipped the joystick, just as Krieger made a wild dive behind the Bofors.

CRABB FIRED, and the bullet ricochetted from the mount, grazing Trent's forearm. The Bofors jerked skyward, belched a fiery torrent into the night. Crabb pitched another shot after Krieger, as the spy raced for the P-39.

"Forget him, Mort!" said Trent. "We've got to run for it now!"

Blood was dripping down his hand, but he caught Crabb's arm and shoved him toward the AT-6. Two mechanics were springing in the direction of the cavern. Abruptly, a machine gun clattered, as Mawson scrambled into the rear pit of the Corsair. A Nazi fell, just as he lifted his pistol for a shot at Trent. The spotlight flashed on, blindingly.

Back in the blue-lighted hideout, an automatic barked twice. Crabb emptied his gun, then vaulted up into the idling trainer. He pulled Trent to the wing and Eric got onto the controls just as the P-39 streaked by for a lightning take-off.

Trent's numbed arm was instantly forgotten. If Krieger got into the air, their chances would be slim against that deadly Airacobra. He hit the throttle and the AT-6 pivoted dizzily to follow. A machine gun back in the shadows opened up and blasted as the Corsair swept by. In the spotlight glare, Trent saw Mawson in the front pit, with Webster trying to swing the rear guns.

The AT-6 lifted quickly and Trent looked hastily for Krieger. The spotlight tilted sharply away, catching the Corsair. And in that moment, by the glow cast back into the cavelike space, Trent saw the launching crew elevate the catapult to send the first black-winged projectile speeding toward Randolph Field. Even in this tense moment, Guden had not forgotten his sinister mission.

Trent threw the trainer into a vertical turn, kicked back at the catapult. Tracers suddenly flamed by the left wing, closed in. Krieger was diving, narrowing the gap. Trent heard, faintly, the pound of the rear cockpit guns behind him. But his eyes were on the steep-tilted track below and the grim black bird poised for its fateful flight.

He tripped the Browning .30s clamped on the wings. But it was an instant too late. There was a flash of gunpowder, as the catapult charge went off. The black torpedo shot upward, straight into the path of the diving trainer.

Trent's guns were blazing, but the torpedo was almost upon him. For one dreadful instant, he thought he would have to crash it headlong. Then his bullets hit.

A mirage of gas danced before his eyes as he kicked aside. The bullet-torn projectile whirled by his wing-tip, with barely a foot to spare. Above the screech of wings as he zoomed he heard a full crash. He leveled out and stared down from the trainer.

Krieger's P-39 was plunging to earth with the cockpit enclosure torn clear off where the torpedo had raked it. Trent had a glimpse of Krieger's huddled figure, one hand before his face. Then the fighter struck with a great burst of flame that swept back over the catapult.

Blazing gasoline roared up, hiding the entrance. But Trent knew that no human being could live behind that wall of flame, not even the blackbirds of death. When that holocaust was done, gas from the torpedoes would take care of any who remained in the ancient tunnel.

He looked down and saw a few scattered figures, the mechanics who had been outside and had escaped. His fingers went to the stick trigger, then he shook his head. Let them go…. The memory of this night would be enough—that and the story they would have to take back to the men who had sent them.

"WELL," SAID Trent, "I guess that just about closes the case of the Disappearing Cadets."

Captain Mawson nodded, looked down at the report on his desk. "Webster cleared up the last angles. He and Dana were taking a little ride below the border when they saw a plane land on that lake-bed. They went down to look—and the plane took-off and forced them down. It was the Caproni. It seems the Nazis and Fascists in Mexico learned about the old tunnel and figured it for a good hideout near our border. Krieger got up the catapult scheme. They flew some of the material in, and finally got ready to wipe us out here at Randolph."

"I still don't get the idea of the crash that vanished," growled Mortimer Crabb. "The AT-6 wasn't crashed."

"That instructor thought it was when he flew over, after Webster tried to radio in an S.O.S. After he flew back, the Nazis simply got the ship in under their canopy, which was a neat job of blending in with the scenery when they let it down."

"That affair at Overman's was a test, according to Krieger," said Trent. "But how did Webster come to send that warning?"

"He heard them planning to send a gas-torpedo there. They'd tried empty ones to get range and speed and drift factors before then. Overman's was right in line with Randolph Field, so it gave them a sighting point. Krieger flew over to check the test, using the Stinson he had for American undercover jobs. Webster got loose while most of the Nazis were at chow, and he knocked the catapult tender cold and sent that plane with the warning, that Overman had better escape before he got killed and to warn Randolph Field that aerial torpedoes were being sent from Mexico bearing 192. He didn't know they'd already sent the gas torpedo. Krieger had gone down to cover up—he set that fire just as you thought, to hide the murder. They were afraid to radio him the truth, so they sent the Caproni chasing after the torpedo."

Trent inspected the piece of stone frieze Mawson was using for a paperweight. "These Air Corps cadets are up and coming lads. Dana had a lot of what it takes, to hide out there four days, half-starved, and then sneak in and steal a ship from a hornets' nest like that."

"Speaking of hornets' nests," said Mawson, looking at Trent's bandaged forearm, "how'd you get stung? Was it during that last air scrap?"

Trent grinned. "No, it was one of Mort's ideas for a new invention. He was trying to shoot a bullet around a curve. I just happened to be on the other side."

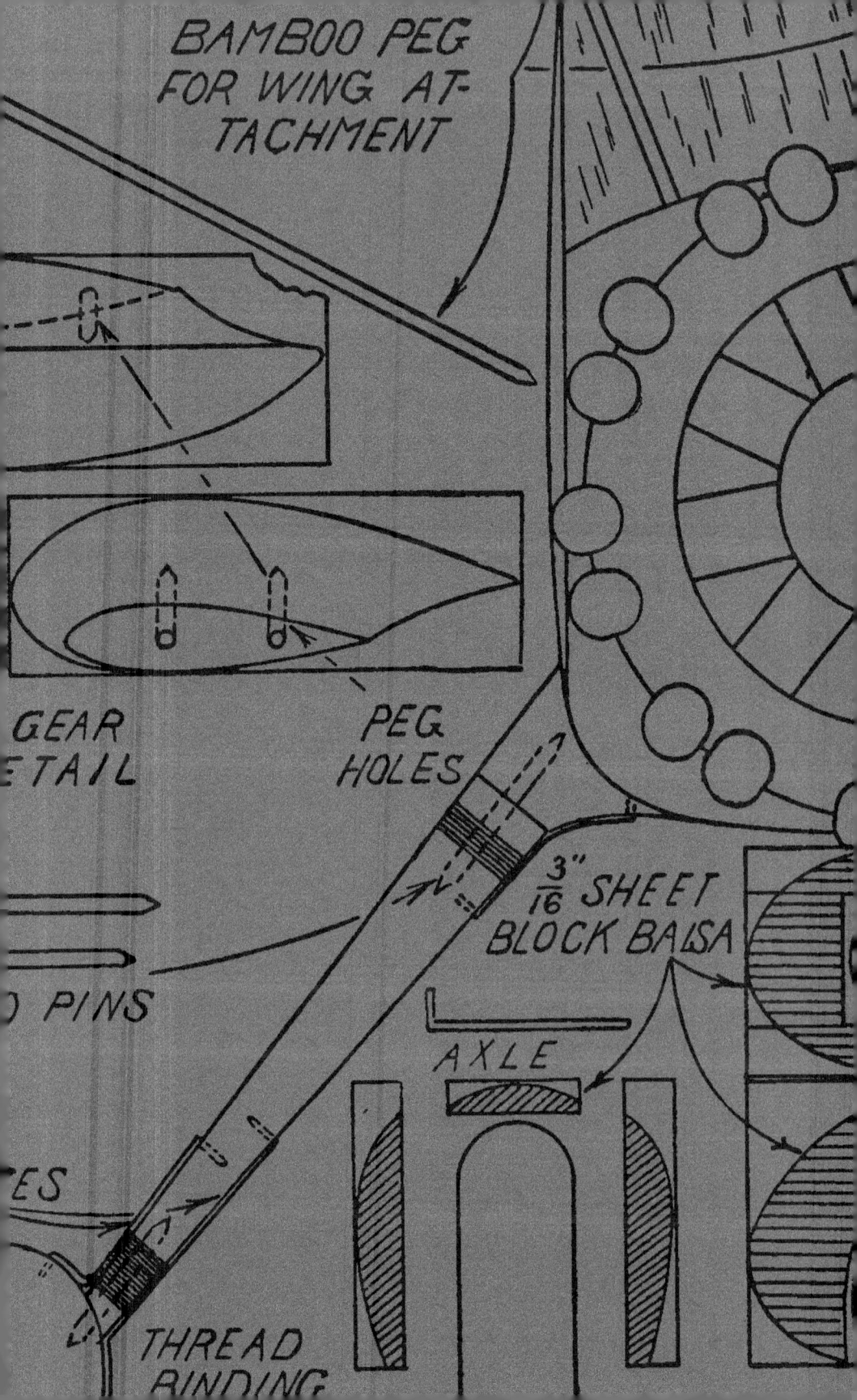

BAMBOO PEG
FOR WING AT-
TACHMENT

GEAR
ETAIL

PEG
HOLES

PINS

ES

$\frac{3''}{16}$ SHEET
BLOCK BALSA

AXLE

THREAD
BINDING

Death Flies the Beam

CHAPTER I
The Message

THE UNSEEN plane was getting closer. Eric Trent peered across the dark flight-deck of the carrier *Lextoga*, to where the machine-gunners squatted, waiting. Beyond them, the muzzles of anti-aircraft guns shone faintly under tropical stars. Trent turned to his perpetually sad-faced partner, Mortimer Crabb, who like himself had been commissioned in the Navy for special duty.

"Well, Mort, if it's a Jap trick, he'll get a hot reception. It's probably young Shelton, though it's a bit odd—"

"What happened?" interrupted Crabb. "I ate early and took a little nap—just woke up when I heard 'battle stations.'"

Trent grinned to himself in the darkness. "The way you were sawing wood, I thought it would take Gabriel's horn—that snore was probably what got the sound-rangers on their toes."

"Ha, ha!" Crabb said acidly. "About as funny as the time you slipped up and broke the admiral's watch, back at San Pedro."

"That was no slip," replied Trent. "The admiral had a weird

notion a magician would make a good aide. I had other ideas—such as being the *Lextoga's* air intelligence officer."

"Hot air's more like it," snorted Crabb. "What about Ensign Shelton?"

"He's an hour overdue. All the other patrols got in at dusk. We'd begun to think he was forced down when the detector-crew heard this ship heading toward us."

"Isn't Shelton's plane one of the three with my new radio-beam receivers?" demanded Crabb.

"Right, old chap, but that doesn't prove—" Trent broke off abruptly. The approaching plane was still invisible, but its lights were blinking as it came down in a wide spiral.

"That's his code-recognition number, all right," muttered Crabb. He jumped as a deep rumble sounded from somewhere above the carrier.

"Don't worry, Mort," said Trent. "The skipper sent off a flight of Brewsters—just in case. Oh-oh, what's this?"

The blinking lights slowly spelled out a word in plain Morse code, dragging out the last letter.

"D-a-n-g-e-r…" There was an interval in which the plane's engine revved up, then fell to idling speed. The ship's navigation lights winked again, and a hush fell over the flight-deck crew.

"F-i-r-e a-t M-a-k-i… s-h-o-r-t l-i-n-e d-i-r-e-c-t-l-y w-e-s-t…"

Again the blinking signals ceased. The plane seemed to be circling aimlessly for a minute, its power now full on.

"Why don't they give him a light and let him land?" Mortimer Crabb said hoarsely.

"It still may be some trick," rapped Trent. "There go his code-signals again."

Slowly, with a hint of something almost painful, the words winked out. "W-r-e-c-k J-a-p-s… h-a-v-e h-i-d-d-e-n c-a-t…"

THE STEADY drone of the plane's engine broke sharply, and a second later a parachute flare blossomed above the dark sea. Anti-aircraft and machine-gun crews tensed as a plane dipped into the glare. It was a Navy Grumman F4F-3 fighter, and it was swaying in toward the carrier, apparently almost out of control. Above it, the Brewsters swooped down, ready for swift action.

With a last muffled backfire, the engine went dead. The Grumman made a wide, skidding turn as the pilot attempted to correct his approach. For a second Trent thought the fighter would drop below the flight-deck and crash the side of the vessel. But with a crazy zoom, the Grumman moaned up above the deck, stalled, and struck with a resounding crash.

Even before it hit, the crash-squad was running toward the spot. Trent reached the group just as the pilot's limp body was lifted out. The blue-white glare of the parachute flare shone with a ghastly light on the face of Ensign Shelton. There was a wide, dark stain across the front of his flying-suit, and another on his left sleeve. At least thirty bullets had drilled the Grumman's wing and fuselage.

A hospital-corpsman knelt beside the pilot's body. As he opened Shelton's flying-suit, two of the *Lextoga's* flight officers pushed through the throng. Trent recognized one, a two-striper, as Lieutenant Biff Jackson, a laconic, blunt-spoken Texan.

"Gangway for the Skipper!" said Jackson. The men stood aside for Captain Bradford, commanding officer of the *Lextoga*. Bradford was young for a four-striper, with an habitually grave expression that contrasted with his plump, ruddy face.

The hospital-corpsman stood up, shook his head in answer

to Bradford's unspoken query. "It's a miracle he was ever able to fly back here, sir."

No one moved for a moment. Trent looked down at Shelton's ashen face, and a lump came into his throat. He was—he had been—only twenty-one. That afternoon, taking off, he had been as eager as a kid; it had been his first patrol in the Jap mandated area.

Captain Bradford looked up, and Trent saw the brief hint of tears in his eyes.

"Take Mr. Shelton below," he said. "Commander Trent, will you and Lieutenant Crabb come to my cabin, please?"

The drifting flare settled into the ocean as Trent turned to follow, but he had time for a quick glance skyward. Except for the circling Brewsters, there was no sign of planes. He saw the landing-officer signal with lighted wand to guide the first plane down.

BRADFORD HAD gone below. Trent glanced at Mortimer Crabb as they followed. The inventor's homely countenance had a grim look.

"I'm beginnin' to hate Japs," Crabb grated.

"I've a head start on you," Trent said. "I've hated them for six years—ever since I ran into some in China and found out what dirty butchers they are."

"What do you think Shelton meant by that message?" Crabb said.

Trent shook his head. "There's an island named Maki in the mandated area—but the last part of the message didn't make sense. The poor devil was probably out of his mind."

A Marine sentry let them into the captain's cabin. Bradford motioned them to seats, offered cigarettes. Trent sat back, absently fingering his clipped black mustache, waiting for the C.O. to speak. Bradford smoked for a minute, staring at a map on his desk, then he turned to Trent.

"Well, what do you make of it?"

"Not enough, captain," admitted Trent. "Maki's supposed

to be deserted, from our latest reports. Obviously, Shelton discovered something and died trying to warn us to wreck it."

"What about 'short line west' and 'have hidden cat'?" asked Bradford.

"I don't know." Trent's dark eyes rested on the map. "But I've a suggestion. Let me fly to Maki tonight, I'll drop flares, see what's up—and get back before they can tag me."

"Wait a minute," growled Mortimer Crabb. "I've got a better idea. Make it a two-seater, and we'll take one of my K-type transmitters. We can flash back word the second we spot anything—I'll stake my life no Jap has a set that will receive those frequencies. If Shelton had had one of my transmitters, he wouldn't have had to worry about radio silence and we'd know the truth."

"He probably tried to use his set, when he saw it was necessary," said Bradford. "I noticed the mike switch was on, but a bullet had gone through the set." He hesitated for a moment. "If we only had time to run tests on that new transmitter—remember, we're only part of a raiding force. If the Japs learned we were in these waters—"

Trent squashed out his cigarette. "They already know at least one carrier is in these waters. Seeing Shelton's fighter would tip them off to that. Why not let us go? We might be able to block some trick."

"Very well, I'll order a Curtiss prepared. You can take one of the ships that just landed. Of course, you realize it's a suicide mission, gentlemen?"

Trent looked at Crabb, and grinned. "How about it, Mort? Tired of life?"

"No Jap's going to knock me off," scoffed Crabb. "Let's go."

WHEN THEY reached the flight-deck, after donning flying-suits and getting their chutes, the K-type transmitter had been brought up from the radio-room. The *Lextoga*, in accordance with Task Force orders, was circling slowly in her assigned area before steaming to her dawn rendezvous with the rest of the raiding fleet. The destroyer escort was invisible in the darkness, but Trent knew the ocean grey-hounds were tirelessly weaving back and forth, to protect the carrier from attack.

The special transmitter had been installed, with a temporary hookup, and Trent was buckling on his chute when from off to starboard came the sudden roar of an airplane engine. Almost instantly, a searchlight flicked out from a destroyer. The rays fell on a seaplane that was bouncing from the waves in a hasty take-off.

"Jap plane!" shouted, a mechanic. Pilots swarmed out of the "island" superstructure, but Trent was the first to reach his cockpit. A mechanic swung his prop, as Mortimer Crabb tumbled into the rear of the SB2C-1. Trent taxied out, and the mechs swung him into take-off position. As he got the signal, he sent the heavy dive-bomber thundering down the deck. The carrier had straightened into the wind, swiftly speeding up. The Curtiss hurtled off, and Trent banked toward the Jap seaplane. The destroyer's searchlight had swung to follow it, and he could tell that it was a Nakajima fighter on a pontoon.

The Nakajima whipped sharply back toward the destroyer, from which a machine-gun began to blast. Tracers streaked from its guns, and the searchlight went out. Trent tripped his four forward guns just as the glow disappeared. For an instant, there was pitch darkness, then three more search-lights came on simultaneously. The Jap plane was climbing steeply, but Trent reached its level with a full-power zoom. The Nakajima frantically renversed. Trent felt the throb of the guns in the power-turret behind him, but a searchlight momentarily blinded him.

"Look out, Eric!" shouted Crabb. Trent chandelled automatically, cast a hurried look to each side. The Nakajima raced by underneath him, heading West. Trent coolly ringed the seaplane in his sights, flicked a burst over the tip of the prop. The Jap pilot skidded, nosed down. Trent stabbed a blast past his left wing tip, herded him back toward the carrier.

By now, the searchlight crews were with him. Dazzling light streamed across the seaplane's path, and for a moment the pilot seemed to be floundering, helpless.

Trent watched, on his guard. Without warning, the Nakajima shot into a tight loop, guns flaming back at the Curtiss. Trent rolled, and the Jap's tracers went into empty space. Before the seaplane was halfway into its dive Trent's tracers were clipping its tail. The flippers and rudder disintegrated like kindling under an axe, and the Nakajima plunged headlong.

THE PILOT went tumbling out as the seaplane dived, and a few seconds later his parachute opened. Two searchlights followed him down, and Trent saw a boat being lowered from the carrier. He circled for a minute or two, looking for the exhaust flare glow of other enemy planes, but saw no sign of any.

"There's a signal for us to land," Crabb bawled from the rear cockpit. Trent made his approach, watching the lighted wands. The Curtiss landed, was quickly snubbed to a stop by the retarding-gear. As they climbed out, Lieutenant Jackson came alongside.

"Skipper's inside the island," he said brusquely. "Wants to see you."

"Trent, did you recognize any insignia on that plane?" Bradford asked, as they entered the superstructure. "Anything to help identify its squadron?"

"Not a thing, captain," Trent told him. "All it had was the rising sun emblem—and it's a pleasure to report that particular sun won't rise for some time."

"That was good work—I saw the last part." Bradford beckoned to Jackson. "When the boat's hoisted aboard, have the prisoner brought down to the ready-room."

Ten minutes later, Jackson and a bluejacket appeared with the Jap pilot. The prisoner wore dripping uniform of a shosa, or major. High protruding cheekbones gave his dark face a brutal look. He moved sullenly into the ready-room at a prod from Lieutenant Jackson's big .45.

"He's been searched, sir," reported Jackson. "We took a knife off of him—I guess he's got rid of everything else."

Captain Bradford sternly faced the Jap pilot.

"Where is your base?" he demanded.

The prisoner glared at him without answer.

"Speak up!" rasped Jackson.

Wakarimasen!" the prisoner flung at him. Trent got up from the chair in which he had sat at one side, unnoticed by the Jap.

"He says he doesn't understand. I might add that he's a dirty yellow liar—and I don't refer to his outside color."

The Jap jumped back, his face suddenly a muddy gray.

"You! I thought you were—" he stopped, lips clamped tight. Trent eyed him with ironic amusement.

"Yes, I know—you thought you'd finished me that night in Shanghai."

"Then you know him?" Captain Bradford exclaimed.

"A little too well," said Trent. "He used to go by the name of Baron Igo Horuti. Don't let the 'baron' fool you. He's one of Japan's higher-class assassins, used by the Kimitsu Kyoku—their Army Intelligence Department. Combines espionage with blackmail and any other pretty little tricks that occur to him. I ran across him while I was learning the language in Tokio—and later, after I got mixed up with his gang of cutthroats in China."

"I refuse to be insulted in this manner!" Horuti burst out furiously. "I am an officer of the Imperial Japanese Army. I demand the treatment of a prisoner of war."

"Japanese style?" said Trent. "I seem to remember a Chinese prisoner whose tongue you cut out—because his screams annoyed your corporal who was practicing with a bayonet on him."

"You saw that, Trent?" Bradford said, with a sickened look.

"And a lot worse, captain. If the situation were reversed,

the easiest we'd get would be a bullet through the back of the head."

Horuti gave him a sneering smile. "Fortunately, you decadent Americans still hold to your foolish ideas of chivalry. That's why we will win this war."

Jackson swore under his breath. "By Heaven, captain, I wish you'd put me in a stateroom with this man—just for three seconds."

"You can't bluff me," mocked Horuti. "I will betray no secrets."

"You don't have to," said Trent. "The Grumman pilot told us about Maki before he died."

The Jap stiffened for a fraction of a second. Then his black slant eyes darted around the ready-room. He showed his teeth in another mirthless grin.

"So he flew to Maki, your pilot? He must have been disappointed—there is nothing at Maki but two or three nipa-roof huts. It is only a fueling station for planes in emergency."

"What were you doing there?" Bradford flung at him.

"My dear captain," smirked Horuti. "I have not seen Maki in three years."

"Then you wouldn't know," said Trent, "about the hidden cat?"

CHAPTER II
The Riddle at Maki

FOR THE second time since his entrance, Horuti's dark face lost color. But he recovered himself swiftly.

"Some American joke, Mr. Trent? I am afraid my poor sense of humor fails to grasp it."

Trent absently reached up, flicked his long fingers. A lighted cigarette materialized, seemingly from nowhere.

"Very clever," Horuti said, in an edged voice. "I had forgotten you were a prestidigitator. But the joke—about the cat?"

"So that worries you?" said Trent. He exhaled lazily. "Don't give it a thought. We're going to take a little trip to Maki. We'll tell you all about it when we get back."

"Fool, you'll never get—" the Nipponese cut himself short, and his face became an inscrutable mask.

"I think that's all we'll need of Mr. Horuti right now," Trent told Bradford. "Of course, later he will stand trial for murder."

"Murder?" repeated the C.O. "But even if he was the one who killed Ensign Shelton, it was in battle—"

"Not Shelton—an American Marine Corps sergeant he murdered in Shanghai. The entire case is on file at Washington, and I have enough evidence to hang him. I happened to see the killing—it was the time when he thought he'd finished me, too."

"Lock him up!" Bradford ordered curtly. Jackson and the bluejacket headed for the brig with Horuti. The captain eyed Trent dubiously.

"We didn't learn much, commander."

"More than he meant us to," said Trent. "Shelton wasn't delirious after all when he signaled about the hidden cat. It must have some significance we don't get. It's a pretty fair guess that Shelton tangled with Horuti somewhere close to

Maki. Horuti followed but couldn't see enough in the dark to finish him off. Or else he wanted Shelton to lead him back so he'd find out how big a force we have. Maybe Shelton suspected he was followed—or else he knew he was dying and knew he wouldn't last long enough to land and give us the message."

The C.O. nodded. "Sounds probable. But why did Horuti land when he could have flown back and escaped?"

"Perhaps he had to know how much that message told us, and if we were going into action because of it. He couldn't fly around without being heard, so he landed. Or his engine may simply have cut out on him while he was gliding in, to see what he could discover. In the dark, he may not have seen the destroyers when he tried to get away."

"We've got to know the truth about Maki—tonight," said Bradford. "I'm going to let you and Crabb go ahead."

"Come on, Mort," said Trent.

"Wait," said the C.O. "I'm going to send Lieutenant Jackson and two other pilots with you in Grummans, to bring back word in case—"

"In case we get liquidated." Trent grinned. "All right, captain, we're ready any time they are."

BRADFORD SENT his orderly to inform Jackson of the order. "One thing you must remember," he told Trent, "if Maki has been converted into a strong air base, the *Lextoga's* present course must be changed. Despite our own planes, dive-bombers might get through and sink us. Either the entire Task Force will have to concentrate for an attack on Maki, or we'll have to by-pass it until our other objective is attained."

"Don't worry, sir," interposed Crabb. "I'll flash word the minute we see the set-up."

The C.O. looked at the clock "Nine-forty... it'll take about thirty-five minutes to reach Maki. I'll have the ship on alert, planes on deck, ready for a quick night attack if you report the island is an air base. Meantime, I'll have a blinker message flashed to one of the destroyers and they can take one of your K-type receivers to the flagship so the admiral can hear your report. If necessary, he can order immediate attack, or one at dawn when we will be closer."

By the time Jackson and his pilots were ready, the destroyer was on its way to contact the flagship. Trent looked around the little group.

"We'll get our altitude and glide in from 18,000 feet. You three men will stay on top until you're sure everything's clear."

"What if the Japs get your ship?" Jackson said bluntly. "How will we know whether you had time to send a message? Our receivers won't catch that new high-frequency stuff."

"I'll flash my lights or fire a Very rocket," answered Trent.

As they went up from the ready-room to the flight-deck, a sandy-haired junior lieutenant caught up with them.

"Commander Trent—I'd like to see you a second."

Trent stopped. "What's the matter, Denny?"

"There's a spy on board!" Denny said tensely. "When Shelton crashed, there was a map in his cockpit. I saw it, but I was helping him get out and I didn't think about it until a few minutes ago."

"Well?" said Trent.

"It's gone. I asked the men who moved the wreck, and nobody turned it in."

"It wasn't clipped to Shelton's knee?"

"No, it had come off and it was caught under a rudder pedal. I think it had something written on it—"

"Then somebody got it right after Shelton was lifted out," muttered Trent. "I looked in there and I didn't see any map. Can you remember who was in that group?"

"The crash squad and Shelton's mech, and a petty officer named Beckett."

"Round them up on some excuse and then search their quarters," directed Trent. "I'm taking off right now, or I'd tend to it myself. Report what you find to Captain Bradford."

THE CURTISS and the three Grummans were waiting, engines idling, when they reached the flight-deck. The Grummans took off first. Trent climbed into the Curtiss' front cockpit, and Crabb settled himself in the rear. At a flick of the control officer's lighted wands, Trent sent the dive-bomber roaring off into the darkness.

It was 165 miles to Maki. Trent climbed to 17,000, leveled out to keep well under the fighters. They were about half the distance to the island when a bright glow, as from an explosion, lit up the horizon. The light quickly faded.

"Now what?" Crabb said dismally through the inter-phones. "I think I'd better report that."

"Hold your horses, old bean," returned Trent. "Wait till we find out what goes on and how come."

A few minutes later a faint, flickering light appeared on the horizon. It seemed to be at the approximate location of Maki.

"I suppose that's a beacon, so we won't miss it," growled Crabb.

"Dig out the binoculars," said Trent.

Crabb passed them forward, and Trent trained them on the island as the Curtiss glided in.

"Looks like a shed on fire," he reported. "I don't see any Japs around.

I wonder how this hooks up with Shelton's message."

"Say, that's right! He said 'fire on Maki.'"

"I thought he meant for us to fire on the island. This may be—"

"What's that beyond the fire? Looks like a plane."

"It is—but it's on its back. Guess we'd better drop a flare and check up on all this."

Trent jerked the release, gunned the engine and pulled up in a climbing turn as the flare blazed. The three-mile, irregular expanse of Maki was brilliantly revealed below. On the east, a cove cut into the island, and the shore beyond rose sharply for about sixty feet, then flattened out into a gradual ascent. A quarter of a mile inland, the palm trees had been cleared to create two intersecting runways. Two thatched huts stood to the west of the north-and-south runway. The burning shed was near the intersection. Aside from a Mitsubishi dive-bomber which lay upside down by the west runway, there was no sign of a Japanese air force. Trent circled lower, watching for camouflage nets, but the island seemed to be barren of defenses.

"If they had any planes here, looks like they pulled them out in a hurry," said Crabb. "Might as well call the *Lextoga* and tell 'em no Japs here."

"Okay," said Trent. "Wait a minute—what's that down in the cove?"

He banked over the shore, spiraled down to a thousand feet. Floating debris covered the water. Some of it looked like charred wood, and on a jutting reef at the side of the cove lay what appeared to be the bowsprit of a schooner.

"Looks like a ship had blown up," said Crabb. "Not long ago, either." Trent stared down at the wreckage. "It could have been that glare we saw. Maybe they had a supply ship here and were afraid it would fall into our hands."

"What are you going to do?" demanded Crabb, as Trent swung back over Maki.

"I'm going to land—as soon as you send word to the *Lextoga*. Report 'Island deserted. Landing to check up.'"

Crabb switched on his special transmitter, tapped out the message. By the time he had finished the flare had gone out, but the flames from the burning shed were enough to mark the runway. Trent blinked his navigation lights until he saw an answering flicker from one of the Grummans above. Then he landed.

The Curtiss stopped, brakes on. Trent looked around carefully, then cut off the engine. The hush that followed was broken only by the moan of the Grummans' wings, as the three fighters circled down.

"Stay here, Mort, and keep your eyes peeled," said Trent,

as he climbed down. "There might be a Jap or two lurking behind a palm tree."

"They'd have to be pretty skinny, from the size of those trees," grunted Crabb. "Know what I think? I think Horuti radioed back that message Shelton flashed us, and the Japs just high-tailed out of here."

"Well, I'll take a look-see, anyway." Trent unholstered his .45, warily circled the burning shed. By now, the flames had died down, and he could see an overturned fuel drum inside. He walked around the two thatched huts, halted abruptly when he saw a dim light shining through the doorway.

TWO OF the Grummans landed as he tiptoed toward the shack. Jackson climbed from the first fighter, leaving the engine idling.

The other pilot went over to the Curtiss, and Jackson came toward Trent.

Trent motioned him to the side of the hut, and Jackson reached for his gun as he saw the light. Trent took a quick step to the entrance, kicked the door wide open. Then he slowly lowered the .45. Jackson joined him, and they stared silently into the hut.

There was no one inside. Cigarette stubs and an old Japanese magazine lay on the floor, and a soiled blanket on a bunk gave evidence of recent occupancy. In the middle of the floor stood a table on which stood a charcoal sketch, lighted by an oil lamp. The sketch, so crudely done that it might have been the work of a child, showed an angular cat with huge claws. Underneath was written: Shima neko.

"What the devil!" said Jackson blankly.

"Shima neko means 'island cat,'" said Trent. He frowned at the sketch, then suddenly wheeled. "Come on, we've got to get off this island!"

"Huh? What's wrong?" exclaimed the Texan.

"This whole thing's a fake—we may have run into a trap!" Trent headed for the doorway. Just as he reached it, he heard a shout, then a roar as the Curtiss' engine started up.

Jackson hastily followed him outside. The pilot of the second Grumman was running toward the hut.

"Japs—I don't know where they came from!" he yelled.

Two Nakajimas on pontoons were charging in at the lone Grumman overhead. As Trent and Jackson raced back to their planes, a third Nakajima zoomed into sight from the direction of the cove. Wheeling into the light of the burning shed, it pitched down at the grounded planes.

Four streams of tracer shot from the Jap ship's cowl and wing. Jackson's pilot crumpled beside his riddled fighter. Mortimer Crabb swung the Curtiss' power-turret, sent a furious blast up at the Nakajima. The Jap hurriedly banked out of the lighted space. Trent shoved Jackson toward the Curtiss.

"Go ahead—get clear and tell Mort to warn the Skipper!"

Without waiting for the Texan's answer, he raced to Jackson's idling fighter. The third Nakajima had joined the others to bring down the beleaguered Grumman. Trent vaulted into Jackson's ship, snapped his belt and sent the fighter hurtling down the runway. The Curtiss was two hundred feet ahead, taking off.

Trent pulled the Grumman into a screeching zoom, caught the nearest Nakajima under his guns. But he was a split-second too late. The Navy pilot, after a valiant battle at odds of three to one, suddenly toppled over his controls. The fighter struck in a clump of palms and burst into flames.

ONE OF the Jap ships was staggering from the Navy man's last burst. Trent savagely drove a blast through the cockpit. The pilot crumpled from view, and the Nakajima went floundering down to a crash. The two other Japs had whirled to attack the Curtiss. As Trent renversed to aid Crabb and Jackson, the tail of the ship quivered under the impact of bullets.

Trent backsticked, threw a swift look behind, expecting to see still another Jap plane. Instead, he saw the flaming muzzles of double-mounted machine-guns firing from a pit in the ground. He turned back to the fight, but the

Curtiss was going down, smoke pouring from its cowl. Trent groaned, but the Japs gave him no time to watch the Curtiss. Separating in quick chandelles, the two Nakajimas darted in to crisscross the Grumman's tail.

On shrieking wings, Trent threw the fighter into a vertical bank. His tail was for an instant directly toward one Jap, but the other plane, ahead, almost blanketed the rear man's fire. Trent thumbed the stick-button, saw the pilot in front of him jump spasmodically. The Nakajima yawed crazily, its guns still spouting. Trent dived underneath, hoping to lead the man behind him into collision with the pilotless ship.

Crackling tracers smoked past his head, as his pursuer nosed down to follow. Trent rolled to throw his prop out of range, but in vain. There was a muffled report, a high-pitched scream, as the unleashed engine revved up. He cut off ignition and fuel, hastily switched on his radio transmitter.

"T-19—Jap planes hidden on Maki!" he shouted into the mike. "All four of flight downed! Look for secret seaplane base on east of—"

Br-t-t-t-t-t! Bullets hammered savagely across his cowl, hurtled splinters of dural and Plexiglas back into his face. He dropped the Grumman in a steep forward slip, away from the glare of the burning shed. Another burst tore through the right wing. With a sudden decision, he whipped back across the island. The Grumman howled into a brief dive, leveled off ten feet above the ground.

The burning fuel shed loomed up directly in Trent's path. Bracing himself, he hurled the fighter straight into the blazing wreckage. A flaming upright flew over the wing, and embers went in all directions. In the abrupt darkness beyond, he could see nothing for a moment, but he knew he was headed for the cove. A second later he felt the wheels touch.

Unsnapping his belt, he climbed out onto the wing, still holding tight to the stick. Unbraked, the Grumman plunged toward a little clump of palms above the water. He waited until the ship was within sixty feet of the trees, then let go.

CHAPTER III
The Hidden Cats

*H*E STRUCK doubled up, rolling. A moment later there was a rending crash, followed by a scraping and a loud splash below. He tumbled against the side of a palm tree, started to slide down the incline to the cove. A few feet below, the slope flattened into what seemed to be a ledge, and he lay there, trying to catch his breath.

Muffled voices came to his ears, and he sat up, gazing around in the dark. There was no one near him, and he was forty feet above the water. He was peering up the slope when to his astonishment the ledge on which he lay began to move. He tried to scramble up, but it was too late. The flat surface was moving slowly sidewise, as was a section of the slope below. Trent started. He was on top of a huge sliding door!

Dim greenish light showed from the space the great door had hidden, and Trent saw that there was another door sliding open on the other side. In a brief glimpse before he threw himself flat he saw a score of Japanese looking out into the cove.

"*Goran nasai*—look!" exclaimed one Nipponese. "There is the tail of the plane sticking out of the water. It must have dived in."

"It rolled over the edge," said a harsher voice. "Turn on a light—make sure the American did not swim free."

"But Captain Kenako, is it safe?" protested the first man.

"Do what I order!" snapped the one addressed as Kenako. "The sound-rangers report there are no other planes within a hundred miles."

A spotlight went on, played across the tail of the Grumman, then slowly covered the surrounding water. It was still traversing the cove when the remaining Nakajima landed and taxied in toward the hidden base. Trent hugged the shelf until the seaplane's engine went off and the ship drifted inside.

"Enough of the light," came Kenako's voice. "The pig was obviously drowned. I should like to have had him alive."

"They are better fighters than we were told," said another voice. It had a shrill, angry note. "The first man was bad enough—but this one was a demon."

"They were both undoubtedly drugged," Kenako said hurriedly. Trent grinned to himself. Then as the spotlight went out he cautiously raised up for a glance into the base. One look, and he saw how it had been built. The original shore had sloped up at a point farther back, and the Japs had merely extended the higher ground by roofing over the low area. Steel uprights supported a trusswork for about as far back as he could see. Apparently there was a fairly deep layer of earth on top of the hangar roof, so that grass and a few smaller palms would grow there.

EXTENDING ALMOST to the entrance of the base were three seaplane catapults, placed parallel so that three planes could be launched simultaneously. The true meaning of Shelton's message came suddenly to Trent… "Have hidden cat" must have been meant for "have hidden catapults," but the young ensign's failing strength had given out before he could finish.

Trent risked another quick look over the top of the camou-flaged door. He could identify Kenako—a short, burly Jap, the only one with a captain's insignia. Kenako was talking with the Nakajima pilot, a young, wedge-faced Jap with a shrill voice. Beyond them a crew of mechanics was hooking a boom onto the Nakajima for raising it onto a cradle. Steel doors at the rear of the launching-chamber stood open, revealing the hangar space in which at least twenty planes were dimly visible. Trent recognized some as Mitsubishi dive-bombers which had been equipped with pontoons.

"The warning was sent by Major Horuti," he heard Kenako

tell the Jap pilot. "He had us prepare the trick in case more planes came to investigate."

"It is as well he did," retorted the pilot. "If all four American planes had been in the air, we would have been lost before you could launch the others. But where is the *chosa* now?"

Captain Kenako looked worried. "He should have been back before this. I am afraid he was shot down after sending the warning."

The pilot turned to look toward the sea, and Trent ducked out of sight.

"Then we do not know how many American ships there are?" he heard the Jap's shrill voice.

"No, but we will be ready for them at dawn—no matter how many," said Kenako. "We have a prisoner from the plane you forced down," he added with an ugly note, "and if he knows anything I shall soon get it out of him."

Trent felt something sick inside. One prisoner... Mortimer Crabb or Jackson? Perhaps, he thought grimly, the dead man was the luckier....

He heard Kenako give an order, and in a moment the huge doors began to slide shut. He waited for a full minute after they had closed, then crawled up the incline. It was fairly easy, for the Japs had stretched canvas over irregular blocks of wood, to create the illusion of a rough coral slope. With the protruding points for handholds, he reached the flatter ground above and stopped for a moment to consider the next move.

His radio to the *Lextoga* might not be acted upon until daylight, if then. In the meantime, the prisoner down in that Jap hellhole would probably be tortured to death.

Trent stood up, estimated the spot where he had jumped from the Grumman. He crawled over the ground on hands and knees, but failed to find his .45. Possibly it had gone over with the plane. He would have to work it unarmed.

He closed his eyes, trying to recall the exact location of the machine-gun "fox-hole" from which the Japs had fired on him. It was approximately halfway between the burned fuel-shed and the cove. That meant it probably served as another entrance to the base, for the hidden hangar extended back almost that far.

Trent bent down, rubbed his hands in the dirt and smeared his face and neck. Then he took off his flying-suit. He was wearing the naval air service forestry-green uniform, which was dark enough for his purpose. By scattering the embers of the fuel-shed he had eliminated it as a guide-point, but he knew the general direction. Again on hands and knees, he made his way toward the fox-hole.

HE HAD gone about two hundred feet when he saw flash-lights off to the right. Several Japs were examining the Curtiss, which had ended up off the runway. Trent crawled closer, stopped short as the flashlights silhouetted a small hut between three palm trees. A Jap sentry stood leaning against one side, watching the men at the plane.

Trent wormed his way back a few yards, then around behind the largest tree. He had barely reached it when the Japs returned from the Curtiss. They deviated around a dark spot in the open ground beyond the hut, and he surmised this was the concealed machine-gun post.

Jabbering with each other, the Japs went into the hut. Trent edged closer, saw the flashlight reflections alter, then shift to the ceiling. He was right. There was a passage leading down into the base, but instead of leading to the fox-hole, it ran to this harmless-looking nipa shack.

The sentry had followed the men inside. Trent got to his feet as the sound of voices died out. He was crouched beside the doorway, hands outstretched, when the sentry emerged. Like a flash, Trent was on him. His hands shot around the Jap's throat from behind, thumbs pressed tight under his ears. The Nipponese gave a convulsive leap, dropped his rifle. Trent toppled to the ground with him, but held on.

For a moment, the Jap's fingers clawed wildly at Trent's hands. Suddenly his head jerked forward and he sagged in a limp heap. Instinctively, Trent started to release his hold. Then he grimly tightened his grasp. Below, an American was facing death—or worse. There was only one way to insure this sentry's silence....

A MINUTE later, he dragged the Jap's body out of the hut. The man's broad-visored cap was a fair fit, but his blouse was too small in the shoulders. Trent struggled into it, smeared his face again, and picked up the sentry's bayoneted rifle.

Inside the hut he found an electric lantern on a chair. He switched it on, inspected the floor. A dirty grass rug had been kicked carelessly aside, and he saw a trap-door. Turning off the lantern, he raised the trap an inch. A faint light showed from below. He lifted the trap higher, saw a flight of steps and a bricked-up passage. There was a turn at the bottom of the stairs and the dim light came from somewhere beyond. Apparently no one else was on guard at this end.

Trent went down silently, closed the trap-door after him. A cautious glance around the turn revealed a bricked vestibule. Two doors led from it, one of which stood open. He could see into a long corridor with doors on the right-hand side. The nearest was labeled "Major Horuti," the second one "Captain Kenako." The others were in shadow, but he surmised that all the officers were quartered in this section.

He put his ear against the other vestibule door, heard metallic sounds of men working on planes. He was about to open the door a fraction of an inch when a scraping sound from Kenako's room made him jump back. He stepped back into the space below the stairs, but Kenako's door remained closed. Then he heard the shrill-voiced pilot.

"If the captain will permit me, I will make this stubborn American speak."

"I am equal to that," came Kenako's harsh answer. Trent gripped the rifle, swiftly reached the captain's door. From inside, Kenako's voice came with a suddenly furious note.

"Light the candle! Now, you American dog, will you tell us or would you prefer blindness?"

Trent's ice-cold hand turned the knob. With a lightning motion, he threw the door open and leaped inside. Kenako was stooping before the bound figure of Mortimer Crabb, a candle flaring close to the prisoner's eyes. The skinny Jap pilot stood at his elbow.

Both of them whirled as Trent entered. The pilot sprang back with his eyes bulging, and his mouth flew open to cry for help. Trent lunged, brought up the butt of the rifle under the Jap's jaw. The pilot's head flew back with a vicious snap, and he went down without a sound.

Kenako had dropped the candle. He gave a frantic jump for the door. Trent sprang in front of him, drove the bayonet toward his throat. Kenako shrank back against the wall, his horrified eyes glued to the shining blade.

"Eric!" Mortimer Crabb said huskily. "Thank God—they were going to—"

"I know, Mort," Trent said tautly. He shoved the bayonet tip under Kenako's chin, held it there while he shot a quick look at Crabb. The Japs had tied him to a heavy wooden chair. Trent's grim eyes came back to the trembling Nipponese.

"Untie him!"

Kenako dropped to his knees, fumbled with the knot. Perspiration dripped from his forehead.

"Watch him, Eric," Crabb said hoarsely. "He'll try to trick you."

"One yip and I'll cheerfully slit his throat," said Trent.

"How did you get in here?" Crabb whispered.

Trent reached back without taking his eyes from Kenako, closed the door. "Never mind about that, old bean. The important thing is getting out."

"We've got to warn the Task Force," mumbled Crabb. "I tried to get a message through with the K-set, but they hit my transmitter."

"It's all right, I warned them."

Crabb shook his head. "No—they jammed the air with artificial static."

Kenako finished untying Crabb, backed away under Trent's savage gaze. For an instant his black eyes went to the Jap pilot's shattered jaw, the odd angle at which his head lay.

"Right," Trent said pleasantly. "His neck's broken. But he died a lot easier than you will if you try anything."

"What do you want?" Kenako moaned.

Trent jerked his head toward the telephone on Kenako's desk. "Order those camouflaged doors opened, and a Mitsubishi moored outside, engine warmed and radio tested. Guns and bomb-ranks are to be loaded."

"You—what are you going to do?" gasped the Nipponese.

Trent smiled coolly. "We're going to blow this place to hell."

CHAPTER IV
The Crooning Crabb

FEAR AND rage struggled together in Kenako's black eyes. "You're insane—you can never escape from here alive."

"Let me worry about that," said Trent. "Pick up that phone. And don't forget I know Japanese air slang, too."

"They will ask questions—they will wonder why I should give such an order," protested Kenako.

"Tell them it's for a possible emergency flight later tonight—something you learned from the prisoner. And get this straight. If you slip up, and anybody comes in here—" Trent made a significant motion with the bayonet.

The Jap cringed, reached for the phone. Trent stepped close, to hear what came through the receiver. Kenako gave the order, sweating profusely as he explained.

"We'll never make it, Eric," Crabb said hopelessly, as the Jap hung up. "They've got lights in the hangar, and men working. That dirt on your face won't fool them for a second."

"That," said Trent, "was only to help me get in here. I've figured a way out. We'll wait here ten minutes, in case they should call back about the ship."

"We must've been blind, not to see what Shelton meant in that message," Crabb said dully. "That wasn't 'short line'—it was 'shore line.' He was half dead, and he dragged out the 'e' into a 't.' He meant for us to fire at the Maki shore line west of a wreck. Remember that stuff we saw floating—"

"I know," said Trent. "I doped out that part, too. There must have been a wrecked schooner on the reef. When Horuti relayed Shelton's message, he told them to get rid of the wreck and stage that monkey-business about the cat. There was a sketch somebody had drawn—"

"Jackson told me, just before the Japs shot him." Crabb's

long hands worked for an instant. "Eric, they murdered him in cold blood after we landed, in revenge because they lost two ships and pilots. They'd have murdered me, too, but this one here wanted to question me."

Trent looked at the candle Kenako had dropped. His face hardened.

"I never thought I'd like killing—until this war. These Japs aren't human—they're even worse than animals."

A flicker of hatred touched Kenako's eyes, vanished. From out in the direction of the cove came the sputtering roar of an engine starting up. It settled into a steady drone, then diminished in volume as the ship was taxied outside. After two minutes it ceased, and Trent heard the rumble of the camouflage doors being closed. He waited another minute, but no call came.

"I guess we're ready," he told Crabb. Then he fixed his eyes on Kenako. "We're going up through the hut and down to where the plane's moored. Your one chance of living depends on our getting to that plane."

Kenako wet his lips, made no answer. Trent raised the bayonet, and Kenako moved toward the door. Mortimer Crabb followed close behind Trent.

"Open it up," ordered Trent.

Kenako turned the knob, and the door swung open. Trent went rigid.

Covering them from the hall were three Japs with tommy-guns!

"A neat bit of planning, Commander Trent," said a mocking voice. Horuti stepped into sight from behind the machine-gunners. For a second, his eyes flitted to Kenako's livid face.

"Major, I was going to trick them!" cried Kenako.

"Of that, we will speak later," Horuti said curtly. He motioned to the machine-gunners. "Bring the prisoners. You will come, too, my dear captain."

Helpless before the tommy-guns, Trent let the rifle drop against the wall. Horuti's gaze passed over the dead Jap pilot.

"Major, I was helpless," Kenako moaned. "But I intended to—"

Sudden fury broke through Horuti's pretense of coolness. "You cowardly fool! If I hadn't come when I did, the Americans would have destroyed all our bases in this area!"

"I thought you—I feared you had been shot down," faltered Kenako.

"I was captured!" snarled Horuti. "Thanks to these two you were helping escape, I was locked in an American brig. But for the German agent, Beckett, I would have been doomed. He killed a guard and let me out, and he helped me get away in a fighter—although I almost plunged into the sea taking off."

THE GUARDS herded Trent and Crabb into the main hangar space, with Horuti and Kenako following behind. At least a hundred Japanese were swarming over the planes, preparing them for flight. The steel doors to the launching-chamber were quickly opened up at Horuti's signal.

"We're attacking tonight—immediately!" Trent heard him tell Kenako. "While I was aboard the *Lextoga*, Beckett told me they had apparently received word from Trent that there was no danger at Maki. The carrier is less than 150 miles from here now, but anything can happen. They may force the truth out of Beckett—and that would mean full attack on Maki. We've got to hit first. Once we've wiped out the carrier, we can concentrate on the rest of their raiding force. Even if some of their planes get off, they'll have no place to return to."

"Major Horuti, let me lead the attack," begged Kenako. "Let me prove—"

"No, you will remain here—under arrest." Horuti coldly turned his back, barked several orders to the scurrying pilots and mechanics. Three Mitsubishis had already been hoisted onto the catapult cars, and the hooks were being transferred to three more for quick follow-up in launching. The big doors were already open, and Trent saw the Mitsubishi he had expected to use in the escape. Several Nakajimas were lined up for launching down the ramp, with the catapults this time reserved for the heavily loaded dive-bombers.

Horuti wheeled after a quick inspection of the preparations. He beckoned to the machine-gunners, and the two prisoners were marched over beside the first catapult. Horuti flicked a sharp glance at Kenako.

"You tried to force these two to speak?"

"Only the lieutenant, Major," Kenako answered, with a venomous look at Trent. "He was very stubborn, though I threatened to put out his eyes."

Horuti looked back at Trent.

"You would not like to die, Commander? You are a man who is fond of life...."

"Major Horuti, if you will let me have a bayonet," began Kenako.

"Hold your tongue!" snapped Horuti. "I've no time to waste with you. There's one thing we still don't know—the number and type of the American raiding vessels. Beckett knew only a few."

"Then we may be running into dangerous odds!" cried Kenako.

"In that case, we'll attack only the carrier—then return here and wait our chance." Horuti turned his mocking eyes on Trent, but behind the sardonic look Trent saw the man's hatred. "You are the *Lextoga's* intelligence officer—you have that information?"

"Tell him to go to hell, Eric!" rasped Mortimer Crabb.

Trent made no answer. Horuti fired an order at a passing mechanic, and the Jap brought a roll of stout cord. The Japanese pilots were waiting nervously in a group at the door to the launching-chamber. Horuti saw them, nodded.

"I will give you your orders in a moment. Meanwhile, lay off a course of 72 degrees, to intercept the *Lextoga*." The pilots went to work on their maps, and Horuti unrolled part of the cord. Deliberately, he tied one end to Trent's right arm, jerked it tight.

"Commander, I am going to have you tied behind the exhaust-port of that first catapult. That is, unless you tell me all that I want."

IN SPITE of himself, Trent felt a cold chill go over him. Three years before, he had seen an officer accidentally step in front of a catapult's exhaust as it was fired. The back-blast had blown off his head and hurled his body overboard.

"I see you understand," Horuti said curtly. "Make your choice—I give you twenty seconds!"

Trent stared across at the catapult crew. Two powder bags had been carried from a magazine behind a steel door, while a hand-truck with more bags was loaded for the other catapults.

"Fifteen seconds!" said Horuti.

The Japs at the catapult had stopped to watch Trent. He raised his sleeve, wiped his face, and the watching pilots roared.

"Mort—they'll find it out, anyway," Trent said hoarsely.

"You—Good Lord, you wouldn't tell them?" groaned Crabb.

Horuti was watching, a look of astonished, incredulous pleasure in his beady eyes.

"Ten seconds, Commander," he said.

"You swear you won't—you'll keep your word?" Trent mumbled.

"Eric—you can't!" shouted Crabb.

Trent whirled, slammed a left to Crabb's jaw. Crabb staggered back, slipped on the wet ramp and plunged backward into the water. Trent spun around to Horuti.

"All right, I'll tell you—I'll tell you!" he cried desperately. He closed his eyes, stumbled against the side of the catapult. "First, the *Lextoga*... heavy cruisers, the—"

Horuti had dropped the roll of cord. He shoved one of the guards aside, snatched a pilot's map and pencil.

"Heavy cruisers—quick!" he snapped.

"Here—I'll write it!" Trent took a step forward, then with a swift leap he sprang to the catapult platform and dived headlong into the water.

"Horuti—the cord!" screamed Kenako.

THERE WAS a deafening explosion, a blinding glare as flame shot back from the open breach of the catapult powder-chamber.

Trent's head was under water as the explosion came. The shock-waves instantly deafened him, and he came up in a weird inferno in which there was no sound. He saw Crabb floundering dazedly a few yards away. He swam to him, pointed to the Mitsubishi, and they struck out together.

Crabb scrambled aboard, and Trent hastily released the mooring-line. At his swift gesture, Crabb signaled the switch was on. Trent jumped onto the tip of the pontoon, jerked the prop and dropped into the water. The already warmed engine caught, revved up. Trent barely caught the pontoon as it swept by, dragged himself up. He felt the engine idle, and a second later pulled himself onto the wing to reach the front pit.

Bright, acrid smoke was pouring out of the base. A spot-light went on, a yellowish blur, and a moment later Trent saw a Nakajima fighter slide out from the ramp to the side of the catapults. Two men on the wing were fighting to reach the cockpit. The blurred yellow light fell on the faces of Horuti and Kenako. Suddenly Horuti stepped back, and a pistol blazed.

Kenako doubled over, fell headlong into the water. Horuti jumped into the cockpit, gunned the idling engine. Trent opened the throttle of the Mitsubishi just as Horuti saw the other ship. A fiendish, gloating look shot into the Jap's face as Crabb tugged at the unfamiliar rear-pit gun-controls.

The Nakajima swerved and Horuti's cowl guns blazed,

almost dead on. Trent kicked hard rudder, and simultaneously he felt Crabb's guns throb.

He stared back, almost into Horuti's spouting guns, Crabb's tracers stabbed across the Nakajima's wing, into the cloud of smoke that hid the secret hangar.

For the second time, an explosion rocked the Japanese base. A sheet of flame shot from the yellow cloud, out over the tossing waves. It was like a red avalanche that swept down over Horuti. When the blast faded, the Nakajima was ablaze from nose to tail. Trent had one fearful glimpse of Horuti's face through the flames. Then it was gone.

Without looking back, Trent sent the Mitsubishi speeding across the cove. As the ship lifted, he closed his nostrils with his hand, blew until his ears had cleared. Mortimer Crabb was shouting something at him, and he climbed until he could throttle back in a flat glide.

"When we land," yelled Crabb, "I want you to give me a good sound kick. I might have known that was an act—but I didn't tumble until you knocked me into the drink. I know a pulled punch when I feel one."

"I was afraid to tip you off," said Trent. "I didn't know it would work."

"What in Hades happened?"

"I managed to slip that cord over the firing mechanism. They had two powder bags in the breech. The flare-back set off the other bags they had on the hand-truck. Apparently you finished the job."

"Me?" ejaculated Crabb.

"Sure. Your tracers hit something in there—probably some gasoline. Nice work—especially as Horuti just about had our goose cooked."

Trent gunned the engine again, climbed out over sea. Suddenly Crabb pulled the rear pit throttle shut.

"How in tarnation are we going to get down without being shot?" he bellowed. "When the *Lextoga* gang spots this Jap ship, they'll make us look like a sieve."

"Simple," said Trent. "Turn on the transmitter and start singing 'Sweet Adeline.'"

"Mort, no Jap in the world could ever sing 'Sweet Adeline' with your inimitable manner. Somebody aboard ship is sure to recognize your unique rendition."

"Well, all right," Crabb said dubiously. He switched on the mike, and began to sing in a sepulchral and slightly nasal voice. After a minute Trent reached down and cut off the transmitter.

"What's the idea?" demanded Crabb.

"Frankly," said Trent, "I'd rather be shot."

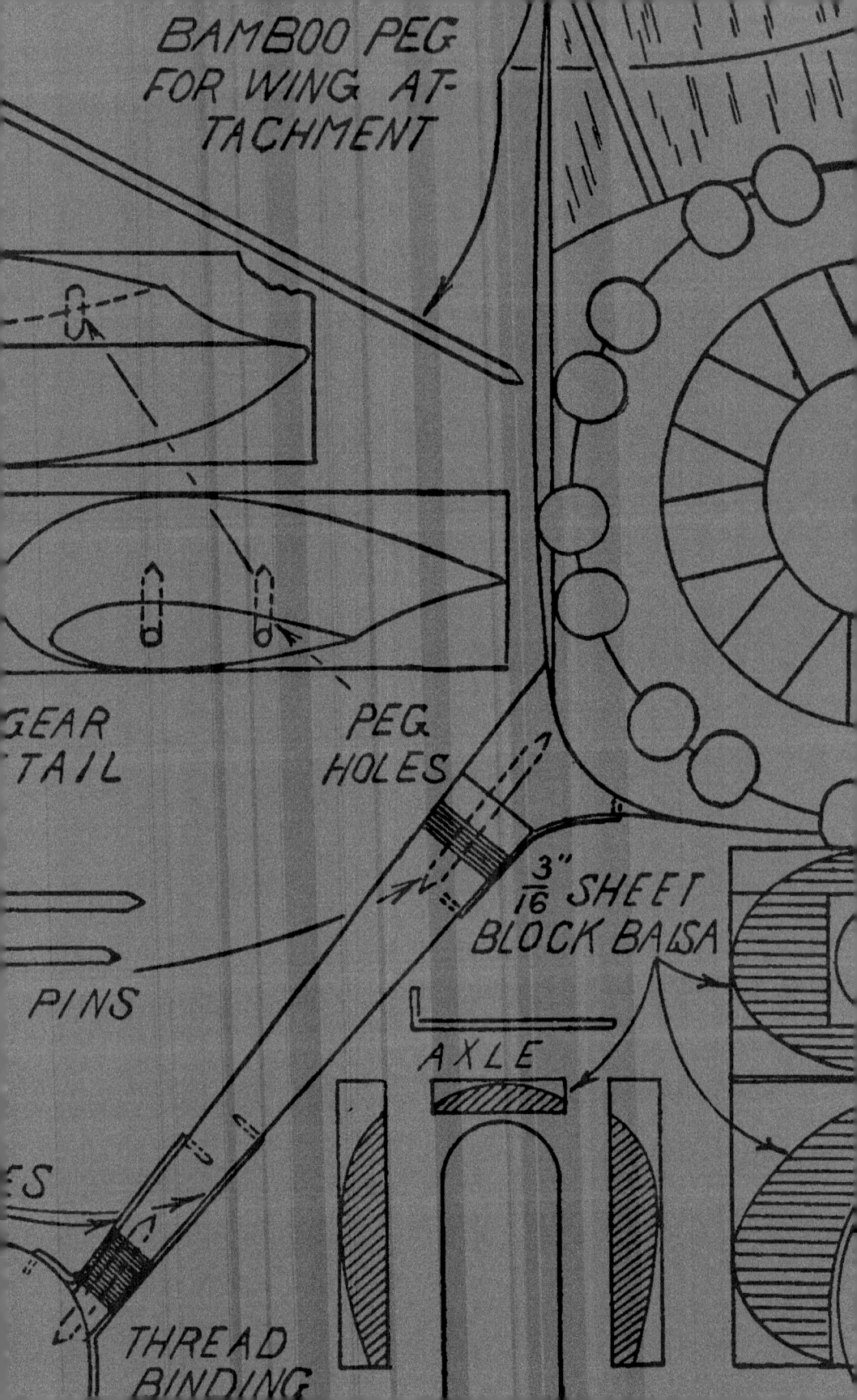

BAMBOO PEG
FOR WING AT-
TACHMENT

GEAR
TAIL

PEG
HOLES

PINS

$\frac{3"}{16}$ SHEET
BLOCK BALSA

AXLE

THREAD
BINDING

On Haunted Wings

CHAPTER I

The Hooded Ace

ERIC TRENT was almost to the phone booths when he saw the three-striper. The Navy man had halted just inside the doorway of the Washington Airport terminal. As Trent turned, the man flung up one hand, hastily shielding his face. Still keeping his face hidden, he wheeled and hurried out.

"Now, what brought that on?" pondered Trent. He stepped out into the night. A mist was falling, and the lights at the entrance were dimmed. The three-striper had vanished in the gloom.

Trent's dark eyes lost their amused twinkle. This began to look more than odd. There had been something tantalizingly familiar about that Navy commander, despite the attempt to hide his identity. Trent thought for a moment. Several officers had been disgruntled at his special assignment in Naval Intelligence. Two or three, he knew, had resented the appointment of Eric Trent, ex-magician and soldier-of-fortune, as senior air agent, with full commander's rank. That might explain cutting him cold—but it would hardly explain the man's precipitous flight or the guilty hiding of his face.

Trent gazed a moment longer into the murky night. A passing airline stewardess gave his tall, uniformed figure an appreciative glance. Trent had a dark, alert face and the smooth poise that comes with hours behind stage footlights. His mouth, under a close-clipped black mustache, had a look of whimsical humor—a look that could, on occasion, become a politely impudent grin.

As Trent turned to go inside, a taxi drove up. Two business men got out, went into the terminal, and the cab rolled off into the night. Trent started on, then stopped. Perhaps it was a faint sound from behind him, or perhaps some sixth sense, the feeling of hostile eyes fixed on his back. He moved from under the dim overhead light, casually took out his cigarette case.

Inside the lid a small curved mirror was secured. Trent extracted a cigarette, tilting the case to look behind him. The mysterious three-striper was stealing toward him on

Trent whipped into a tight bank, tripped his forward guns at the Stuka while Crabb drove off the Curtiss. The hooded pilot gave an agonized jump as the tracers pounded him!

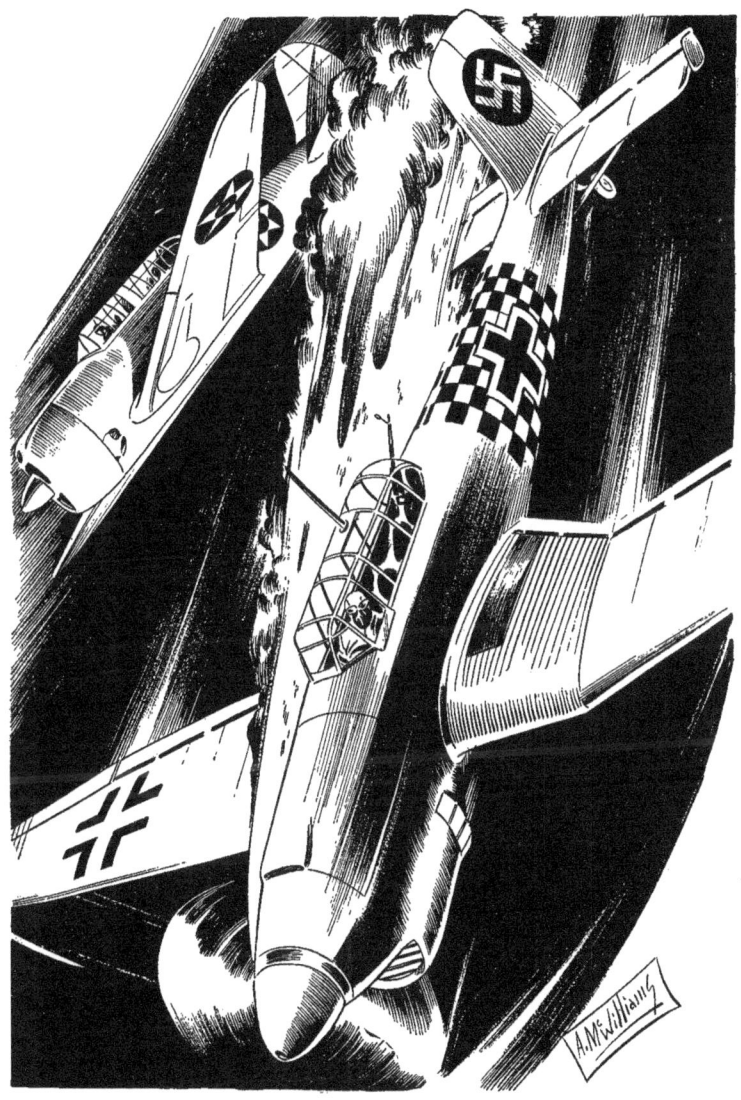

tiptoe. In his right hand was an automatic with a silencer.
His features were still obscured in semi-darkness.

Trent idly dropped the cigarette case into his coat pocket.
He bent his head as though about to light a cigarette, then
spun around and dived in low. The other man jumped back
with a stifled oath. Trent seized his wrist just as he pulled
the trigger.

THE AUTOMATIC made a muffled grunt, but the bullet went into the air. Trent gave his assailant's wrist another hard twist. The three-striper dropped to his knees and Trent deftly flicked the gun from his loosened fingers.

"You don't mind, old chap?" he said amiably. "Now, let's have a look at you."

The captive silently got to his feet. Trent pursed his lips in a soft whistle.

He was gazing on an exact duplicate of his own face!

At first glance, he could hardly discern a flaw. The clipped mustache was the same, the set of the lips underneath. Hair and skin had the same almost Latin darkness. Except for slightly higher cheekbones, and the murderous light in the other man's eyes, Trent might have been facing a mirror.

"My compliments," he told his double. "That's really an excellent job of make-up. You almost fooled *me* for a moment."

The impostor stared at him. "I must say you take it rather coolly."

"Why not? I have the gun."

"I should have shot you at once," muttered the captive.

"Oh, I wouldn't blame myself too much," said Trent. "Some one might have come out. It would look a bit odd, Trent dragging off his own corpse. Probably spoil the impersonation act."

"Very funny," the impostor said bitterly.

"I wonder how long this has been going on," mused Trent. "Mort and I have been away for a month. By the way, you haven't anybody impersonating Mortimer Crabb? That *would* be something."

"You'll learn nothing from me," snapped his captive. "Not even if—" He broke off as a blurred figure came toward the entrance from a car that had just stopped very close to them.

"Get back out of the light," ordered Trent. The impostor obeyed, and Trent turned so that the pistol would not be visible. The approaching figure was a short but powerfully built man, with a close-cropped head that seemed to grow right out of his shoulders. He was making for the doorway when he saw Trent. He wheeled back, and his heavy, brutal features took on a quick relief.

"Von Zenden!" he said hoarsely. "I just got the message from—"

"Hermann—it's Trent!" the impostor burst out. "Use your blackjack!"

Hermann's jaw dropped, then he leaped at Trent. With a quick sidestep, Trent landed a left to the stomach. Hermann doubled over and let go his blackjack, but the false three-striper had seized his opportunity. Hurtling against Trent, he knocked the pistol aside.

The silenced automatic grunted again, twice. Glass crashed from the nearest swinging door, as the bullets went wide. The impostor was clawing at the weapon when a clamor of voices arose from inside. An armed airport guard charged out into the vestibule. The tall masquerader instantly fled, with Hermann at his heels, wheezing for breath. Trent started after them, the gun shining faintly under the light.

"Halt, you!" bawled the airport guard. Trent stopped, but Hermann lurched around, and a snub-nosed revolver blasted. As the guard fell, Trent pitched a shot at Hermann, now only a shadow in the night. The German's gun blazed again, and a bullet smacked the stone wall behind Trent. The next instant he was hidden behind the car he had driven up.

The impostor was already at the wheel. Trent sent a bullet after the machine, heard the slug ricochet from metal. The car was swallowed up in the darkness before he could aim again. There was no sign of Hermann. Evidently he had jumped onto the running-board and escaped.

Three or four frightened porters were bending over the wounded guard. Trent hesitated, out in the screening mist, then he saw a crowd swarm out from the huge waiting-room. He made his way swiftly around to the north door, near the luggage room. The guard would be given full attention without him; and to appear there now would only delay action.

Trent put the gun in his belt, so his uniform blouse hid it. Then he straightened his cap and went into the terminal. Everyone was running toward the south entrance. He trailed along until he saw the mournful visage of Lieut. Mortimer Crabb, the engineering expert of Naval Intelligence. Crabb, a New England inventor, had been his reluctant partner in numerous tricks against the Axis before the war. After Pearl Harbor, Trent had signed up with the Navy, and Crabb, though still dolefully complaining, had followed him in the Service.

MORTIMER CRABB was about forty years old. Even in a two-striper's uniform, he was still a gawky figure, thick-waisted, legs a trifle too short, long arms dangling. His face was long and gloomy, and his general philosophy was to expect the worst.

Trent found him at the edge of the phone-booth alcove. Crabb eyed him with dismal suspicion.

"And just where have you been?" he demanded. His voice had a sepulchral sound, as though it came from the bottom of a well.

"Oh, I dropped up to see Johnny Groves, the airport manager," Trent said blithely. "What's going on here? Some celebrity arriving?"

"Somebody shot a guard," growled Crabb. "Shot the glass out of that door, too. Nobody seems to know what it's all about."

"How badly is the guard hurt?"

"He got it below the right shoulder, one of the porters said. They just carried him down the hall."

"Say anything about who shot him?" queried Trent.

"Nope," grunted Crabb. "Say, why are you so anxious?"

"Never mind. Did you get Captain Blaine?"

"He wasn't in," Crabb said testily. "Here he yanks us back

from Australia on rush orders, and then doesn't even leave word—"

"Calm down, old bean. I think I've spotted the leak in Air Intelligence."

"Ha!" scoffed Crabb. "I suppose you pulled it out of your hat, like one of your stage rabbits."

"My dear Mort, the rabbit-and-hat trick was passe years ago. During my career as the Great Mysto I never once produced a bunny."

"Skip it," snorted Crabb. "I want to get home, where I can sleep in a real bed once more. I suppose it's too much to hope the garage people sent our car out here. And there won't be any taxis, a rainy night like this."

Trent grinned as they went outside. "Good old cheerful Mort. You'll never know how you buoy up my spirits on dark days."

They found the car, a big convertible coupé, parked in the officials' reserved section. Trent climbed in behind the wheel, took the silenced automatic from his belt, and laid it on the seat.

"Where'd you get that?" exclaimed Crabb. "Don't tell me that's the gun that shot the guard?"

"No," said Trent, "this one just drilled the door."

"I knew it," groaned Crabb. "We aren't in a place five minutes before we're in a jam. What have you done now?"

Trent started the car. "Mort, remember that quick-change artist we saw in the Pintzstrasse Theater, in Berlin, back in '39?"

"The German who did all the impersonations? Sure— what of it?"

"His name was Kurt von Zenden. His father was Karl von Zenden, the notorious World War spy who was stopped so often by Capt. Philip Strange. Karl von Zenden was also a professional before that war broke out; he used to call himself the 'Man of a Thousand Faces.' It's obvious he's trained Kurt to follow in his footsteps and serve Hitler."

"What's that got to do with tonight?"

"Quite a lot. I met the gentleman back there. We had a little argument. He was using my face, and I'm a bit particular about those things."

"He was *what?*" sputtered Crabb. "You mean he was made up as you?"

"Right. And a good job, too." As Trent swung into the airport road leading toward Washington and Arlington he gave Crabb a brief summary of the encounter.

"This is terrible," moaned Crabb. Lord knows what he's done, posing as you. You'll probably—"

He jumped, and Trent put on the brakes as the rising howl of air-raid sirens filled the air. The airport lights began to go out. Ahead, the misty glow from the Memorial Highway faded into blackness. Across the Potomac, where the wail of Washington's super-sirens was now audible, street and house lights hastily went dark. Trent cut off his headlights and ignition, climbed out.

He had stopped on the crest at the west side of the airport. Below and back nearer the terminal he could see Army mechanics starting three Airacobras, by the faint glow of shielded lanterns. Just beyond, two Navy ships were briefly illuminated by the flitting lights. One was the Brewster SB2A-1 dive-bomber in which Crabb and he had flown from the West Coast. The other was a Curtiss SB2C-1. Apparently it was not kept there for defense, like the Airacobras, for it was not being manned.

"I'd give a month's pay to get into this," said Trent. "That is, if it's a real raid."

"You'd get your pants shot off," Crabb said sourly. "Those Army guys will be firing at everything but their own ships."

The Airacobras roared down a darkened runway, swept up into the murk. From across the Potomac came the thunder of other interceptors taking off from Bolling Field."

"Probably just a test," grunted Crabb. "Bombers couldn't see to hit anything, a night like this."

THE DRONE of engines diminished, as the Army fighters climbed on up to get on top of the overcast, Trent took three small hollow steel balls from his coin pocket, began to juggle them in the darkness. It was one of his habits when thinking over some problem—juggling, palming coins, while his brain kept pace with his fingers. He looked back at the terminal, remembering Hermann's tense expression and his reference to a message.

"Mort, I've a hunch this isn't a test. That gorilla of von Zenden's acted as though something were about to pop."

"Maybe so," Crabb said, staring up into the night. "Sounds like something right now."

The drone of an unseen plane had changed to an angry snarl, as it suddenly picked up speed. Trent thought he heard a muffled pound of guns. The snarling roar abruptly died out. A few moments later ground guns hammered, somewhere across the river. A searchlight angled through the dark, jerked back.

"What's that?" ejaculated Crabb, as the beam caught something in the mists.

"It's a Stuka!" said Trent. Even as he spoke, the ground guns cut loose with a furious barrage. Tracers from five directions flamed toward the Nazi dive-bombers. But the Stuka never swerved. Slowly, almost majestically, it glided over the Highway Bridge. But no bombs fell. One wing tilted under a machine gun blast, then, with a sharp dip, the Stuka plunged into the river.

Searchlights were focused on the spot before the seething waters had time to settle. The Stuka's tail was visible for a moment in the glare, then it slowly went under.

"The pilot must've been dead or out cold, the way it came in," muttered Crabb.

"Notice anything odd about that ship?" said Trent.

"Only the way it came down."

"It didn't have a landing gear. Either they dropped the

wheels or—" Trent swiftly put the steel balls in his pocket, turned to the car.

"What's up?" erupted Crabb.

Trent pointed up into the gloom. The faint glow reflected from the searchlights on the water revealed a descending parachute, with a figure dangling beneath it.

"He's going to land near the edge of the field." Trent started the engine. "If we move fast we'll nab him before he can run."

He sent the coupé racing toward the junction of the airport road and the boulevard. The searchlight from the terminal, probing toward the Stuka, was barely enough to guide him.

"Slow down, you lunatic!" howled Crabb. We'll hit something."

Trent gazed up through the windshield-wiper arc. The man in the chute was a hundred feet from the ground. He was going to land near a boundary light standard, about ninety yards from the boulevard.

"Hang on, Mort." Trent skidded off the road, up onto the flat earthen dyke which formed the airport boundary. The descending figure struck the ground, and the chute soddenly collapsed over him. Trent braked the car, jumped out with the silenced gun in his hand. Crabb helped him pull aside the folds of silk.

"Well, burn my breeches!" Crabb said in amazement.

The Nazi airman's head was almost completely covered by a black hood. It had been pulled sidewise, twisting upward so that the goggle lenses sewed into it showed the man's forehead. On his neck, above the Luftwaffe uniform collar, was a scratch from the opened buckle of the strap which secured the hood.

Trent bent over, removed the hood. The German's head rolled back, his blue eyes staring glassily into the sky. His face was a mottled, unnatural color, and Trent saw a broad red band on his throat, where the strap had been pulled tight.

There was no trace of a mortal wound, but he knew, even before he listened for a heartbeat, that the man was dead.

"Looks like he was strangled," Crabb said huskily. "But why was he wearing that hood in the first place?"

Trent shook his head. "It reminds me of a hangman's hood, the kind the Germans used back in the sixteenth century." He stopped, bent for another look at the dead man. "Mort, do you know who this is? It's Wilhelm Grussen—the Nazi ace!"

"First von Zenden, and now Grussen! Eric, this thing's getting hot."

"Help me put him in the car," said Trent. "We'll take him back to the airport and search him."

He unbuckled the parachute harness, and Crabb helped carry the body back to the car. Trent unlocked the luggage compartment and they shoved the corpse inside, doubled up. Something made a metallic thud. He opened the German's flight jacket, saw a pistol in a shoulder harness. It was the same make as the silenced gun in his coat pocket.

Trent started to close the top of the compartment. Suddenly there was a scuffing sound behind him, and Crabb gave a startled exclamation. Trent made a lightning movement.

"Look out, Eric!" moaned Mortimer Crabb. Trent turned, bumped his hat against the raised lid of the luggage compartment. Crabb's hands were in the air. Twenty feet away stood Hermann, the dimly reflected glow of the searchlights gleaming from a tommy-gun.

CHAPTER II

"For Murder and Treason!"

"**D**ON'T MOVE!**" rasped the German. He side-stepped to cover them better. Back in the shadows Trent saw the dark shape of another car which had crept up silently. A uniformed figure circled around behind Crabb, and Trent recognised Von Zenden, still made up as his double.

"Put up your hands, Commander," ordered von Zenden. As he spoke, he quickly ran his hands over Crabb in search of a weapon. Finding none, he strode over to Trent.

"The left-hand coat pocket," Trent said pleasantly.

The impersonator felt on that side, then with a scowl took his silenced gun from the right-hand pocket.

"So! Still trying your tricks, *Herr* Trent. Another like that and—" he drew in his breath sharply as he saw the corpse. He took out a pencil flashlight, cupped his hand around the end and hastily inspected the dead ace.

"*Lieber Gott!* He wasn't shot, Hermann. The hood must have—" von Zenden bit off the words, straightened up. "We must act quickly. Some one else may have seen the parachute."

"Why not have them move the body to our car?" said Hermann gruffly.

"No. We'll use their machine and save time. The police may have the number of the other car, also." Von Zenden opened the door of the coupé. "Commander, you and this sour-faced *Leutnant* will put the body on the rear seat. Then you will climb into the luggage compartment—both of you."

"Why not shoot us now?" Mortimer Crabb said gloomily. "That's what you're aiming at, anyway."

"Speak for yourself, Mort," said Trent. "Personally, I'll string along with *Herr* von Zenden. We might make a deal."

Von Zenden smiled sardonically. "A deal? Perhaps so. Now, the body—*mach Schnell.*"

Trent pivoted, hands still raised to the level of his hat. Suddenly he flipped it aside and snatched out Grussen's pistol, which he had concealed underneath it. Flame jetted from the muzzle and Hermann tottered back, dropped the tommy-gun. Von Zenden leaped into the coupé, pumped a wild shot at Trent from his silenced pistol. Trent hurtled against Crabb, knocking him flat. Crouching back of the raised compartment-lid, he sent two bullets through the coupé's rear window. The engine started with a roar and the car plunged crookedly along the top of the dyke.

Crabb jumped up, lifted the tommy-gun. Its tracers blazed close to the fleeing car, but before he could correct his aim von Zenden drove the coupé off the dyke and went racing down onto a runway. Trent flung a look at Hermann. The Nazi was crawling off, groaning, one arm dangling.

"Come on, Mort!" Trent sprinted to the spies' car and Crabb tumbled in after him. The airport searchlight whipped back from the Potomac, spotted the two cars. Trent sent the spy machine bouncing over the side of the dyke, with von Zenden now a hundred yards ahead.

The impersonator was making for the Curtiss SB2C-1. He stopped, his tires screeching, car and plane silhouetted in the glare. Trent pounded the horn button, but his attempted warning was drowned as the scout-bomber's engine started. Von Zenden stumbled toward the rear pit, Grussen's body slung over his shoulder. He dumped it in, sprang up into the front cockpit. The Curtiss lurched ahead, its wing tip knocking a mechanic flat.

"That dirty Hun!" bawled Crabb. He sent a burst from the tommy-gun after the fast-moving Curtiss. But the ship did not swerve. Trent brought the car to a violent halt beside the Brewster. Crabb jumped out and seized the inertia-starter crank, and the engine, still warm, caught at Trent's first try.

Two Army sentries were running toward the Brewster, an airline pilot behind them.

"Pile in, Mort!" Trent said swiftly. "No time to explain now."

A rifle bullet drilled the hatch-cover as he taxied out. He kicked around, into the wind, and the Brewster thundered away, with rifles blazing behind them.

The Curtiss was a hundred feet in the air, climbing fast. Trent took-off, zoomed the instant he had speed. A quick blast over the Curtiss brought it around in a furious turn. Four tracer streams shot back at the Brewster. Trent crouched as the Plexiglas-shattered overhead. His own guns were pounding again. He lifted his tracers, saw them gouge near the tail and jerk forward.

Von Zenden started to roll out of the burst. Grussen's body lurched, his arms hanging down from the rear pit. The spy hastily chandelled, to keep the corpse from falling out. Trent was almost in line for another attack when a Bolling Field searchlight flashed across the Brewster.

By the time he could see again, the Curtiss had disappeared. He swung across the Potomac, banked to turn back from the pursuing searchlights. The tip of the Washington Monument showed through the misty sky ahead. He twisted to pass south of it.

"Watch out!" bellowed Crabb. "There's another Stuka!"

The Nazi ship came riding in with a searchlight at its back. Trent pulled up in a half-roll, barely in time. The Brewster quivered from the impact of bullets near the tail. Crabb cut loose with the rear guns, and the Stuka hurriedly renversed. Trent saw the pilot in the shifting light beams. The Nazi's head was covered with a black hood, just as Grusson's had been.

CRABB'S TRACERS abruptly shifted, and Trent saw the Curtiss reappear on his left. He whipped into a tight bank, tripped the forward guns at the Stuka while Crabb drove off the Curtiss. The hooded pilot gave an agonized jump, then

Trent's blazing tracers stabbed on past and into the Stuka's cowl. Flame puffed out and the Stuka nosed down, streaking groundward like a huge torch hurled from the sky.

Trent turned sharply, but the Curtiss was only a blur, swiftly vanishing. He circled for a minute or two, waiting to see if there were any more Stukas. Then he turned back toward the airport. The burning plane had struck in the upper end of Potomac Park, and its lurid glow lit up the low-drifting clouds.

"What do you make of it, Eric?" Crabb said, as Trent cut the throttle to land. "That hangman's hood business, I mean."

"Your guess is as good as mine, old bean. Too bad we couldn't hang onto Grussen's body. Might have told us a lot."

Trent flashed his recognition signal with the Brewster's running-lights, got an answer from the tower. He landed, taxied in on an approach runway. An Army sentry was talking with a civilian at the spot where the Brewster had been parked. The sentry started out as Trent stopped the ship, but the civilian motioned him back. Trent swung the Brewster around, pivoting on one wheel.

"You stay here, Mort, and leave the engine running. That looks like our old F.B.I. friend, Red McBride. He might have some cockeyed idea—"

"Here we go again," Crabb said unhappily.

Trent chuckled, opened bullet-torn greenhouse, and swung down. McBride waited, the sentry a few yards behind him. The light from the burning Stuka gleamed from the sentry's fixed bayonet. The F.B.I. man stood with his hands in the pockets of his raincoat, a limp felt hat cocked over one ear, revealing a thatch of bristling red hair. McBride was above medium height and a trifle on the thin side. He had dark-brown, unblinking eyes, and a deadpan face.

"I want to see you, Trent," he said curtly.

"Delighted, Red, old top," replied Trent.

"Don't call me Red," growled the F.B.I. man. "Come on inside."

"I'm quite comfortable here." Trent idly reached out, produced a lighted cigarette seemingly from behind McBride's ear. "Thanks, don't mind if I do. Would you care for one?"

"Lay off that magician stuff," McBride said tartly, while the sentry gaped at the cigarette. "I want to know what's going on out here."

"Well, of course, you know planes go in and out. That's the first thing. Then there's the de luxe dinner in the main restaurant, short orders in the coffee shop."

"Cut the comedy," said McBride. "Just exactly where were you at ten o'clock—"

"On the night of January twenty-eighth? I know that one; I always have an alibi for that night. Very lovely one, too. Remind me to introduce you some time."

"Look here, Commander," McBride said coldly, "I'm the senior agent covering airports around Washington. So don't try pulling rank on me."

"My dear fellow, I'm completely at your service." Trent took out the three little steel balls, began to juggle them. "You don't mind if I practice a bit while you give me the third-degree?"

McBride scowled. "A guard was shot out here tonight. Know anything about it?"

"Certainly." Trent juggled for a moment. "I was in the crowd when they brought him in—poor fellow."

McBride said something under his breath. "All right, let that go for a minute. When I got here somebody said you dragged a stiff into your ship and beat it."

"I think Mort would resent that." Trent grinned. "Though I'll admit there's a touch of rigor mortis about him at times—somewhat the same expression you have, now that I think of it."

McBride lost his dead-pan look. "Say, are you trying to make a monkey out of me?"

"I never compete with Nature," Trent said amiably. "She always does a better job."

"I don't like you, Trent," the F.B.I. man said grimly.

TRENT SIGHED, juggled the balls around behind his back. "I was beginning to suspect that. I guess I just don't know how to win friends and influence people."

"According to the evidence," McBride said doggedly, "you heaved a stiff into your ship and then ran down an Army mechanic. Right after you hopped off a German plane came along to help you—"

"Oh, so that's what it was doing," Trent cut in.

"Uh—beg pardon, sir," the sentry said to McBride. "But it was the Curtiss, not this ship. That's what the sergeant told me."

"They told me the pilot was a Navy three-striper with a black mustache," McBride asserted flatly. "If that isn't Trent here, who is it?"

"Sure, I changed ships in mid-air," said Trent. "And there's the stolen corpse—or is it just a reasonable facsimile?"

McBride strode toward the Brewster. Mortimer Crabb looked mournfully over the side at him, and the F.B.I. man swore.

"All right, Trent, somebody got mixed and saw you in this ship. Then you were chasing that other plane. Why—and what about the stiff? And who was the pilot?"

Trent kept the balls moving, but his glance shifted for a second. A hatless airport attendant was running toward McBride, with what looked like a message in his hand.

"It's a Naval Intelligence job, but I'll let you in on it," he told the F.B.I. agent. He put the balls in his pocket, motioned McBride closer. But the messenger broke in: "Mr. Groves said to see that you got this right away. That guard came to, and he recognized—"

McBride snatched the envelope, ripped it open. Trent tried to get a glimpse at the scrawled message, but the light was too dim. McBride held it close to his eyes and his face went dead-pan again. He slowly folded the paper, reached inside his raincoat as though to put it in his pocket. Trent suddenly caught the upturned collar with both hands. A swift yank, and the coat was down pinioning McBride's arms to his sides.

"Sorry, old top!" Trent whirled, raced for the Brewster.

"Stop! You're under arrest!" shouted McBride. "You fools, get this coat loose!"

A pistol made a faint report as Trent shoved open the Brewster's throttle. Mortimer Crabb ducked, and Trent saw his lips working soundlessly. The ship slued around, onto a cross-wind runway. Trent brought the Brewster up to flying speed and sent it hurtling out over the misty Potomac.

"You lunatic!" moaned Crabb. "Now we are in a mess."

Trent slid the hatch closed. "Why, Mort," he said reproachfully, "I couldn't let McBride lock us up and leave that juicy mystery about von Zenden unsolved could I, old man?"

He reached for his head-set, slid the phones over his ears.

"What are you going to do?" Crabb demanded through the interphone.

"I want to give McBride a bum steer. I'll call Naval Air at Anacostia and tell them we're landing there. Then we'll shoot for our old field."

Trent switched on the set. Before he could cut in the transmitter, words crackled into his phones:

"P-39 Patrol, Bolling. Force down Navy Brewster just taking off from Washington Airport… Men in it wanted for murder and treason… If unable to force down, use your guns."

"Eric—the Airacobra!" shouted Crabb. "We're finished!"

The nearest P-39 flipped into a vertical bank to follow the Brewster. Trent zoomed and the Airacobra pilot sent a burst past his wing tip.

As though submitting, Trent nosed down. Then with a lightning renversement he dived under the P-39 and instantly climbed at full gun. The Airacobra hastily followed through, but another P-39 was charging in to force the Brewster down. Both fighters veered out to avoid collision, and Trent lifted the two-seater up into the shrouding mists.

The Bolling Field operator was still calling the P-39 Patrol, repeating the order. Trent got a radio bearing, glanced at the compass. Easing down to three hundred feet, he closed the throttle and began a shallow glide.

"Are you crazy?" howled Crabb. "We'll crack into Arlington radio towers."

"We'll sit down right in the middle of our private field," Trent said, unperturbed. "I've offset the Bolling Field station, and we're practically on a beam."

THE BREWSTER settled through the murk. Trent waited, ready to open the throttle. Something brushed past the right wing tip. He flattened out, held it, and the Brewster hit, bounced, and rolled to a quick-braked stop. Trent switched off the engine.

"We just missed a tree by a hair," Crabb said gloomily as they got out. "Not that it would make any difference. We're doomed men—thanks to you."

"Have I ever let you down?" Trent countered.

"Only about a hundred times," grated Crabb.

Trent laughed. "You're still able to put away three square meals a day, I notice. I got us out of von Zenden's little trap tonight, and I'll get us out of this."

"You and your magician tricks! Where'd you get that gun, anyway?"

"A variation of the rabbit-in-the-hat trick, my dear Mort. That was Grussen's pistol. I put it on top of my head for emergency use when I heard our friends arrive."

"Not bad," Crabb admitted grudgingly. "At least you finally found some use for that thick skull of yours."

"You're just trying to be nice." Trent grinned. "Come on. We'd better get over to the house. If I can reach Captain Blaine I'll explain everything and he'll head off the F.B.I."

"A fat chance." Crabb morosely trudged after him. "That

Army operator said 'murder and treason.' The guard must have died, after implicating you. Unless you can find von Zenden and make him confess, it's going to be bad."

Trent pushed through a turnstile in the fence. "You're clear, old man, anyhow. The phone girl can testify you were in there when the shooting happened."

"I don't know," Crabb said dismally. "She might not remember me."

"One look at that distinctive countenance and nobody could ever forget you," said Trent.

"Never mind about my face," snorted Crabb. "Open the gate, if you can remember the combination."

The stone wall of the old Harrington estate loomed up darkly as they crossed the road. Trent and Crabb had leased the mansion and the adjoining meadow some months before Pearl Harbor. Crabb had fitted up the basement as a laboratory, where he developed his inventions for the Army and Navy. The meadow had proved usable as a landing field, even for the military planes which were sometimes loaned to Trent for semi-official missions before he signed up with the Navy. To safeguard his inventions, Crabb had installed special electric-charged barbed wire on top of the high wall. Inside the massive iron-studded gates were electric locks operated by secret buttons or from a radio-relay under the instrument board of Trent's coupé.

Trent peered up and down the road, to be certain no one was approaching. He removed a small stone from the right-hand portal, felt for the two buttons recessed there. He pressed the left one twice, the other one four times, and the heavy gates began to grind open. Floodlights under the eaves of the mansion came on automatically. Trent replaced the stone, followed Crabb inside.

"Better disconnect those lights, Mort, or we'll have an air raid warden on our necks."

"They'll cut off when the gates shut," said Crabb. "I'll attend to that later."

Trent glanced toward the gloomy old mansion. In the walled yard to the left he saw "Leaping Lena," the autogyro which had come into their possession during a brush with Axis spies. Then the gates clicked shut and the lights went out.

They went on up the winding drive, to the porte-cochere entrance. Crabb produced the key, and they went into the dark hall. Heavy velvet drapes shut out all light, and for a few seconds there was pitch blackness, until Trent switched on the chandelier.

"I'll phone Blaine," he told Crabb. He went into the drawing-room, dialed the Intelligence chief's private number. In a moment he heard Blaine's dry, precise voice say, "Hello."

"Captain, this is Eric Trent. I'd like to report—"

"Where the devil are you?" rapped Blaine. "I've just had a cockeyed telephone call from the F.B.I. about Crabb and you."

"I'll explain everything, Captain. But first, you'd better get a warning out about Kurt—"

There was a sharp click. Trent rattled the cradle, then slowly replaced the phone.

"What's the matter?" asked Crabb.

"The line's gone dead," said Trent.

CHAPTER III

The Man of a Thousand Faces

"YOU MEAN somebody's cut the wire?" Crabb said, alarmed.

"Sounded like it. Blaine would hardly have hung up."

"That means the F.B.I. is already headed this way," Crabb said hopelessly. "Our phone and light cables run underground and nobody could cut the wires. The G-men must've been tapped in at some exchange, and they cut you off."

Trent grinned. "Don't let it get you down, Mort. We've still got our transmitter downstairs. I'll contact Blaine through Navy radio, and I'll use code so F.B.I. won't get it."

The basement stairs opened off the rear hall, opposite from a large study which Trent had converted into a repository for his magician's paraphernalia. Magic cabinets, trick tables, illusion mirrors, and scores of special effects all but filled the room.

Trent started on past, then he stopped abruptly. Only a dim light shone in from the hall, but his trained eye caught something unfamiliar in the shadows. Taking out Grussen's pistol, he motioned Crabb to keep back while he reached for a light switch.

The lights flashed on. Mortimer Crabb let out a croaking gasp, and Trent looked down in astonishment.

He was gazing on the mottled, ghastly face of Wilhelm Grussen!

"Lord help us," Crabb said hoarsely. "How did this body get in there?"

"Von Zenden must have carried him here; that's the only answer." Trent took a quick glance into the hall. A muffled sound came from somewhere behind him, and he wheeled with the gun poised. Crabb pointed at a tall red-and-gold illusion cabinet.

"Somebody's in there, Eric!" he whispered.

"Get over to the side," Trent said in an undertone. He touched a recessed catch, and the front of the cabinet came open.

Crabb's eyes bulged as the half-dressed body of a man toppled out on the floor. "Another corpse! I'm getting out of here, Eric!"

"Hold on," muttered Trent. "Let's see who it is."

He bent down, gingerly rolled the dead man over. Then something went up his spine like the touch of an icy finger on an August afternoon.

"Grussen!" He spun around, with a sudden understanding.

"Drop it, *Herr* Trent," said the man in the chair. He sat up with an ironic smile, the muzzle of his silenced gun pointed straight at Trent's heart.

Trent looked into the black hole at the end of the silencer. Then he slowly-laid his pistol down on a table.

"Very neat, von Zenden." He gazed from the dead ace back to the impersonator. "Considering the lack of time, an amazingly good job."

"And why not?" the Prussian said sardonically. "I was not called 'The Man of a Thousand Faces' for nothing. Move back!"

Trent stepped back from the table. "So you inherited your father's trade name, along with the spy business, eh?"

Von Zenden's made-up eyes narrowed. "Be careful, *mein Freund*. My father was the finest impersonator who ever lived—and the greatest agent of the Corps d'Elite. If I can but approach his deeds, in serving our *Fuehrer*—"

"Never mind the 'heil Hitler,'" Trent cut him off. "If it will make you feel any better, I'll admit the von Zendens seemed to be fairly bright boys."

"Very kind of you, *Herr* Trent," the spy said mockingly. "The German mind is always superior to low Yankee cunning—such as that trick with the gun in your hat."

"That was pretty crude, wasn't it?" Trent said apologetically. "I'm afraid it can't compare with this—" he stopped and picked up a small clockwork device which had fallen out of the cabinet with Grussen's body. It was one of the timers used to set off various delayed-action magic apparatus. Von Zenden had evidently set it to release the trip against the side of the cabinet, making the noise which Crabb and he had heard.

"The mechanical effect was of small importance," von Zenden said disdainfully. "But only a master could have made up to pass for Grussen."

"True Prussian modesty," said Trent. He set the timer beside a cuckoo clock, motioned to Crabb. "Might as well sit down and be comfortable, Mort. This hymn of praise may go on all night."

VON ZENDEN'S lips tightened. "You will not be listening to anything much longer, either of you. When my aides arrive, it will be my privilege to even the *Fuehrer's* score against you."

"Well, Eric, I hope you're satisfied," Crabb said mournfully. "At least the F.B.I. would have given us a fair trial."

Trent looked down at the dead Nazi ace. "Sorry, Mort. But, anyway, we've wrecked their plans, whatever they were up to."

"You think so?" sneered von Zenden. "You fool, by tomorrow morning Washington will… Ach! So you think you'll get me to betray the secret and then somehow escape to warn them."

"That was the general idea. Trent smiled indolently, as he eyed himself in one of the full-length mirrors. "You know, Kurt, now that modesty's the keynote, I think I cut a better figure than you did when you were Commander Trent. At least, I don't have to put lifts in my shoes."

The spy's hand tightened on his gun. "Keep a civil tongue in your head, or I'll finish you here and now! My impersonation was perfect. In three weeks, no one has suspected—not even your contacts in G-2 who have been so obliging."

"So that's it. You've not only been making this place your headquarters, but also doing a termite act over in town."

"Precisely," von Zenden smirked. "I planned the whole thing even before you left Washington. My agents watched this place every night for two weeks, until they learned about the hidden buttons at the gate. We tried the various mathematical combinations until we hit the right setting."

"Damned burglars!" grated Crabb. "Eric, you realize what that means? They've had access to the radio, our Naval Intelligence teletype, all my confidential files!"

"*Cuckoo!*" The front of a small clock suddenly opened and a little yellow bird popped out. There was a bright flash, a puff of acrid smoke, and both clock and cuckoo vanished.

Trent had been waiting for the flash. He jumped back through the smoke, in front of the illusion mirrors. Six other Eric Trents instantly became visible.

"Halt!" shouted von Zenden. He jerked the trigger and a slug crashed through the glass. Trent laughed.

"Try again, Nazi!" He sprang toward the center panel, shoved. The mirror revolved, and he was through in a twinkling. Another bullet shattered glass back of him. He ducked, snatched up a nickel-plated prop revolver.

"Keep back, Crabb!" he heard von Zenden cry tautly. The Prussian's voice came from the middle of the room. Trent pressed at the back of the cabinet where Grussen's body had been hidden. The rear section swung in on silent hinges. Trent leaped through into the room, fired the prop pistol at the back of von Zenden's head.

The Prussian gave a wild leap as the revolver roared. Dropping his gun, he staggered sidewise, clasping both hands behind his head.

"I'm shot!" he groaned. "I'm dying!"

Trent picked up Grussen's automatic from the table where he had laid it. Mortimer Crabb had dived for von Zenden's silenced pistol.

"Well, I guess you saved me the job," Crabb said sepulchrally.

"Much as I hate to disappoint you two," said Trent, "that was only a blank."

VON ZENDEN turned around, ashen through the already corpse-like make-up. His shaking fingers removed the blank-cartridge wadding from the back of his neck.

"*Schweinhund!*" he said thickly, "I'll kill you for that."

"Take it easy," advised Trent, "or the Master Mind's superior brain may spring a sudden leak. This one has real bullets."

"Let's get him out of here," Crabb urged. "He said he had his gang coming."

"Calm down, old bean," said Trent. "I fancy we can handle a few Nazi muscle-men. While we're waiting, go through his pockets—also that Navy uniform he discarded behind the cabinet."

He covered von Zenden while Crabb searched. The inventor laid a wallet and a folded paper on the nearest table.

"Watch it," said Trent. "That'll fall through the cuckoo-clock trap."

"That thing scared the liver out of me," grumbled Crabb. "I never knew it was a trick clock."

"My dear chap, if I explained all my effects I'd never have any surprises left. Think how dull life would be for you and our friend Kurt."

Von Zenden's eyes watched intently as Trent unfolded the paper. It was a map of the Washington area, including a section of Virginia. An easterly course-line had been drawn from their estate to a point beyond the capital suburbs. There it ended in a circle with "1,000 meters" written beside it.

"H-m-m," mused Trent. "This begins to clear up. You're using our short-wave transmitter as a beam to guide the Stukas. Take a look at this, Mort. What does that circle and the '1,000 meters' suggest?"

Crabb eyed the map while Trent covered von Zenden. "My guess is they've made a radio marker-beacon out there, intersecting this beam, and when the Stukas hear the signal they're supposed to start a set glide from 1,000 meters."

"Sounds likely." Trent glanced at the spy's grim-set face. "Feel like talking? It might make it easier for you on that murder charge."

Von Zenden laughed harshly. "You're the one they accused. I heard them radio the Airacobra pilots." Trent looked amused. "My dear Kurt, you Nazis are so naive. Haven't you ever heard of a frame-up?"

"What do you mean?" snapped the impersonator.

"Very simple. First, Mort knocks you cold while I keep you covered. Then we dress you in that three-striper uniform again. After that, I take off your make-up, replace the black mustache, and put the silenced gun in your hand—after wiping off Mort's prints. A little smear of grease-paint and cold cream on your face—and the stage is set."

"It won't work!" snarled von Zenden.

"When we call in the F.B.I. and Naval Intelligence, I'm afraid you'll have a rude shock. That make-up kit you left behind the screen will be hard to explain. In a pinch, I might even do your face over in a passable imitation of your making-up as myself. I'm not entirely a stranger to grease-paints."

Von Zenden glared at him, then a crafty light came into his eyes. "Very well, *Herr* Trent. What do you want to know?"

"What killed Grussen?"

"The hood must have strangled him," replied the Prussian. "It probably caught on something when he jumped."

"Most unfortunate. And why was he wearing that hood?"

"Because he was in disgrace," von Zenden said rapidly. "He and other pilots were to be executed, but they were given a last chance—"

"You really should study the fine art of lying," observed Trent. "Suppose I tell *you*. Grussen was poisoned. He was given that hood to keep from inhaling gas or poison dust. It probably had an oxygen tube leading into it so he could breathe. But he either left it off until the last moment or it wasn't tight enough. He bailed out to save himself and tried to get the hood off, but it stuck and he died. His throat swelled up and the strap made the red mark on it."

"Eric, you really think they were going to gas Washington?" Crabb said, appalled.

"No. They couldn't gas a whole city. But they might gas some vital spot. Maybe we can figure it out. Their target must be on this courseline—"

OUT IN the hall a buzzer-signal sounded and Trent heard the more distant grind of the gate-motors; he saw a gleam come into von Zenden's eyes.

"How many bullets left in that gun?" he asked swiftly.

"Three," said Crabb, after a hasty inspection of the magazine.

"Good. Get our friend Kurt behind that Chinese screen... on the floor, face down. Hold a gun at his head. If he tries to warn them, shoot. Nobody's likely to hear it, so don't hesitate."

"I won't," grated Crabb. He shoved von Zenden behind the screen and Trent hurriedly shifted the illusion mirrors, leaving only one shattered frame in sight to explain the broken pieces. He closed the trick cabinet, tossed Grussen's Luftwaffe jacket over the dead ace's body, and put the prop revolver away.

In a few moments he heard the front door open. He picked up the impersonator's make-up kit, snapped it open. Small cakes of special greaseless paints were arranged on one side, like blocks of water-colors. Tufts of crepe hair, prepared mustaches, lining pencils, and adhesive tape were on the other side. Small scissors, powder puffs, special overlay teeth, and other make-up accessories were clipped in between, and in the lid was a mirror.

Trent laid down his gun, quickly smudged a bit of flesh color along one cheek. Muttered voices became audible and he heard footsteps coming nearer. He took the pistol and stepped to the doorway.

"Wo ist es?" he rapped out, imitating von Zenden's voice.

"Von Zenden—*Gott sie Dank!*" came the mumbled answer. Trent hid a start as he saw Hermann's brutal features. The Nazi's coat sleeve was ripped open and a red-stained bandage showed on his forearm. Behind him were two men; both wore dark suits, although it was late Spring. They slid guns to their inside arm-pit holsters when they saw Trent's face. The first was a young man, with a big, hulking body. He had a low forehead and thick, protruding lips. The other was about thirty-two, small but wiry. He had little darting black eyes, so dark that the pupils were all but invisible.

"Excellenz, we thought you were killed," said the little Nazi. "Ludwig said the Curtiss was shot down in flames."

"I said it looked like it," the hulking youth said, sullenly. "Don't always try to blame me—"

"There's no time to waste in arguing," snapped Trent. "Are you sure you weren't followed here?"

Hermann shook his head. "The blackout's still on. It was all I could do to find Max and Ludwig. We drove without lights." His heavy features took on a resentful expression as he eyed Trent's immaculate uniform. "You saved your hide without a scratch, I see. For all of you, I might have been killed back there."

"Don't be a fool," Trent said sharply. "I had to get Grussen's body away, didn't I? The cause is more important than anyone's life!"

"You had better get out of that make-up," Hermann said in a gruff voice. "They're sending a description by radio to all Intelligence and police offices. We caught it on the short-wave in the ear."

"Did you learn anything else?" demanded Trent, stepping back into the doorway.

"We caught the U-boat flotilla's signal, *Herr* von Zenden," Max said eagerly. "The rest of the Stukas will take off to reach the marker-intersection point at exactly twelve o'clock!"

CHAPTER IV

Double fob Death

HERMANN NODDED. "This time there will be no mistake. Washington will be a mausoleum in twenty-four hours."

Trent felt a prickling at his scalp, but he managed a gloating smile. "*Gut,* but the time is short. You know what to do, while I change?"

"Then you landed the Curtiss here?" returned Hermann. "The transmitter in the gyro is still not working, May says."

"The Curtiss is across the road," answered Trent. "I brought Grussen's body in it. A doctor's examination might have given everything away."

Max and Ludwig stared at the dead ace.

"I still don't understand how he got poisoned," Ludwig said stupidly. "Hermann said the only danger was if they got in each other's slipstream. They couldn't have been releasing the dust, because the radio wasn't on to guide them."

"One of the Airacobras must have punctured the tank, or maybe Grussen opened the dump valve trying to gas the pilots," offered Max. "That's my guess. Grussen probably had to make a sudden turn and he flew into the stuff before he could get his hood tight. Then he took to his chute, hoping to get into clear air—"

"*Ja,* only it was too late," Hermann said stolidly. "Well, he was a fool. Anyone knows cyanide dust is not a child's toy."

"Maybe it killed some Americans down in the city," Ludwig said hopefully.

"No such luck," replied Max. "By the time it floated down it would be too much dispersed."

"*Himmel!*" Ludwig said suddenly. "What happened here?"

He pointed at the shattered glass across the room.

"I ran into a mirror in the dark," said Trent. He rubbed the paint spot on his cheek. "Forget about that—go down and turn on the transmitter."

Max and Ludwig started out. Hermann stared at a piece of mirror-glass on the floor, then with another glance at Grussen's body he followed the two Nazis. Trent waited until he heard them descend the basement stairs, then he quickly closed the door. As he turned back his eyes fell on the glass fragment Hermann had noticed.

A shadowy face was reflected there. In dismay, he realized it was a double reflection from one of the standing mirrors to von Zenden's made-up face, back of the screen. Before he could seize the gun he had put down to allay suspicion, the hall door burst open. Hermann charged in, pistol leveled, Max and Ludwig behind him with their guns ready.

"Get back!" Hermann rammed his gun against Trent's ribs. "Max, pull that screen away!"

IN ANOTHER second the light shone down on von Zenden and Mortimer Crabb. The impersonator threw himself back, one hand knocking Crabb's gun toward the ceiling. Max and Ludwig leaped in, tore the weapon from Crabb's grasp.

"Why didn't you shoot when you had the chance?" said Trent, as Crabb was dragged to his feet.

"What good would it do?" croaked the inventor. "They'd have finished you; I could see they had you covered."

"At least, you'd have knocked off von Zenden. Now they'll kill us anyway."

Von Zenden gave him a savage look. "Right, my smart Yankee. Hermann, that was good work."

"I almost gave it away, when I saw the glass," said Hermann. "Then when Max said the telephone fuses were pulled out, I knew it wasn't just some funny angle with the mirrors."

"I took out the fuses." Von Zenden explained in brief words how he had been captured. "I had to catch them off guard; that's why I made up as Grussen when I heard them open the gates. But this *Teufel*, Trent, with his infernal magician tricks—"

"But how did they get here, *Excellenz?*" exclaimed Max.

"They must have landed in that Brewster. Fortunately it was too dark for them to see the Curtiss unless they almost ran into it. Hermann, go over and set the radio in the Curtiss to the Stukas' wave-length. Ludwig, plug in those fuses, so I can telephone while Max starts the transmitter downstairs. I want to make sure our men are ready to take over at—"

"What about weather reports?" interrupted Hermann.

"I got the latest Navy report an hour ago," said von Zenden. "We'll fly out on the beam from here and circle down low at the 'marker' location. It won't be as easy as landing there in the gyro would have been, but it will be enough to guide the Stukas."

"All this could have been avoided if the U-boat operators had kept tuned in for any changes," complained Hermann. "I called them for an hour after Max found the gyro transmitter wasn't working. By one o'clock we could have had it going, and there would have still been time—"

"Lucky, they sent off only two Stukas before they caught our warning," von Zenden said brusquely. "But it's too late to wait for the gyro now. Go ahead with the Curtiss. Max, you wait here a minute—we have a little work to do."

Hermann went out and Trent heard the front door open. Ludwig had already gone down to put in the fuses. There was a moment's silence, while von Zenden smiled mirthlessly at Trent. He had picked up Grussen's pistol, and Max had his gun carefully trained on Mortimer Crabb.

"I should thank you for coming here, Commander," the impersonator said silkily. "Your Government—what there is left of it—after tonight will be looking for what you call the 'Master Mind.' Your unexpected return from Australia proves fortuitous, after all."

"So you're going to pin it on me?" said Trent.

"On you and your Gloomy Gus comrade. Or they may

think you fooled *Herr* Crabb and he tried to stop you at the last moment. Yes, that would be better. Murder and suicide… and I'll leave this little map to show how you planned—"

The buzzer in the hall sounded as the gates started to open. Trent heard three pistol shots in rapid succession, then a man cried out hoarsely.

"Watch those two!" von Zenden flung at Max. He ran toward the front door. Trent saw Ludwig out in the hall, his face taut with sudden panic. There was a thud as though some one had fallen inside the vestibule. Then he heard Hermann's labored voice.

"Von Zenden… it's the F.B.I… they got me!"

"The basement—over the wall!" shouted von Zenden. Ludwig dashed by the door of the magic room, the Prussian close behind. Von Zenden cast a hasty look at the prisoners.

"Shoot them, you *Dumpkoff!*" he snarled at Max, and raced on by. Max jumped back toward the doorway, raised the gun.

"If you do, you'll get the chair!" said Trent.

A CLAMOR of voices sounded outside the mansion. Max, deathly white, jerked a frantic glance up the hall. Trent dived behind Grussen's body, with a yell at Mortimer Crabb. Max whirled, fired twice. The bullets hit the corpse as Trent held it up before him. With an oath, Max swerved the gun toward Crabb. Trent dropped Grussen's body, seized the leg of a small magic table.

He hurled the table at Max's shins, and the Nazi fell on one knee with a howl. Both Trent and Crabb lit on him at once. The pistol went off, searing Trent's sleeve. Mortimer Crabb snatched the gun out of his hand, brought it down hard behind the German's ear.

"Well, I guess that'll hold him a while," Crabb grated. "What happened to von Zenden?"

"He must have escaped through the basement," said Trent. He ran into the hall.

"Stop where you are!" bawled a familiar voice. Trent

wheeled. McBride strode in through the vestibule, three F.B.I. agents behind him.

"Get some men around back," clipped Trent. "Two Nazis just went down through the basement."

"It's no use, Trent, I've got you cold," barked McBride. "Take his gun, Williams."

A blond young G-Man obeyed. McBride stared into the magic room, where Mortimer Crabb sat astride Max's unconscious figure.

"What in Pete's name—" he blurted out. "So that's the stiff!"

"No, he's merely *hors du combat*," said Trent. "Your long-lost corpse is over in the corner. I had to use him as a barrier, but you can ignore the bullet holes."

Out in the walled garden an engine sputtered, went dead. Two of McBride's agents streaked outside, and in a few seconds Trent heard a muffled command, "Halt!" A pistol shot followed like a punctuation point. One of the agents came back panting.

"Big fellow; tried to get over the wall with an insulated ladder when he couldn't get the gyro started."

"Well?" snapped McBride.

"Sorry, but I had to shoot. He was about to drill Peterson."

"That," said Trent, "would be *Herr* Ludwig, one of the muscle-men. I suppose it wouldn't interest you that the leader is probably outside the wall and making a clean getaway."

McBride looked uncertainly at Max, then at Grussen's body. "Williams, scout outside the wall. With those flood-lights on maybe you can spot him—if there *is* any leader," he added tartly, turning back to Trent.

"Suppose you listen for a minute," Trent said calmly. "It might also interest you to know there's a plot to use gas against Washington—tonight."

McBride started. "Gas? Talk—and talk fast!"

Trent crisply gave him the salient points. McBride sent an uneasy glance at Grussen's mottled face, then went behind the magic cabinet and brought out the Navy uniform von Zenden had worn.

"For Heaven's sake, man, make up your mind!" snorted Crabb. "Those devils are planning to strike within forty minutes! At least warn the Interceptor Command."

"There's only one way to be sure they don't reach their target—whatever it is," cut in Trent. "Leave the transmitter going downstairs, so they can ride in on the carrier beam. Have the Airacobras out there, waiting at that intersection point on the map."

McBride hesitated, staring at the map. "All right, where's the phone?"

Trent led the way into the hall. "It's in the drawing-room, through that arched doorway. Wait until I see if Ludwig put the fuses back."

"And to save time," Crabb said morosely, "you'd better let me try that transmitter, to be sure it's set on the right bearing."

"Williams, go down with them," ordered McBride. "Watch what goes on. I still wouldn't bet on that guy Trent, even if Captain Blaine did say…" The rest was a mumble as McBride went on into the drawing-room.

THE BASEMENT was brightly lighted, the outside doorway wide open. Trent saw a ladder leaning against the wall, Ludwig's body at the bottom, doubled up.

"Anybody guarding those ships across the road?" he asked Williams. The young agent nodded.

"McBride left a man over there. He spotted the planes when the floodlights went on."

Crabb finished checking the beam angle, and in a few seconds McBride hurried down the steps. "All right, Trent. They'll have the interceptors there. But I'm going with you— just in case you've got some trick up your sleeve."

"It's a pleasure, Red, old top," said Trent. "Of course, it's usually the chap in the rear seat who gets shot first."

McBride pulled his hat down with both hands, in a defi-ant gesture. "You can't scare me. Get going."

"I was only thinking of your weak stomach," Trent said maliciously. "You see, Red, Lieutenant Shafer told me about that bumpy trip you had with him last Fall."

McBride gave a sickly smile. "Don't worry about my stom-ach. Come on—I've got the map."

"Just a second." Trent crossed the lab to Crabb's desk. He scribbled a note, came back. "Mort, give this to Captain Blaine when you see him," he said.

"Let me see that," snapped McBride. He read the words. "So! 'Ignore all charges by that fathead McBride!' We'll see about that, Commander—when I get back!"

"You shouldn't read private notes," chuckled Trent. He patted Crabb on the shoulder. "So long, Mort, in case my guardian angel slips up."

"I'll help you get started," Crabb said gruffly.

Later, with McBride ensconced in the rear cockpit, Trent sent the Curtiss roaring up into the night. The floodlights, still on despite the blackout, enabled him to miss the trees, and he quickly swung onto the course the Nazis had mapped. He ran his eyes again over his instruments, cartridge-belt indicators, on down to the Pyrene fire-extinguisher and his flare releases.

"Turn on the radio!" McBride shouted, his voice barely audible over the engine. "How do you know we're heading right?"

Trent switched on the receiver. "Give me the map, while you check the beam."

McBride shoved it over into the front cockpit, put on the rear-pit headset. Trent swiftly inspected the course-line, which he had already traced through downtown Washing-ton. Oddly, it touched no important buildings. Then he saw it, an all but invisible dot on the line at the edge of the main reservoir.

The reservoir—Washington's water supply! It hit him like

a blow. Cyanide powder dumped into the reservoir… von Zenden's hint of men taking over some point—undoubtedly the water testing-station—to prevent any warning… and in the morning, unsuspecting thousands drinking—and dying!

"Trent, we're off the beam!" McBride's shout broke in on Trent's tense thoughts. "You circled too far before you set your course."

Trent put on his headset, banked into a climbing turn until he had maximum volume. He straightened out, holding an altitude of four-thousand feet. The low clouds were thinner on top and he could see occasional stars.

"Switch on your transmitter," roared McBride. "Hurry up!"

Bending over, Trent flicked the switch. The Curtiss skidded as he lifted his foot from the left rudder pedal. He heard McBride yell for him to swing back and start the circle, at the marker-intersection point. But before he could start his turn, the red and green lights of a plane appeared, ahead and about five-hundred feet below. Trent jerked open the front cockpit enclosure, fired a red rocket into the sky.

"What are you doing?" screamed McBride.

A brilliant light burst overhead, and against the blinding glare Trent could dimly see the diving planes.

"It's a trap!" McBride cried wildly. He whirled the rearpit guns up at the leading ship. Trent snatched the Pyrene loose from its clamps, slammed it at the other man's head. It caught McBride behind the ear, and he slumped down in the seat.

The diving ships materialized, under the flare, as Army P-39's. Trent whipped aside, to clear their path. Below, three black Stukas were zooming wildly to get out from under the light. A faint, smoky haze, like a mirage, suddenly appeared behind the leading Stuka, as the black ship flicked its tail toward a plunging P-39. Trent stood the Curtiss on its nose, cut loose his four forward guns.

The Airacobra veered off hastily, to miss Trent's tracers. Before the Stuka could swerve, Trent's guns stabbed their blazing death into the pilot's cockpit. He held the trip against his stick until the tracers ate forward into the cowl. The Stuka fell off, in flames.

AS TRENT chandelled he saw another black Nazi ship explode in mid-air. Four P-39's converged on the last Stuka before it could flee. With its tail cut off, the Nazi dive-bomber started a headlong plunge. Trent dived after it, holding his breath. If Mort had not understood…

The first flamer had burned its way through the mist, and he saw, as the last one struck, that it was open country. With a long breath of relief, he leveled out and headed back toward the Potomac.

The floodlights were still on at the old mansion, and he landed without difficulty. Mortimer Crabb and the young agent, Williams, came to the side of the ship.

"Eric! We just got word about the Stukas!" exclaimed Crabb.

"They hardly knew what hit them," said Trent. "But I had a casualty. Our friend here didn't like the way I was handling things, and I had to bop him. Help me lug him inside."

It took the three of them to carry the senior agent into the mansion. He began to stir as they laid him on a sofa in the drawing room. One of the other F.B.I. men brought some ammonia from Crabb's medicine chest.

"He's coming out of it all right," said Trent. "But I'm afraid he's going to be a little peevish."

Their patient sat up, gasping and sputtering. He put up one hand and felt the bump on his head, just under the brim of his hat.

"Sorry I had to lay you out, old chap," Trent said amiably.

The other man staggered to his feet. "You—you traitor! You're under arrest. Take him out of here, Williams."

"What charge?" said Williams. "He led the Interceptor Patrol to those German planes and helped wipe them out."

"He's lying! He signaled the Nazis… he tried to kill me. I know now he was one of von Zenden's spies. Trent let the Nazi escape!"

"That's right," said Trent. He smiled as the other man gaped at him. "But you see—I brought him back."

He reached out, suddenly jerked off the agent's felt hat. A mass of red hair, glued inside the band, came off with it, revealing the man's natural blond hair, plastered close to his skull. A strip of white skin, devoid of makeup, showed at the hairline, where the tight-drawn hat had concealed it.

"Gentlemen," said Eric Trent, "permit me to present the Man of a Thousand Faces. This is known as Face Number 13, by courtesy of McBride."

For an instant von Zenden stood as though turned to stone. Then he made a fierce lunge at Trent.

"You fiend! I'll kill you for this."

The F.B.I. men hauled him back, and Trent glanced toward the hall. "Okay, Red, you can come in now."

"Don't call me Red!" snarled McBride as he stalked in, a comical figure with half of his hair snipped off. "Put the cuffs on that Nazi, Williams. He'll pay for this night's business." Von Zenden stared incredulously at Trent. "You knew, even before we took-off?"

"My dear Kurt, you gave yourself away when you pulled that hat down, in the basement. When I called you 'Red' it evidently reminded you of the hair you had so hurriedly fastened in there after—er—borrowing it from—"

"Never mind about that," snapped McBride. "And don't think I let him do it. He got me in the dark when I went to phone. Next thing I knew, I was trussed up and gagged in that closet where Crabb found me. If you knew it then, why didn't you grab him and look for me?"

"I wasn't sure what else he'd done. I made positive it wasn't you, by inventing a bumpy ride with a non-existent mutual friend. Then I wrote two notes, one for him to see; the other I slipped to Mort telling him it was von Zenden and to look for you, warn the Interceptor Command, and bend the beam so the Stukas wouldn't get over Washington. I knew if I took von Zenden along he'd make sure we contacted the Stukas.

Otherwise, they might drop the stuff before the P-39's could get them."

McBride glowered at the impersonator. "I traced that call you did make, my fine Nazi. We've rounded up the mob that seized the Bryant pumping station and the testing lab, and that gave the show away. We've enough to burn the lot of you."

"I shall never sit in the electric chair," von Zenden said haughtily. "*Der Fuehrer* will see to that."

"Damn if I'm going to have my own face talking back to me!" roared McBride. "Trent, can you get that stuff off?"

"Sure, but I'd leave it on until you photograph him over at the Bureau. Then at least you'll have him for impersonating an officer."

"Thanks," growled McBride. He slammed the felt hat over his cropped hair. "Take him out of here, Williams, before I make another egg grow by that one Trent gave him."